"What an untidy household you keep, sir, that everyone disappears on you."

"You can see why I need you."

Richard needed her? Oh, how Claire wanted to be truly needed, a helpmate instead of an ornament to be trotted out to impress but forgotten otherwise. Yet, would it be any different with him? Wasn't she, even now, just a means to an end for him?

"So you think it's safe here?" she asked.

"No harm will come to Samantha," Richard said softly. "Or you. I promise."

Richard was standing so close, Claire found herself longing to lean against him, let his arms come around her, sheltering her. Instead, she took a step back.

"I shall hold you to that promise, Captain Everard. Now, if you'll excuse me, I should check on your cousin before retiring."

Claire turned for the stairs.

"Good night, Claire," he called. "Pleasant dreams."

Dreams? Once he'd embodied her dreams of the future. Now she didn't know what to think. For, no matter his promise, she was very much afraid she was in danger at Dallsten Manor—in danger of losing her heart.

Books by Regina Scott

Love Inspired Historical

The Irresistible Earl
An Honorable Gentleman
*The Rogue's Reform
*The Captain's Courtship

*The Everard Legacy

REGINA SCOTT

started writing novels in the third grade. Thankfully for literature as we know it, she didn't actually sell her first novel until she had learned a bit more about writing. Since her first book was published in 1998, her stories have traveled the globe, with translations in many languages including Dutch, German, Italian and Portuguese.

She and her husband of more than twenty years reside in southeast Washington State. Regina Scott is a decent fencer, owns a historical costume collection that takes up over a third of her large closet and she is an active member of the Church of the Nazarene. Her friends and church family know that if you want something organized, you call Regina. You can find her online, blogging at www.nineteenteen.blogspot.com. Learn more about her at www.reginascott.com.

The Captain's Courtship

REGINA SCOTT

Love Inspired

Recycling programs
for this product may
not exist in your area.

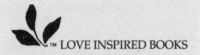 ™ LOVE INSPIRED BOOKS

ISBN-13: 978-0-373-82924-8

THE CAPTAIN'S COURTSHIP

Copyright © 2012 by Regina Lundgren

Do not judge, and you will not be judged.
Do not condemn, and you will not be condemned.
Forgive, and you will be forgiven.
Give, and it will be given to you. A good measure,
pressed down, shaken together and running over,
will be poured into your lap.
—*Luke* 37–38

To all the captains I know:
Scott Doyle, captain of the Cape; Larry,
captain of my heart; and the Lord, captain of my life

Chapter One

London, England, Spring 1805

A man was standing in her mirror. Lady Claire Winthrop didn't turn to see if he was real. He couldn't be real. Even with that neat auburn beard and mustache, the face of her dreams was unmistakable. Richard Everard had sailed out of her life ten years ago. He wasn't likely to return now, just because she'd never needed him more.

She regarded the massive gilt-framed mirror hanging on the wall of the sitting room in the town house that would be hers for a few days more. The reflection gave back a picture of the perfect society widow—every honey-colored curl sleeked back into a bun behind her head, face suitably wane and pale against the black of her silk gown. Nothing about her appearance had changed since the day her husband had died nearly a year ago. All the changes were inside of her.

She turned to regard the portly tradesman standing beside her. "I'm afraid, Mr. Devizes, that ten pounds simply won't do. Surely you can see that a mirror of this size is worth so much more."

Mr. Devizes sucked in his chubby cheeks and peered

at the glass. Like everything else in Claire's life, it was elegant and ornate and tarnished around the edges. "M'customers aren't so much impressed by size as pedigree," he mused in a rusty voice. "Were it owned by someone famous, then?"

She had no idea. The mirror was one of the last pieces left that had belonged to her late husband. Nearly everything else had been returned to his family seat and the possession of his heir, or sold to pay off debts. The remaining pieces were sadly inferior, which was why she'd had to go to less reputable dealers to find a buyer.

Claire waved a hand. "Well, certainly it was owned by the affluent and powerful. Very likely, kings have regarded themselves in this glass."

"Or at least those who fancied themselves royalty," said a warm bass voice.

Words froze on her tongue. Mr. Devizes turned to glance behind them, then took a step back, closer to the mirror. "I thought you said this was to be a private sale. I didn't come prepared to bid."

Lord, please help me! Is he truly here? Every muscle in her body protested as she turned to find out. Just one look at that tall, powerful frame, and she felt her knees buckling.

No! She would not faint. Richard Everard already held her in the utmost contempt. She refused to let him see her least weakness. She did what she'd done since the day he'd abandoned her. She smiled—not too effusive, not too sweet—just a gentle upturn of the corners of her mouth, which most people took as approval.

"Good day, sir." Her voice was equally calm and distant. Excellent. Surely she could do this. "Mr. Everard, isn't it?"

One russet brow went up, whether in surprise or

amusement, she wasn't sure. Once she'd been able to read every thought in those deep brown eyes, every quirk of that gentle mouth. He had obviously grown skilled at hiding his feelings.

"Captain Everard," he corrected her, but his nod was for the tradesman beside her. "Forgive the interruption, sir. The footman who answered my knock seemed to think I was expected."

A logical assumption. Jones knew his mistress was expecting any number of furniture purveyors to make offers on the last items. The footman and her cook were only staying on at the house until they secured other posts. Claire was thankful for their loyalty, especially since she could no longer afford to pay them for their help.

Devizes licked his flabby lips, then glanced between Claire and the towering stranger. "Friend of yours then, your ladyship?"

How could she answer? Once she'd hoped for so much more.

"No," Richard Everard said, and his gaze hardened. "I have business with the lady."

"Twenty pounds," Devizes barked out to Claire. "I was here first. I have rights."

Claire glanced at Richard. So he would not even claim a friendship. Why did that hurt so much, after such a long time apart? And she certainly couldn't imagine what business they had, unless he'd come about one of the other pieces. How absurd! What interest could a privateer turned merchant captain have in things like an old walnut secretary and a tarnished mirror?

But she'd also learned in the last few years to make the most of every opportunity, never knowing when another door would close. Richard might not be a friend, but he could be of use to her. Desperation made for strange companions.

"Fifty," she said to the dealer.

"Fifty?" Devizes fairly ̲uttered. Then his eyes narrowed. "Thirty."

Captain Everard was staring at her, but she didn't care, much. She needed that money. It was the only way she might start over. "Forty-five."

"Forty."

"Forty-three, and I shall have it delivered."

The dealer eyed her a moment more, then inclined his head. "Done. Payment when it is delivered."

Claire gave him her reasonable smile. "But, sir, surely you don't malign my character. Payment now will allow me to arrange delivery."

"You might have her put that in writing," Richard Everard said.

Why, the nerve! Well, she wouldn't give him the satisfaction of knowing that he'd hurt her yet again. "What an excellent suggestion, Mister...Captain Everard. I have parchment and a quill on the secretary." She made her way carefully across the nearly empty room, hoping she was the only one who heard the angry footsteps under the whisper of her skirts against the bare wood floor.

"No, no," Mr. Devizes protested, following her. "No need. I'll take you at your word. I heard your father was an earl."

Yes, he had been, though little good that had done her. Earls had expectations about whom their daughters should marry, expectations of how their daughters should comport themselves in society. And earls could not leave their titles or entailed property to anyone female in the line. That was one reason she was in such difficulty at the moment.

She turned once more, and the dealer, with a side glance at Richard, met her in the middle of the room. He took a bag from inside his rumpled brown coat and handed it to her. "That should cover it."

And she was expected to be a lady and take him at his word as well. After all, ladies did not haggle with tradesmen. Sordid matters like finance were far below them. Unfortunately, too many gentlemen of her acquaintance had failed to live up to their words, and they had claimed to love her. Claire had no one to protect her but herself. *And You, Lord. Thank You for never failing me!*

"Oh, how kind," she said to the dealer. "Let me just make sure. We wouldn't want you to overpay, now, would we?"

Richard Everard crossed his arms over the chest of his black greatcoat as if she was inconveniencing him, and Mr. Devizes fairly danced with impatience. But she counted every coin, made sure the amount added up to the forty-three pounds he'd offered, slipped the money into a corner of the secretary for the moment and returned the bag to the dealer. The gold and silver glowed against the dark wood, but the gleam only reminded her of the future she'd planned, far away from her beloved London.

"I'll have the mirror to your shop later today," she promised as she walked Mr. Devizes to the sitting room door and out into the parquet-tiled entryway. Jones was elsewhere, so she opened the front door and watched the dealer descend the short flight of stairs to the Mayfair street. Outside, life went on. Ladies in flowered and ribboned bonnets strolled past, attended by strapping footmen; gentlemen rode by on horses with lineages better than hers. Soon, if things went as planned, she would leave them all behind.

But first she had to get rid of the past that had suddenly loomed up in front of her. She held the lacquered green door open and eyed Richard Everard where he stood in the doorway of the sitting room. That long, straight nose always made him look as if he were leaning forward, ready for anything. She didn't feel nearly as ready.

"Please don't let me detain you, Captain Everard," she said. "Surely you have something more important to do than to accost me."

He strolled toward her, and she stood taller. There— she'd succeeded in insulting him, and he'd leave as quickly as he'd arrived. She wouldn't have to learn why he'd shown up at her door, what he thought he could say to her. She wouldn't have to take the chance that her heart would break all over again. She could go back to dreaming of him and waking in the night wondering what might have been.

He reached up over her head with one large hand, took hold of the door and pulled it easily from her grip. It shut with a click.

"We must talk," he said.

Richard watched as Claire's blue eyes widened. Such a pale blue, as clear and bright as the sky on a winter's morn. And just as cold, like the heart that beat in that silk-covered chest.

"Fah, sir," she said with an elegant wave of her long-fingered hand. "I cannot imagine what we have to say to each other."

Couldn't she? He'd thought of little else on the long ride from Cumberland. What did you say to the woman who'd jilted you, now that you needed her help? He'd hoped to apply to her husband first, even if he had to clench his fists at his sides to keep from planting the fellow a facer.

But the few discreet questions he'd asked to locate Claire had yielded surprising news.

Lord Colton Winthrop was dead and in the ground nearly a year. And that fact made any conversation harder still.

"I came here to seek your help," he told her. "I've a cousin set to make her debut, and she needs a sponsor."

"I see." She tilted her chin and gazed up at him. Time had been kind, but he thought she was one of those women who would only grow more beautiful with each passing year. Though how she'd tamed her soft curls into that stern bun was beyond him. The style narrowed her face, called out the line of cheekbone and chin. But her lips were as pink and appealing as they'd been when he'd first longed to steal a kiss.

"You will forgive me, sir," she said. "I've been in mourning, so I am not completely *au courant* on the social scene. But I don't recall your having a cousin the proper age, and certainly not a female."

Trust her to know. She'd always been fascinated with the lineage of every one of the ten thousand individuals said to make up the *bon ton*. No doubt her late viscount had a title dating to the conquest. Richard's family title was far more tenuous. He had to go carefully. His cousin Samantha could ill afford the gossip. "My uncle, Arthur, Lord Everard, has a daughter. She's sixteen."

"Indeed," she replied.

He'd forgotten how she could stop conversation with a single word. If he'd had any doubts as to her feelings on the matter, the narrowing of her crystal gaze would have convinced him of her skepticism.

"But I believe I heard your uncle passed on recently," she continued. "Surely his daughter must be in mourning."

She would understand that as well. Her slender figure

was swathed in black, from the high lace collar to the ruffled hem of her graceful skirts. And she hadn't worn a single piece of jewelry, not even a wedding ring. He remembered a time when she'd refused to go out in anything less than pearls. She must have loved her husband a great deal to give up so much to mourn him. The thought brought less comfort than it should have.

"My uncle instructed that she forgo mourning," he explained. "He believed in living to the fullest."

"Yes, so I recall." She refused to take her hand off the brass pull of the door, as if she'd throw it open and order him from the house at any moment.

Her attitude grated on his nerves, already too high for his liking. In fact, his cravat seemed to have tightened since he'd arrived in the house, and he tugged at it now. "Perhaps we could sit down."

That oh-so-proper smile did not waver. "I fear I've nothing to offer you, Captain Everard, by way of seating or assistance. I'm sure you'll find another lady far more suited to your purpose. You should go."

So she *was* throwing him out. Why had he even considered asking her for help? She was more high-handed now than she'd been as a girl. Nothing he'd said back then had mattered. Why should today be any different? *If I needed a lesson in humility, Lord, this is it.*

"No doubt you're right, Lady Winthrop," he said with a bow. "As I recall, you had the annoying habit of always being right. I bid you good-day, madam." He took the handle from her grip and swung open the door.

She sighed. It was the smallest of sounds, hardly audible, because of her own good breeding and through the noise from the busy street. But the dejected breath cut through his frustration—awakened something inside him he'd thought long dead. His foot on the step, he turned to gaze back at her.

"Are you all right, Claire?"

An emotion flickered across her oval face. Was it because he'd used her given name, or was she truly in trouble? Still, that infuriating smile remained pleasant. "Certainly, Captain Everard. I have all I need. I am quite content."

Content? The Lady Claire he remembered had never been content. The latest fashion, the fastest carriage—she had to have them all and much sooner than half of London. She had ridden with more skill and danced with more enthusiasm than any other woman he'd ever met. He truly hadn't been surprised when she'd chosen a wealthy, titled peer over a second son of a second son of a newly minted baron. Just crushed.

She shifted as if eager to have him leave, and he caught a clear view into the entryway. For the first time, he noticed the darker rectangles on the papered walls where paintings must have been removed, the scuffs on the parquet floor where large pieces of furniture had no doubt been scraped as they'd been carried out. A house this size ought to boast a half dozen servants at least, but no maid had attended her during her conversation with the tradesman, and no butler came hurrying to see him out now.

"You don't have a sofa to sit on, do you?" he asked.

Her smile slipped at last. "That, sir, is none of your concern."

He put a hand flat on the door, shoved it wide and strode back into the house. "It may not be my concern, madam, but it is to my advantage. I have a proposal for you, and I advise you to listen."

Chapter Two

A proposal? Claire stared at him, mouth dry. No, he couldn't mean a proposal of marriage. She'd destroyed any tender feelings he'd had for her. And her own feelings had been folded away like a favorite gown, tucked between sheets of tissue for safety. Some might say that a marriage would solve her problems, but she couldn't believe that. And marriage to Richard Everard? Never.

But he didn't wait for her response. He strode to the sitting room door, the slap of his brown boot heels echoing against the wood floor, and glanced inside. Apparently disliking what he saw, he stalked across the space to glare into what had been her husband's library.

"You really don't have a sofa," he declared, as if that was somehow a moral deficiency.

Claire tugged down on her sleeves, careful to keep him from seeing the edge she'd so carefully patched. Her mother would never have imagined the ends to which Claire would have to put the embroidery skills she'd been taught.

"The sofas in this house were shabby pieces," she told him. "I am well rid of them."

He returned to her side, dark eyes narrowing. "So you'd have me believe you merely tired of all your furnishings."

It was close to the truth; she'd tired of any number of things. Claire waved a hand. "I've grown weary of the whole, tedious social whirl. The town house has been sold, and I plan to leave London before Easter. I thought perhaps Bath, or Italy. I have yet to decide."

She had hoped her tone was as breezy as her wave, but he shook his head. "The Claire I knew would have crawled to London over broken glass rather than miss the Season."

"Then perhaps, sir, I am not the Claire you knew."

He laughed as if she'd said something remarkably clever. He had no idea how difficult the last ten years had been, how much she'd changed, how much she'd had to mature. *At least that much good has come of it, Father.*

"We'll see about that," he said. "But I can't keep you standing about like this. Is there nowhere in this house we can sit down?"

She thought about turning him away more forcefully, but truly, did it matter? He would say his piece, she would decline, and he would be gone. If he told anyone about her constrained circumstances, she'd be miles away before the gossip grew to any magnitude.

"We still have a table and chairs in the kitchen," she told him. "This way."

She led him down the corridor beside the stairs toward the little kitchen at the rear of the town house. Her right knee twinged just the slightest, protesting all this moving about. *Not now, Lord. Please, keep it strong until I'm finished with him.* She refused to see pity or, worse, pleasure at her pain. Though, who could blame him for thinking she deserved what she'd gotten from her marriage? She was the one who had broken her promise.

Shoving the memories aside, she pushed through the

kitchen door with Richard right behind her. Mrs. Corday looked up from the potatoes she'd been peeling, hand frozen on the knife.

"This is Captain Everard," Claire said, as if she normally entertained guests in her kitchen. "He wishes to have words with me."

Her cook blinked bleary blue eyes wreathed in wrinkles. "And would you like me to stay, your ladyship?"

Claire glanced at Richard, who looked surprised she'd think twice about trusting herself alone with him. Claire focused on her cook. "Please go about your duties. Don't let us disturb you."

The cook's snowy brows went up, but she ducked her head and set about whipping the peelings off the crusty vegetables as if her life depended on finishing.

Claire hadn't spent a lot of time in her kitchen until the furnishings had been taken, but she'd been surprised to find it a dark and dismal place, with a gray stone fireplace that took up one entire wall and oak cabinets painted a lacquered black that had dimmed with time. The only bright spots were the copper tools hanging from the walls around the hearth and what was left of her china, creamy white with rosebuds along the edges, piled haphazardly on the sideboard for packing.

Still, she could remember how to be the proper hostess, even if she had to take the role of servant. "May I take your coat, Captain Everard?"

"Thank you." He shrugged out of the multicaped greatcoat and folded it over one arm to hand it to her. Under it he wore tan breeches and a tailored brown wool jacket. An emerald-striped satin waistcoat peeked out through the lapels. She could find no fault in his clothing or the elegantly tied cravat at his throat. In fact, he looked every bit the gentleman.

"Please, have a seat," she said, motioning him to a ladder-back chair farther down the oak worktable. She went to hang his coat on a curved-arm hall tree by the kitchen door. "Would you care for some tea?"

She turned in time to see that he had pursed his lips as if he doubted she could produce the brew. "Certainly, if it's not too much trouble."

Meeting Claire's gaze, Mrs. Corday jerked her head toward the fire. "Kettle's already on the boil, your ladyship. There's enough for a few more cups in the caddy."

"Thank you," Claire murmured. Fully aware that Richard's gaze followed her every step, she went to the fireplace and took the kettle off the hook. Carrying it to the sideboard, she set about pouring the steaming water into one of her china cups.

She nearly sighed aloud when she peered into the satinwood tea caddy. This was the last of her bohea. Funny how little things had come to mean so much now. Would she be able to get the mellow tea in the little town where she hoped to retire? For, regardless of what she'd told Richard and a few close friends, her funds would never extend to Bath or Italy. She was considering a two-room cottage in the tiny village of Nether Crawley, a day's ride from London. Of course, with no carriage or horse, the distance was immaterial. Very likely, she would never see London again.

Help me remember why I made that choice, Lord. It does no good to wish it otherwise now.

She returned with Richard's tea and set it in front of him. Lifting the cup to his mouth, he took a cautious sip. Now, why did that smile please her so much? She'd have thought she'd played a complicated Mozart sonata in front of the king.

"Are you certain you want to leave London?" he asked as he lowered the cup.

"Quite," she replied. She turned her back on his frown and went to pour for herself.

"What if I could give you another Season, all expenses paid?"

She could not even reach for the teapot. Stay in London? Enjoy the balls, the parties; reacquaint herself with her friends, with no thought of tomorrow?

Ah, but she'd learned there always came the time to pay the piper. Tomorrow, however much she wished otherwise, would come. He only offered a reprieve. She would have to leave London regardless, before the Season, after the Season, for the same small house at the back of beyond. In the meantime, she would have to continue to pretend that her life was perfect, that she was perfect. No, not that. *Lord, You know I am so tired of that.*

She poured the last of the brew, the steam curling up to her face. "I fear my mind is made up, sir."

"Then it's my duty to change it."

She turned to find him regarding her, his cup sitting in front of him, his hands braced on either side of it as if he meant to keep it captive.

"Sit down, Claire," he ordered.

Mrs. Corday's hands were moving so fast Claire thought the potato might fly across the table and embed itself in Richard Everard's waistcoat. She left her cup on the sideboard and went to lay a hand on her cook's shoulder.

"It's all right, Mrs. Corday. Our guest is a sea captain. He's no doubt forgotten that it isn't polite to give orders to people who are not his subordinates."

Mrs. Corday cast Richard a quick glance. "As you say, your ladyship."

He had the good grace to incline his head, and the light from the lamps overhead made a halo on the crown of his auburn hair. "Forgive me, Mrs. Corday. You are the captain of your kitchen. I should have asked permission to come aboard."

The older woman's rosy lips quirked as if she were fighting a smile. "It's no trouble, sir. Would you care for a biscuit to go with your tea?"

"If you made it," he said with a smile, "I'm sure I'd enjoy it."

She set down the potato and hurried to the pantry.

So, he could be perfectly charming to the staff, but not to Claire. Well, she wasn't going to allow him to order her about, either. She swept back to the sideboard and busied herself adding sugar to the tea. Normally she preferred three teaspoons, but she had to economize. She took a sip of the flavorful brew, even as she heard Mrs. Corday murmuring to their guest and the clink of porcelain on oak as she set the plate of the last biscuits on the table.

"Please sit down, Lady Winthrop," Richard Everard said quietly. "I have a great deal to explain."

Claire steeled herself, picked up her cup and turned. His smile was contrite, his face composed. She couldn't trust what lay beneath that fair surface, but she went to join him at the table. Her cook began cutting the potatoes into a copper pot.

"I should probably start with expressing my condolences on your loss," he continued in that gentle tone.

"And mine on yours," she acknowledged. "Though, as I recall, you and your uncle were no longer close."

He rubbed a long finger along the wood grain of the table. She'd always thought he should play the piano with those hands. Certainly he could have managed the octave-and-a-half reach that still eluded her. And he'd definitely had the fire to play with enthusiasm, once.

"Uncle had changed recently," he said. "Tried to make amends, to me, my brother and cousin, as well as his daughter."

"So he really has a daughter?" Claire could not see the pleasure-loving Lord Everard as a doting father. His exploits—from duels at daybreak to wagers at one in the morning—were legendary. "Where has she been all these years?"

"Cumberland, in an old manor house. She was raised to be a lady, Claire. You need have no worries on that score."

She should protest the way her first name kept coming so easily to his lips, but the sound of it was sweet. With her father and husband dead, no one called her Claire anymore. "You intend to bring her out this year?"

"Right after Easter. She'll need a coming-out ball or some such, I suppose—clothes, of course—oh, and presentation to the queen."

So that was why he needed her. He could have found someone to cater an event, issue invitations, and certainly any dressmaker could have gowned the girl. But to be presented to the queen, Richard's cousin needed someone who had already been presented, a lady of some social standing, a lady like Claire.

Which meant that Richard Everard needed her help, almost as badly as she needed his. Was it possible she could parlay his request into more?

Is this a door You want me to walk through, Lord?

Aloud, she murmured, "I imagine she has her heart set on this Season."

"She's actually a bit intimidated by the prospect," he confessed with a fond smile. "She needs a good example."

Now, that would be pleasant, serving as an example

to a young girl, helping her avoid Claire's mistakes. But did she really want to relive those mistakes any more than she already had?

"Perhaps you should wait a year, then," Claire replied. "She's only sixteen, you said. Plenty of time."

He shifted on the chair, spine straightening, chin lifting. Sitting beside him, she could see the physical influences of his profession—the golden tan of his skin where the sun had caressed him, the lines at the corners of his eyes where he'd gazed across the horizon.

"It must be this year," he said.

Interesting. Why was he so insistent? She'd been pushed to do her duty too many times to force it on another, particularly a girl fresh from the schoolroom. "Nonsense, sir. I assure you a maiden needs a certain level of maturity to do well in London. Would you pluck a peach before it had ripened?"

"Lady Everard is hardly a fruit."

Claire sat taller. "*Lady* Everard? Then she has the title.. Oh, your brother must be beside himself."

Even with his close beard, she could see the tension in that square jaw. "My brother Jerome is delighted with the turn of events. He was married four days ago and is busy setting up his household."

"Indeed. I must send him a note in congratulations. Who is the lucky bride?"

He leaned back from the table. Oh, but he didn't want to give her the information. Claire kept her smile polite. A lady did not gloat in triumph at discomfiting a troublesome guest, however sorely she was tempted.

"Her name is Adele Walcott," he said.

Claire tapped her chin with one finger. "Adele Walcott. I don't believe I've had the pleasure. Is she related to Admiral Walcott?"

"Not that I know of."

"The Walcotts of Gloucester, then."

"No."

"Daniel Walcott, the Parliamentarian from Dover?"

"No. She's from Cumberland. Until recently she was Lady Everard's governess."

The story improved by the moment. But it would do his cousin no good. One could only dine on gossip for so long. Claire took a sip of her tea. "So, your brother married the girl's governess, and you need another suitable female willing to play tagalong so your cousin can join Society. Naturally you'd think of me."

"I thought of you," he gritted out, "because you are the only lady known to the queen and perhaps willing to help my family."

"My dear Captain Everard," Claire replied, "I have no idea what gave you that impression."

As if she'd pushed him too far, he rose, dwarfing the table, dwarfing her. "Oh, you'll help us, Claire, and I'll tell you why. You want to stay in London, and I can give you that."

"Indeed." Did he truly think it that easy? Richard Everard wanted her in London, therefore in London he expected her to be. Well, London, she had learned to her sorrow, exacted a price from its residents. She wasn't sure she was willing to pay it any longer. But if she was going to stay, it would be on her terms.

She glared up at him. "Staying in London does not come cheap, sir, and neither do I. I have any number of requirements that must be met before I would even consider changing my plans. And I would need to know that your intentions are serious this time. Just how much are you willing to invest to guarantee your cousin's success and my goodwill?"

Chapter Three

~❧~

Why was it only money that made the rose bloom in those fair cheeks? Once Richard would have given anything to be the one who made Claire smile. Now he was tempted to wring her neck.

As if she could see trouble brewing, she raised her chin. "Sit down, Captain Everard," she said. "We have a great deal to discuss."

He wasn't so frustrated that he didn't recognize she was turning his own words against him. Perhaps he *had* been too demanding. But the subject was a difficult one, with so many aspects that he could not confide in anyone outside the family, especially not a woman who'd proven particularly unfaithful in the past.

Still, Claire was their only hope. He had a duty to his cousin Samantha, a promise to keep.

Funny. He'd only known of the girl's existence for a month, after the family solicitor, Benjamin Caruthers, had informed Richard, his brother Jerome and their cousin Vaughn of the contents of their uncle's will and the fact that his daughter would inherit the bulk of the estate. Jerome had been certain it was all a lie, some game of Uncle's, even from the grave. But after riding to Cumberland and spending a fortnight in the girl's company, they were in agreement. Samantha was an Everard through and through.

Richard had never come to care for anyone so quickly, except for Claire. His new cousin deserved his loyalty and his best effort as she embarked on this Season, which would mark the triumph or doom of his family. If humbling himself in front of Claire would help, he'd simply have to do it. They had nowhere else to turn.

Samantha must be presented at court, and only a lady like Claire could sponsor her. Given his uncle's wild ways, few ladies were willing to risk their reputations by associating themselves with the Everards. But Claire posed an opportunity, and he'd be mad not to take it.

He returned to his seat and made himself pick up the fragile teacup like the polished gentleman he was. "We're not lacking in funds," he assured Claire, with a quick glance at Mrs. Corday. The woman had moved to the hearth and was arranging her pot on the fire, her broad back to him, but he had no doubt she could still hear every word that was said across the room. He couldn't risk any hint of scandal, for Samantha's sake.

"I'm delighted you're prepared," Claire said beside him. She was too proper to show her triumph at his apparent capitulation, but he thought he heard it in her voice. She had a siren's voice, warm, low, compelling. He'd found it hard not to heed ten years ago, and it wasn't any easier to ignore now.

She eyed him speculatively, as if calculating just what it would take to break him. "Very likely, your cousin will need an entirely new wardrobe, and that will be pricey."

"Fripperies," Richard scoffed.

Her smile grew. "You'd be surprised at the cost of

fripperies, sir. You'll need to refurbish the Everard town house as well."

Richard frowned. "Why? It's good enough for the rest of us."

She sniffed, a mere tightening of her nostrils. "I'm sure it was quite sufficient for your uncle and the three of you, who rarely entertained among your class. For a young girl with a score of suitors and acquaintances coming to call, no."

She had a point there. He wasn't sure when a fresh coat of paint had been slapped on the light green walls. And Uncle's tastes in decor might give some people pause. Some years ago, he had purchased a fifteen-foot-tall marble statue of a naked woman holding out a golden apple. It currently resided in the entry hall. Samantha would no doubt be intrigued by the piece, but he could imagine how any other lady entering the house might take it.

"We can redecorate," he agreed.

"And increase the staff," she insisted. "Your uncle was rather famous for plaguing the help. What was the record, four valets in one year?"

She was right there as well. The fourth, Repton, had disappeared the night Uncle had died in what the authorities persisted in calling a duel, even though his opponent was unknown. The other servants had found Uncle's whimsical approach to life, forever haring off after a new interest, equally frustrating.

"I'll see that the town house is adequately staffed," Richard promised.

She picked up her teacup. "If you require a footman or cook, I can give you recommendations."

Mrs. Corday paused in washing her hands to gaze at her mistress with worshipful eyes. Did the woman need a position, then? The current cook at Everard House had given notice just last week, saying his skills were wasted on men who were so seldom in residence. On the other hand, Claire's cook seemed competent, and the biscuit had been nicely done.

Richard nodded in her direction. "Consider yourself hired, Mrs. Corday."

Eyes widening, she bobbed a curtsy. "Oh, God bless you, sir, your ladyship!"

But Claire wasn't finished. "You'll need a town carriage, too, I think," she said, gazing off in the middle distance. "You all go on horseback far too often. And a matched set of horses in black or white. Nothing looks more slovenly than to arrive at a ball with a ragtag set of nags."

Samantha would be through her inheritance in hours. "And I suppose you'd like several teams to match her gowns."

She gave him one of her elegant waves. "We needn't go so far as all that. Though I will expect a respectable coachman and a groom. And a decent riding horse." She paused to frown. "She does ride, does she not?"

"Like the wind, I'm told," Richard said with a grin. "She's an Everard."

"A matter of considerable concern," she replied, then continued before he could take umbrage. "Tell me about her other skills. Does she play an instrument?"

"The piano, with enthusiasm." Richard knew he sounded defensive. Samantha was a darling, no matter what anyone thought of her family name. Any man would be lucky to claim her heart and her hand in marriage.

"Sing?" Claire persisted.

"I haven't heard her, but her speaking voice is pleasant enough."

"Paint?"

He raised a brow. "Paint?"

She pursed her lips, and he had to look away as memories flooded in like a high tide. What was wrong with him? Even after ten years, he found it far too easy to remember how soft those lips had felt against his, how easily they could form words that cut him to the quick.

"Well," she said, blithely unaware, as usual, of the turmoil she was causing inside him. "I suppose painting is optional. She is versed in the latest dances?"

Richard struggled to focus on her questions. "I wouldn't know."

Her frown was back. "Has she ever attended a local assembly?"

He hadn't realized such things would be important. "Not to my knowledge."

"A party at her own home, then."

The party his uncle had held every year came to mind. Samantha and her governess, Adele Walcott, who had married his brother Jerome last week, spoke of an event each summer, when his uncle entertained all his neighbors, great and small, on the grounds of Dallsten Manor in Cumberland. While the locals toasted his health, he'd met with other men inside the manor, and no one knew what they had discussed or who had been invited, except for his uncle's closest friend, the Marquess of Widmore. But Adele had made it sound as if Samantha had always been sent inside in the evening, when the locals held a dance.

"I suspect she's never danced with a partner," Richard told Claire.

She shook her head at such a ramshackle upbringing, and one of her curls came free from her bun. It hung between her ear and cheek, a strand of silky sunlight in the dark kitchen. He grabbed his cup of tea and made himself take a sip of the cooling brew rather than reach out to touch the gleaming gold.

"Then she must have a dance master, before she reaches London," she declared. "I'll write to Monsieur Chevalier immediately."

"Chevalier?" Richard asked, setting down the cup but keeping his fingers anchored to the handle.

"Henri Chevalier, a dance master of some note. He's trained any number of young ladies the last few years, including a foreign princess."

Just what he needed, a swell-headed fop teaching Samantha to take on airs. "We can put an ad in the Carlisle paper and find someone in Cumberland."

She raised a delicate brow. "Certainly we could do that, if Lady Everard was coming out in the wilds of Cumberland. As she is making her debut in London, under my tutelage, only a London master will do. Chevalier is the best, the son of a deposed French count. I'm sure you wouldn't want your cousin to make do with less."

And how was he to answer that? Of course he wanted the best for Samantha. That was one of the reasons he hoped Claire would sponsor her. "Very well," he conceded. "See if your fancy London fellow is available to come with me to Cumberland. I planned to leave tomorrow morning."

"That," she said, "we shall discuss in a moment."

"So you even intend to dictate my travel, madam?" Richard challenged.

She tsked. "Come now, sir. If you wish to bargain, you must be willing to put everything on the counter."

"Bargain, madam?" What more did she want? Ready for the worst, he braced his hands on the hard wood of the table.

"A turn of phrase, sir," she assured him, but she

straightened in her ladder-back chair as if making a decision. "Allow me to sum up our discussion for you. You wish me to sponsor an untried girl of indeterminate skills, a girl I have never met, and shepherd her through her first Season, including being presented to Her Royal Majesty."

"And be welcomed everywhere," Richard added, remembering the requirements of his uncle's will, which his cousin Samantha was trying so hard to fulfill. "And garner at least three offers of marriage from suitable gentlemen."

She trilled a laugh. "Why stop at three, sir? Why not a dozen?"

Richard gritted his teeth. "Three will be sufficient. Then you'll do it?"

She held up a hand. "Perhaps you should hear my requirements first."

"I heard them—a new wardrobe for Samantha; a carriage and team with coachman, groom and riding horse; the town house refurbished and staffed; and the services of a dance master."

"The services of Monsieur Chevalier," she corrected him. "And all that you will need for your cousin regardless of who sponsors her. I'm sure you'll agree that I deserve something for my struggles."

So she truly would bargain with him, just as she'd done with the tradesman. He wasn't sure why that so disappointed him. She was right. He was asking her to change her plans, risk her reputation. Yet he couldn't help thinking that Claire was the one who had gone back on her word ten years ago. It seemed only fair she do him this favor now.

"What struggles?" he protested. "Samantha is a beauty. Your work will not be onerous."

"You, sir, have never been a girl on her first London Season. Besides, beauties often require the most effort from their sponsors. I will need a new wardrobe."

Richard eyed her black dress. "What you're wearing ought to scare off obnoxious suitors."

Her smile remained polite, though he thought he saw her eyes narrow just the slightest. "Doubtless. But I'm certain you'd like me to reflect well on Lady Everard in public. You did say I was to be an example. Or do you intend to gown her in black as well?"

Neither his uncle nor his cousin would have stood for it. "My uncle insisted that she enjoy her Season," he told Claire.

She inclined her head. "And I shall see that she enjoys it thoroughly. I will also require a maid. French, I think."

Richard gaped. "What possible good can that do?"

She tapped her finger on the table by his cup. "Think, Captain Everard. Your cousin has been raised in the wilderness. Her personal maid cannot possibly be versed in the latest styles."

"As far as I know, she doesn't even require a maid!"

She shook her head. "Every lady requires a maid. You, sir, have never had to pull on a ball gown alone. Having a maid to serve your cousin and me will solve that problem, won't it?"

He hated it when she sounded so reasonable about such a triviality. "Very well."

She nodded as if pleased by his answer. "And when the Season is over, you will set me up in a house, anywhere I want to go."

A house? She had to know what she asked. Any lady who took such an offer from a gentleman would no longer be welcomed by the *ton*. Besides, he couldn't believe she truly wanted to leave London, or that she lacked the funds to do so herself.

"That's a tall order," he returned. "Who knows where you'll wish to settle? Shipping a household to Italy can cost a fortune."

"Which you claim to have," she pointed out.

More than he'd ever dreamed, if Samantha managed her Season as planned. But he was no longer so willing to lay that fortune at Claire's feet. "My cousin inherited a great deal of the legacy," he said. "I can't in good conscience make promises against it without her approval."

She gazed at him in obvious wonder. "An Everard taking orders from a slip of a girl. That must have cost you a great deal to admit."

"Not as much as once." He pushed the tea away. "If it's a new house you fancy, I'll agree to setting you up somewhere in England, Claire. No more. And your reputation will take a beating if our agreement ever becomes public knowledge."

"Then we will keep it private," she said. "I'm a longtime friend of the family, who is delighted to sponsor the new Lady Everard. That is all anyone need know."

He hoped it would be so easy. "So, we're agreed. A new wardrobe, a French maid and relocation in England at the end. Anything else?"

Her smile broadened. "Yes. If you'd be so good as to deliver the mirror in the sitting room to Mr. Devizes, I think I might be ready to journey to Cumberland to meet your cousin by this time tomorrow."

Richard blinked. "Cumberland? Why would you go to Cumberland?"

"To meet your cousin, of course. To make sure she's ready."

"I planned to bring her to you after Easter."

Claire's smile was kind. "Nonsense. I've already sold the town house, and you just hired my cook. Where did you expect me to live until Easter, sir?"

He could only stare at her as she rose and collected the cup. "Now, then, go about your business. I shall see you on the morrow, and we will have several days to discuss matters on our way north."

Several days with Claire? Some part of him brightened at the thought, and he immediately squashed it. What was wrong with him? Lady Claire Winthrop was entirely too good at manipulating his feelings. If she could get him to agree to a new wardrobe, a French maid and a new house in the space of a quarter hour, what more would he end up conceding after several days in Claire's company?

And he still couldn't entirely believe she had agreed to help him, constrained circumstances or not. Besides, how had her circumstances become so constrained? Her father had been wealthy; he'd been the one to insist that Richard find a way to care for Claire in style. Richard had always assumed her late husband was wealthy, otherwise, why not fulfill her promise to marry Richard? Surely her father and husband had provided for her in their wills or arranged some marriage portion. Had she gone through the money in a year's time? Given their conversation, he could almost believe it.

But worse was the idea of what she might do to his purpose and plans. Over the last ten years, he'd navigated through waves as high as mountains, defended his cargo from bloodthirsty pirates and steered a convoy of merchant ships safely through treacherous passages. Yet, thrilling as those adventures had been, the idea of being with Claire the next few days thrilled him more.

And that fact concerned him greatly.

Chapter Four

Richard had little time to consider his feelings as he left Claire's town house. He stopped at Everard House only long enough to leave his greatcoat and issue instructions about their plans to journey to Cumberland. He'd have to deal with Claire's requirements later. Right now, he had another commission to complete before he left London.

His older brother Jerome and younger cousin Vaughn, who with him stood to inherit a fortune from their late uncle once Samantha successfully navigated her first Season, had pressed him to contact the Marquess of Widmore.

"The last note from Uncle said the marquess would know why he fought that duel the night he died," Vaughn had insisted when the three met in the library of Dallsten Manor before Richard headed south. "Widmore can help us track Uncle's killer."

"And determine who else knows our secrets," Jerome had reminded Richard. There was a new light in his brother's blue eyes, a new surety in his step, now that he'd married his Adele. Richard envied him that.

"I cannot feel comfortable sending Samantha to

London," Jerome had added, "until I know what she's facing."

Richard had agreed. Ever since their uncle's death, when the three of them had learned about Samantha's existence, more and more secrets had come to light, like a flotilla of ships appearing out of a fog, and he didn't think they had faced the last.

His uncle, Arthur, Lord Everard, had lived by his own rules and only late in life had realized the importance of family and faith. He had attempted to make up for his previous misdeeds by leaving the considerable Everard legacy—which included lands in six counties, sizeable investments in the Exchange and a fleet of sailing ships—to his daughter Samantha, with generous bequests to Jerome, Richard and Vaughn, which they could receive only when they had helped their new cousin enter Society.

Launching a lass wouldn't be so daunting in other circumstances, Richard was sure. But the rumors surrounding Samantha's birth and upbringing would be enough to set tongues wagging. The way his uncle had hidden her and her mother away, in the north of England, would raise questions about Samantha's legitimacy. Yet Jerome had found a marriage certificate from Gretna Green in Scotland that indicated that her mother and Uncle had legally wed.

Still, questions remained. Why had his uncle kept his daughter a secret from the rest of the family and Society until his death? Why had he fought a duel the last night of his life without having one of his nephews act as his second, as was customary as well as his habit? And why had one of Samantha's servants recently endangered Jerome's life to steal a porcelain box that had been emptied of its contents?

All roads of inquiry had eventually led back to the

Marquess of Widmore. But Richard wasn't even sure the powerful lord would see him. Though the marquess had been a good friend of the family, he and Lord Everard had seen little of each other of late, according to Vaughn, as if their uncle had distanced himself from the fellow in the last months of his life. And Richard hadn't seen the man since starting on his most recent sea voyage two years ago.

Besides, the marquess's schedule would be full of appointments and social events. He wasn't likely to find time for a sea captain he hadn't seen for years. But at least Richard could leave his card.

He glanced at the pearly rectangle as he climbed to the door of the ornate stone house set off from the street. *Captain Richard Everard,* the card read, the letters embossed. Like the marquess, Richard was the ruler of all he surveyed, but his power extended only to his ship. There, he was used to relaying orders, having them followed without question. Funny how one look from Claire made him feel like a schoolboy again, staring across a crowded ballroom at the most beautiful girl in all of London and hoping she might notice him.

"Sir?" the footman asked, brows drawn down under his powdered wig. Richard hadn't even heard the door open, much less remembered knocking.

He straightened to his full height, looking down at the black-clad fellow, and boomed in his most commanding tone, "Captain Richard Everard to see the Marquess of Widmore."

The footman accepted his card with a respectful bow. "Please wait inside, Captain Everard, while I determine whether his lordship is at home to visitors."

Richard followed him into the house and glanced about as the footman made his stately way up the stairs. The entry hall was tall, with pale blue walls rising to a veined dome of glass in the ceiling. Already the light was fading with the afternoon. On one wall hung a massive oil painting of sailing ships in the middle of a battle, cannons coughing smoke.

Richard shook his head. The artist was clearly in love with the idea of the sea but had never sailed. No captain would waste powder on the air, the target already past. And the flying flags should be pointed in the same direction as the sails. But then, he'd seen sailing as just as romantic when he'd headed out as a youth.

He clasped his hands behind the back of his brown wool coat and balanced on the balls of his booted feet. Standing about, riding in carriages, felt odd after so many days at sea. At times he missed the order of things; at others he was glad for the good food, a company that included women. Even the sounds of London were different from the roll of the sea, the calls of his crew at work. Here in the house, someone was playing the piano, with a great deal more precision than his cousin. The scent of a woman's cologne, sweet and flowery, hung in the still air.

Claire hadn't been wearing any cologne. He snorted at how easily his mind returned to thoughts of her. She'd always smelled of roses before. The scent had reminded him of the formal gardens his mother had enjoyed at Four Oaks in Derby, the estate where he'd been born. But then, perhaps he'd always wanted to associate Claire with thoughts of home.

"Everard," the marquess called, descending the stairs with a lively step, as if he'd kept the prince waiting and not the nephew of an old friend. "Good to see you."

Richard shook the hand the lord offered as he drew near. He was a little surprised to find that the marquess's hair had gone all white, kept back in a queue like Vaughn's. He looked a little leaner than Richard remembered as well, in his dove-gray coat and black breeches, as if the weight of his responsibilities had worn him thin.

But his grip remained firm and strong as his gray eyes regarded Richard solemnly. "A shame about your uncle. A bit of color left the world the day he died."

"Thank you, my lord," Richard replied, releasing his hand. "And that's what brought me to your door. Do you have a moment for private conversation?"

The marquess frowned. "Certainly. This way."

He led Richard down the silk-draped corridor. As they passed the open door to what was obviously a music room, Richard caught sight of a young lady with close-cropped chestnut curls and a scowl of determination on her lovely face.

"My daughter, Lady Imogene," the marquess offered as if he'd noticed Richard's look. He made no move to introduce them formally. "Join me in the library, if you please."

Richard followed him into the next room. The library was paneled in satinwood; built-in bookcases with leaded-glass fronts lined opposite walls. Oriental carpets ablaze with color lay across the polished-wood floor. The marquess went to a straight-backed settee by a wood-wrapped fireplace and took a seat, nodding to Richard to sit on one of the Egyptian-style chairs across from him.

"Now then," he said, "what can I do for you, Everard?"

Richard braced both hands on the thighs of his tan breeches. "My uncle left us a letter, apparently written the night he died."

"Oh?" the marquess said. He leaned back as if making himself comfortable, but Richard could see the tension in him, like a sail stretched against the wind. Had he known about the letter?

"In it," Richard continued, watching him, "he advised

that if we questioned anything about his death, we should apply to you for answers."

His lordship raised his silvery brows. "How extraordinary. But I would assume you would know more than I would. Which of you seconded him that night?"

"That's one of the things we find questionable, my lord. He didn't ask any of us to second him. The first we knew of the duel was the physician returning with his body."

He leaned forward, eyes narrowing. "And did this physician have nothing to report?"

"Nothing of use to us. He claimed he'd been retained by my uncle's valet to oversee the duel, but he didn't even know the name of the fellow Uncle fought. And Uncle's valet has never returned to the house."

"Naturally you've made inquiries."

Richard inclined his head. "Naturally. But the fellow's gone to ground. We had business in the north, so we haven't been able to investigate further until now."

A smile thinned the marquess's lips. "In the north? Then I suppose you've finally met your cousin Samantha."

Richard nodded. "I understand you knew about her long before we did."

He spread his hands before his tastefully embroidered waistcoat. "Your uncle and I were once closer than brothers. I knew all about his marriage to that Cumberland girl, and why he chose to keep her daughter a secret."

"Oh?" Richard cocked his head. "Then tell me, for I confess, the need for it eludes me."

His smile softened. "Oh, come now, Captain Everard. You know how many adventures your uncle survived by the skin of his teeth. Having a daughter watching would have made life far messier."

That he could not deny. "He could have told us."

"He could have. He chose not to. Only you can determine the reason."

Richard didn't like the implication that he, his brother and Vaughn were somehow a threat to Samantha. "Then you know nothing of the duel itself."

"Alas, your uncle ceased confiding in me a while ago. I suspect he was converted to that evangelical nonsense Wesley used to preach."

Richard had heard of the minister who had at times fought the established Church of England to ensure that all who wished to know Christ might be saved, but he found it difficult to associate the devoted preacher with his uncle.

"Uncle wasn't known for his piety," he replied.

"It seems you've been at sea too long, Everard. Things change." He rose. "Now, if you have no other questions, I have more pressing matters to address."

Richard rose as well. "Only one question, my lord. Have you ever employed a servant with the last name of Todd?"

The marquess frowned. "Todd? The name doesn't sound familiar, but he may have worked on one of my estates. Why do you ask?"

"He recently left our employ and took something of value along with him. His letter of reference said you'd been his previous employer."

"A liar as well as a thief, it seems," the marquess replied with a sad smile. "I'll mention the fellow to my steward, but I doubt anything will come of it. Give my regards to your brother and the new Lady Everard." He started for the door.

"I will," Richard promised, following him, "but you'll likely see them yourself soon enough. Samantha is coming to London for her Season."

He stilled and glanced back at Richard, gray eyes

thoughtful. "Is she indeed? Do you think that advisable? After all, I imagine she's grieving the loss of her father."

"Of course she is," Richard acknowledged, choosing his words with care. He didn't dare trust anyone, not Claire, not even the marquess, with their family secrets. "But you know Uncle. He couldn't abide any sadness. He intended her to come out this Season, and she's determined to honor his wishes."

Widmore shook his head as if doubting the wisdom of the approach. "Surely you could dissuade her, Everard. I cannot think it seemly."

Richard imagined the marquess was used to instant obedience, too, but he obviously didn't know Samantha well. And he couldn't appreciate how much depended on her meeting the requirements of the will.

"I fear she has her heart set on it," Richard replied, with a shrug to show the matter was out of his hands.

The marquess's lean face tightened, but his manners were too good to allow him to show his pique otherwise. "I certainly hope you've found someone to sponsor her properly, then. Imogene is about to start her second Season, with a ball tonight, and I don't know how her mother manages. You have no such lady, if I remember correctly."

"You're right," Richard said, "but an old friend has agreed to help."

He cocked his head. "Anyone I know?"

"Lady Claire Winthrop." Odd that the name felt easier to say than it had earlier.

The marquess straightened. "Excellent choice. She's an exceptional female. I knew her husband. But isn't she still in mourning, or do you plan to challenge that, too?"

Richard wasn't sure what he was asking or how much he remembered of Richard's courtship ten years ago, but he wasn't about to claim a courtship now. "I understand her mourning will end just before the Season starts in earnest."

"Ah," he said, "well, I wish you all the best of luck."

Richard somehow thought they'd need it.

The marquess excused himself, and Richard followed the footman waiting outside the library toward the front door, passing the music room again as they went. Lady Imogene had evidently finished practicing; she was arranging her music neatly on the stand. She must have heard his boots on the floor, for she glanced up and offered him a kind smile.

Now, why couldn't he be interested in a woman like that? True, she was some years his junior, perhaps nineteen years old, if memory served. But she was lovely and talented and seemed to have a pleasant disposition with no sign of pretensions, if her smile was any indication. Considering her father's affection for the Everard family, Richard might even be able to convince him to allow Richard to court her. There was only one problem.

She wasn't Claire.

As he left the town house, he sighed. The weather was fair, his tasks nearly accomplished, but his spirits remained dismal.

Lord, I thought I'd put this behind me. I thought I'd forgiven and forgotten. Now a short time in her company, and all the old emotions come back to plague me.

The peace he'd hoped would flow from his prayer eluded him. Perhaps he was meant to act instead. He'd swept Claire from his mind before; he could do so again. They had a bargain, nothing more. He wasn't offering her his heart this time. The only promise between them was to see Samantha safely through her Season. That was where his duty lay.

He ran several more errands, including commissioning an interior decorator, before returning to Everard House to learn that the mirror had been delivered. But that information wasn't the only thing waiting for him.

"What's this?" he asked, as their most recent butler handed him a piece of paper. Mr. Marshall had only been working for them a few months. He was tall but thin, with thick, graying hair. He reminded Richard of the mops his crew used to swab down the deck, except for that hook nose and a disapproving mouth.

"I believe that is a receipt from a dressmaker, Captain Everard," he replied now, as they stood in the wide entryway of the Everard town house.

"So it would seem," Richard replied, glancing at it again and feeling staggered by the sum. "But somehow I don't see you in apricot silk."

"Certainly not, sir." That formidable nose was in the air. "I believe the gowns are for a certain person of the female persuasion." He wiggled his bushy gray brows up and down.

Richard attempted to hand the bill back to him. "If Uncle arranged this before he died, I fail to see how it's my problem. Send the bill to our solicitor. If Caruthers refuses to pay it, Uncle's lady friend is out of luck."

Mr. Marshall cleared his throat. "I believe, sir, that the lady is a particular friend of yours."

Claire.

All his good intentions sailed out to sea. They'd had a bargain, true, but somehow he'd thought he'd be the one to manage the funds. She would suggest items to be purchased; he'd graciously agree or send her out for more reasonable alternatives. Yet, once again, Claire had taken matters into her own hands without waiting for him.

Richard stared at the bill. "Five hundred pounds! She spent five hundred pounds in one afternoon?"

"Actually, sir, I believe that's just the first installment. See the note?" His finger, looking boney even through his white gloves, pointed to words at the base of the bill. "The other half will be due in a fortnight when the dresses are delivered."

Richard snatched his tricorne off the hall table and clapped it on his head. "Then perhaps those dresses won't be delivered. I'll have words with the lady immediately. Don't expect me until late, Mr. Marshall. And there had better not be a bill waiting for a new carriage!"

Chapter Five

Claire could not help but feel pleased with her afternoon. Not too many Society ladies, she was sure, could have accomplished so much in so little time. Already she'd written to Monsieur Chevalier to ask him to travel to Cumberland to teach Lady Everard to dance. He had returned a note with his regrets, explaining that he was already committed elsewhere, but she was certain she could find a way to change his mind. She'd also interviewed two maids and accepted a young lady, who would return this evening to start her position and pack Claire's things for the trip to Cumberland.

Sadly, the current dresses were black, but Claire took heart that her new wardrobe was on its way, courtesy of one of the most coveted dressmakers in London. Madame Duvall took commissions by appointment only. That she'd cleared her schedule to see Claire this afternoon was a mark of Claire's continued standing on the *ton*.

"And the apricot silk," Claire had said as she wandered through the shop, "for the day dress." She ran her finger along a counter covered with frothy laces and shiny satin ribbons. Madame Duvall's establishment was designed to appeal to elegance, with walls papered in pale pink and white, dainty white chairs for customers, and the largest standing looking glass in London, strategically positioned in one corner. The room always smelled of lavender.

"Your ladyship has exceptional taste," the plump modiste murmured, making notes in pencil in a little clothbound book. Her shrewd brown eyes glanced up. "May I recommend the emerald satin as well?"

Claire eyed the expensive fabric draping the nearest dressmaker's form. "Too dark. I am quite tired of darkness. The sprigged muslin for the morning dress."

"Exquisite," she agreed, making another notation. Her bronze skirts rustled as she followed Claire toward the drawers holding buttons and embroidery floss. "I cannot tell you how pleased I am that you will be staying with us in London this Season, Lady Winthrop. You were planning to leave for Italy, were you not?"

Claire kept her smile hidden as she fingered a poppy-colored skein of floss. She'd long ago learned that the French émigrée charged outrageous sums for her creations, all the while conducting a lucrative side business feeding tidbits of her clients' lives to the gossip sheets. "Well, of course I had to stay," she told the woman. "I couldn't disappoint dear Lady Everard."

She recognized the sharp light in Madame's brown eyes. "Oh, *non, non,*" the dressmaker said, as if she hadn't just heard the Everard title used for a woman for the first time in thirty years. She licked her coral-colored lips. "I do hope I shall have the pleasure of gowning her ladyship."

Oh, but she was good at fishing. "My dear Madame Duvall," Claire said, turning to her with a gracious smile, "would I take the girl I am sponsoring anywhere else? I'll bring her to see you as soon as we return from her winter home in Cumberland. What do you have for Brussels lace?"

Claire smiled now as she hung her pelisse in the closet under the stairs. By this time tomorrow, half of London would know a new lady was coming to town, and Claire would be bringing her out in style. Richard should be quite pleased.

Someone slammed the knocker into her front door. Claire stiffened. Not another dun! How many more of those bill collectors would she have to bear? She'd been stunned when the first fellow had arrived, bills in hand, oily smile on his narrow face.

"Your husband promised payment but, sadly, was unable to provide remuneration before his untimely death. And your solicitor seemed to think there were no funds to be had." His smile had broadened, revealing crooked, yellowing teeth. "I was sure you'd see reason."

Of course she'd seen reason. She'd always found the aristocracy's willingness to ignore bills appalling. God had blessed them with resources. They should not withhold such resources from people who had given service. Besides, what would her neighbors and acquaintances think if men like this kept showing up at her door? She'd paid the first few bills out of her pin money, what was left of it. But as the debts mounted, she'd been forced to take other measures.

She squared her shoulders and marched to the door. She'd let Jones go this afternoon, with a glowing recommendation she could only hope would help the footman find other employment. She had nothing left to pay this new challenge but her mourning clothes, and she was ready to give them away.

She pulled open the door, and Richard barreled into her house. It had begun to rain, and the drops clung to his greatcoat, peppered his russet beard with silver. She had to clench her fists to keep from reaching up to brush them away.

"Did you even wait until I was down the street before spending my money?" he demanded.

How rude! Claire shut the door with shaking hands. "Moderate your tone, if you please. I'm certain you would not want my neighbors to think you had me under your protection."

He turned to face her. "I will moderate my tone, madam, when you offer me an explanation."

Claire raised her chin. "I believe you are referring to the gowns I commissioned this afternoon. Clothing takes time, sir. I thought you'd prefer that I make the most of yours. Surely you wouldn't want Lady Everard sitting at home for her first two weeks in London, waiting on me."

"Perhaps not," he allowed, though the stiffness in those broad shoulders told her that he was not mollified. "But a thousand pounds, Claire!"

She spread her hands. "I told you fripperies do not come cheap. If it makes you feel better, know that I plan to spend twice that on your cousin."

"Twice!" He yanked his hat from his head, disheveling his hair. "Madam, strike your colors!"

Claire raised her brows. "I will not pretend I know that expression. But I stand by my plans. If you want the girl to be a success, you must do things correctly. I can explain the entire process on our trip north tomorrow. Now, if you'll excuse me, I need to change. My carriage will be here shortly."

He stared at her. "I knew it! You *did* buy a carriage!"

"Certainly not. I meant the carriage I hired to take me out this evening. I must keep a promise to a friend."

His eyes narrowed, and he took a step toward her, glaring down at her. She imagined the sailors on his ship would quake at the sight. "Friend?" he asked, voice low and deceptively calm. "What friend?"

She felt the polite face slipping into place again. Habit. It had seen her through Winthrop's drunken tirades, his denials the day after that he could ever be less than a gentleman. For ten years, she'd been at one man's beck and call; for seventeen years before that, she had done her father's bidding. She was not about to let herself be put in that position ever again.

She tilted back her head to meet his gaze, so dark, like the sky on a stormy night. "You did not purchase a slave, Captain Everard. I promised to bring out your cousin for a reasonable compensation. I did not give you permission to question my acquaintances."

"We have an agreement, madam. I have the right to know whose company you keep. I will not have your behavior reflecting poorly on Samantha."

Another woman might have felt slapped by his words, but she'd taken harder blows. Claire turned and reached for the door. "I believe you've made a mistake," she said. "If you leave now, you might find another lady to serve as sponsor. I suggest you treat her with considerably more respect."

He frowned as if not understanding. "You're throwing me out?"

"Certainly not, Captain Everard," she said, opening the door. "I hope I am a better hostess than that. But London is rather thin of company as yet. If you want to find another sponsor, you'll have to start looking this very moment."

He sighed, shoulders coming down. "I don't want another sponsor. I want you." He swept her a bow. "Forgive me, Claire. I'm a jealous fool."

Jealous? He was jealous? She should take no pleasure in that ugly emotion, yet some part of her trembled with the knowledge that he might actually still care a bit for her. Immediately she chided herself. He couldn't care for her. Very likely he was only jealous of the time any friendship might take away from her attentions to his cousin. He knew nothing of what she'd become. Perhaps he was right to wonder about her associations.

"I will do my duty as sponsor," she promised. "Please trust that I have your cousin's best interests at heart."

He inclined his head. "Very well. I will hold you to your word."

He did not add *this time,* but she heard it nonetheless. "Good," she replied. "Now, I bid you good-night, sir."

He made no movement toward the door, where the sound of rain rose louder. Cool air rushed into the entry, chilling her.

"May I ask where you are going this evening?" His tone was considerably kinder, but she still could not like his interference.

"You may not."

"Cut line, Claire," he said with a sigh. "I'm only trying to determine whether I can join you."

Claire raised her brows. "Join me? You mean, you want to escort me to the ball?"

He made a face. "A ball, is it? Ah, well, I suppose I'd better get used to it, for Samantha's sake. Yes, if you'll have me. I'd be honored to escort you."

Did he have any idea of the ramifications of what he had suggested? A gentleman generally escorted a lady to a ball if he was considered a member of the family or intent on courting. Some in London would remember how she'd jilted him ten years ago. She knew what they would assume now that she was widowed, and he was still unmarried, from the gossip she'd heard. But she wasn't ready to be the object of the captain's courtship, even if that courtship was only a fiction in the minds of her friends.

"I'm attending Lady Widmore's ball," she told him. "If you don't already have an invitation, I sincerely doubt you will endear yourself to her by showing up at the door."

A light came to his eyes. "Widmore, eh? That shouldn't be a problem. Give me a few minutes to go home and change, then I'll return for you."

She peered closer, and he arranged his face in a charming smile that did not fool her. "She will expect you to dance, you know," Claire warned him. "A presentable gentleman cannot stand along the wall like a girl fresh from the country."

He laughed, and the sound warmed her. "Then I'll be fine. No one ever considered me a presentable gentleman." He bowed again. "I'll be back shortly." He dashed out into the rain.

Claire shut the door behind him and leaned against it. Feelings swirled around her like pigeons on the steps of Saint Paul's. A handsome gentleman wanted to escort her to a ball. She should be in alt. But having Richard beside her all night was a sure way to go raving mad.

How would she achieve her purpose when all she could think about were other balls, other nights when he'd refused to leave her side? The only thing that had mattered then was being together—listening to him talk of his dreams for glory, sharing her wishes to marry for love rather than position or wealth. How young she'd been! She felt as if she'd aged a lifetime.

And why was it men never saw the difficulties in their sweeping statements? So the Widmores would be no problem, eh? She knew his uncle had been a particular friend of the marquess, but one did not attempt to enter a ball uninvited. Perhaps she needn't worry after all; perhaps they'd simply refuse him entrance.

Claire shook her head as she made her way carefully up the stairs. Even after three years, the first turning still made her body clench in memory and set her knee to throbbing. She did her best to ignore it, continuing on up the marble flight for the chamber story, where Mrs. Corday was waiting to help her.

The cook curtsied as Claire entered the bedchamber that had been hers since her marriage. Stripped of most of its furnishings, save the great bed and her dressing table, the pale blue room felt no more welcoming than it had when it had been stuffed with fine woods, costly fabrics and delicate porcelain.

"I know more about baking than buttons," her cook murmured, as she helped Claire into the black evening gown she hoped would be suitable for the ball. The bodice was covered in black lace, and the back was gathered to spill from her shoulders in graceful folds. Had it been any other color, she might have delighted in it. Still, she was lucky Lady Widmore was an old friend and had been gracious about Claire's last-minute decision to attend, sent only this afternoon.

"Any fingers strong enough to knead bread are strong enough to fasten these infernal tapes," Claire replied. "And I thank you, so much, for all your help. I don't know what I would have done without you."

"There's strength, and then there's strength," Mrs. Corday said, stepping back to smile at Claire. "And you've strength aplenty, your ladyship, if you don't mind my saying. I've seen it."

She had indeed, but Claire didn't want to remember that dark day when her cook had had to intercede for

Claire's life. "We've been through a lot together. And I appreciate everything."

Mrs. Corday's eyes were bright with unshed tears. "That captain's a better man, your ladyship. I'd bet my life on it."

Claire merely smiled. She'd already bet her life on a man's character, and she'd nearly lost. She thanked Mrs. Corday again and sent the woman back to her other duties.

Claire's standing looking glass was long gone, so she bent to peer at herself in the glass on her dressing table. The square-cut neck of the gown demanded a necklace. A shame that in the last months she'd had to quietly sell every piece Winthrop had given her, just to pay bills. Even the jewelry box was gone. There was only one piece left, one she hadn't worn in ten years.

She slid open the little drawer on her dressing table and reached far to the back. The amber cross came out in her hand, its sterling chain turning dark with age. No more than an inch long, the stone glowed in her hand. She should have returned it when she'd accepted Winthrop's offer. But, like her memories, she simply couldn't part with it. Did she dare wear it now that Richard Everard had returned to her life? Would he see it as an admission that she still cared for him?

Very likely, he wouldn't notice or even care. He hadn't returned to her, not really. He was here merely because his cousin needed someone like her. If he'd known any other suitable lady, he would never have come knocking on Claire's door. When the Season was over, he would leave her life as quickly as he'd entered it. And she would be left with memories again.

Memories, and a chance for a future. She was certain he'd keep his word. If she brought his cousin out in style, she could lay claim to a house, some place snug and safe, anywhere in England. The bit she'd managed to save to purchase a cottage could go instead to keeping her clothed and fed. With a little garden, she might be able to eke out an existence. True, she'd forfeit her standing on the *ton,* but she'd gain security. She had to focus on that hope.

She fastened the chain around her neck, feeling the cool weight of the stone against her skin. She'd had a purpose for attending this ball tonight; she must look like a proper lady to achieve it, and the necklace would help. If Richard remembered the day he had given the cross to her, she would simply have to deal with his reaction.

And pretend her own didn't eclipse it.

Chapter Six

Claire had barely finished the last touches on her toilette when the knocker sounded again. This time, Mrs. Corday beat her to it. Claire was still descending the stair when the cook opened the door. The white-haired woman stared a moment, then bobbed a curtsy.

"Goodness, Captain Everard, sir. I barely recognized you!"

Claire felt the same way. Richard's reddish hair had been brushed nearly smooth and pomaded until it shined. His white cravat was spotless and elegantly tied. The black evening coat hugged his shoulders, just as the white satin breeches brushed his thighs. Gone were any vestiges of the eager boy she'd known. This was a gentleman born to command, accustomed to obedience.

But he could not expect hers. She raised her chin, determined not to be easily swayed.

"Even an old sea dog knows how to polish the brass before escorting an admiral, ma'am," he told Mrs. Corday with a smile.

Claire reached the bottom step. "Hardly an admiral, sir."

His gaze met hers, and the admiration in it nearly

stopped her progress. His smile broadening, he offered her a bow. "My mistake. Clearly royalty."

His tone was teasing, so she decided to take the statement as a compliment. "And dare I hope you managed some suitable conveyance as well?"

He stepped aside so she could see down to the street. "Will this do?"

Claire was at the door before she remembered moving. "Oh, Richard, she's a beauty! Where did you find her?"

"She belongs to my cousin Vaughn," he said, gazing down, with almost as much admiration as he'd shown her, at the sleek blue chariot and its pair of matching white horses. "It appears the Everards have a carriage after all. I'd offer to let you take the reins, but I wasn't sure you'd want to arrive at the ball in that sort of style."

And why was she so disappointed by that truth? She hadn't driven her own carriage since she'd married. Winthrop had always insisted on either driving his phaeton himself or having their coachman drive the larger carriage. At first, she'd thought he was merely being a gentleman, but he'd been aghast the day she'd asked to try her hand at his sporty carriage.

"My wife will not be seen behind a team of horses like some farmworker."

Even now the remembered contempt on his face cut her. She realized her hands were clenched at her sides and opened them. "Quite right," she said to Richard. "I've outgrown such antics."

For a moment, she thought she saw a disappointment matching her own flicker in his dark eyes. Then Mrs. Corday stepped forward with Claire's black velvet evening cloak. "You'll be needing this, your ladyship."

"Allow me," Richard said, and took the cloak from her

to drape it over Claire's shoulders. The brush of his hand against her cheek as he drew back was as soft as a caress.

Claire's fingers trembled as she fastened the cloak at her neck. She looked up in time to see him erase a frown from his face. The amber cross seemed to press against her skin. But if he'd noticed it before the cape had covered it, he made no mention of the fact as he took her arm and escorted her down to the carriage.

Lord, now what do I say to him? she prayed, as they sat beside each other on the leather seats. No ideas popped into her head, but she was thankful that Richard seemed just as indisposed to talk, as he gazed out the windows at the lighted town houses they passed. She was also thankful the ride to the Widmores' on Park Lane was mercifully quick, and the coachman was adept at maneuvering the chariot right up to the door.

Climbing out was always a gamble, and Claire prayed that her knee would oblige. But Richard stepped down first and fairly lifted her from the vehicle, his hands strong on her waist. She wasn't surprised to find all her limbs trembling as he led her to the door.

The Widmore home was large, with a full ballroom on the second story. Soon Claire was in the receiving line with Richard, their cloaks taken by a strapping footman, the finest of London society around them. Music drifted from the ballroom beyond, flowing down the stairs. Already the murmur of voices threatened to drown it out, so numerous were the guests in their satins and velvets.

Claire wasn't sure what to say about her escort to her friend Lavinia Devary, Lady Widmore, who stood with her husband and daughter outside the ballroom doors. All three were dressed in velvet, from the white of young Lady Imogene to the raisin-colored gown of her mother and the black coat of her father. As Claire and Richard approached, however, Lord Widmore spoke first. "Ah, Everard. I'm glad you sent that note about attending. You remember my dear wife and daughter?"

Richard bowed to the tall, slender, gray-haired woman standing on the lord's left and the curvaceous young lady with short-cropped curls beside her. "Ladies, a pleasure. I believe you all know Lady Claire."

Lady Widmore's blue eyes widened, but Claire groaned inwardly. As the daughter of an earl, Claire was entitled to style herself by her first name, but as a married woman, even now widowed, she should be using her husband's title. The Widmores had to know that, yet they murmured greetings like polite hosts, and only the marchioness's look told Claire that her friend expected a full accounting soon.

This would never do. Claire and Richard would be a seven-days wonder before she even introduced the idea that Lord Everard had a secret daughter.

"We must talk," Claire said to Richard, as he led her into the ballroom. Pale blue walls rose all around her, adorned by Grecian columns and potted palms in marble urns. Already the golden light from the twin crystal chandeliers was warming the air. She tugged on Richard's arm, and he followed her to a set of gilded chairs along one wall.

"A problem so soon?" he asked.

Claire smiled to an elderly couple who were promenading past. "We must decide what to tell people about this situation with your cousin if we are to use the gossip to our advantage."

He frowned. "What gossip?"

"The gossip that will start the moment everyone realizes that your brother did not assume the title." Claire leaned back in her chair, spreading her skirts around her.

"I planned my strategy for this ball, but I can see that your being here complicates matters."

"Strategy?" he asked, but a man drew up beside them just then. She recognized Sir Geoffrey Plantier's lanky frame and artfully tousled blond hair.

"Lady Winthrop!" he cried, fairly prancing in his dark evening clothes. "What a pleasure to see you! Dare I hope for the honor of a dance later?"

Claire knew what her response must be. "I regret that I am not quite out of mourning yet, Sir Geoffrey. But I'd be delighted to hear of your latest triumph on the Thames. Beat *The Falcon* by a full length, I hear."

"If you don't count the bow spit," he agreed with an embarrassed smile, slender cheeks flushing. "I'll return for you shortly, then."

"The Falcon?" Richard asked, as the baronet toddled away.

"A rival yacht," Claire assured him. "Sir Geoffrey was ecstatic about the win, according to *The Times*. Now, sir, our strategy. I came here tonight with an express purpose."

His look darkened. "I surmised as much. Who is he?"

Claire frowned. "I have no idea what you're talking about. Will you pay attention, please? We must make sure to meet as many people as possible and share the story of your cousin's tragic circumstances."

"Tragic circumstances? She just inherited a barony!"

Claire laid a hand on his arm. "And that will be enough to shock most people. Do you know how few lines can descend from a daughter, sir?" She released him. "Now then, I suggest we paint Samantha as an innocent, kept pure from the scandals your family so enjoys."

She thought he might choke, his look was so choleric. "My uncle didn't think of the consequences and didn't seem to mind the scandal that resulted. I assure you, the rest of the family has more restraint."

"Lady Winthrop!" The *ton*'s favorite dandy, Horace Hapheart, stood in front of them, hands on the hips of his pink-satin breeches. "What a surprise! We must have a nice, long coz!"

"We certainly must," Claire agreed with a ready smile. "I'll look for you at supper, shall I?"

He nodded so vigorously he nearly smashed his high, pointed collar. "Of a certainty! And I hear they're serving those lobster puffs you so enjoy."

"I shall look forward to sharing them with you, sir." As he dashed off to meet another friend, white coattails flapping behind him, she turned to Richard, only to find that his frown had turned to a scowl. "Your family is not at all in the common way," she told him, "and you know it. Your cousin Vaughn writes poetry that sets the town ablaze, and you were a privateer."

"Claire!" Lord Peter Eustace seized both her hands and bowed over them, every line of coat and breeches perfection. "My word, but I'm glad to see you out and about again. Say you'll partner me at whist. I so long to give Thurston and his set a drubbing like we did last year."

"She's taken," Richard snapped, rising and glaring down at the fellow. Lord Eustace dropped Claire's hands and scuttled away with a squeak of apology.

Claire patted the seat beside her. "And that is precisely why we must talk. You cannot go around pretending you own me. Like it or not, I am Lady Winthrop."

"*He* called you Claire."

He sounded like a little boy annoyed his older brother had been given a treat. "He is related to my late husband," Claire explained, "and I've known him for years."

"You've known me for years, too."

"I knew you years ago. There's a difference. And any number of people here will remember that tale if we give them cause. I prefer that they forget."

"I haven't."

The words were soft and sad. Something inside her wanted to cry over the matter as well. But she couldn't sit here, letting near strangers see her sob. *Lord, lend me Your strength.* She put on her polite smile.

"Be that as it may, Captain Everard, you have charged me with a task, and I intend to do it to the best of my ability. For now, I suggest you find some other lady and ask her to dance. Our hostess is bearing down on us, and I need to plant the seeds that will bring your cousin Samantha a rich harvest."

She was afraid he'd argue, but one look at Lady Widmore's determined face, and he stood and headed toward the opposite side of the room, for a group of older gentlemen who were, no doubt, discussing politics.

Lavinia dropped onto the chair he had vacated. She and Claire had met socially and, despite the differences in their ages, had taken to each other at once. "I cannot tarry, dearest," she said now. "I have too many duties as hostess. Quickly, tell me all! Why are you here with Everard? I thought you loathed the fellow!"

"Nonsense," Claire said with an airy wave, hoping to brush aside her past as easily. She went on to explain about Samantha. Lavinia was quickly in sympathy for the poor child, raised alone in the wilderness. So were any number of ladies with whom Claire shared the story as the night progressed. And of course, the gentlemen were ready to believe anything she said as she chatted and played whist and supped. Everything would have gone quite to her satisfaction, except for two gentlemen who did not behave as she expected.

The first was the Marquess of Widmore himself. Claire had known him through Winthrop, who had had visions of rising to a more prominent place in society. She'd wondered whether marriage to her might have been part of his plan. However, shortly before his death, her husband had refused to have anything to do with the marquess, saying that Widmore had odd notions for a nobleman. She wasn't sure what that meant, given what her husband considered normal.

She'd been raised by a father with strict propriety, and she'd certainly grown up trying to please him. But nothing had prepared her for her husband's lengthy list of requirements. Some she found easy to manage, like his desire for her to be a leader in fashion and a welcoming hostess. Others made her chafe. Lord Winthrop's wife was not supposed to have an opinion, it seemed, on politics. She wasn't even supposed to have an opinion on the opera or the latest book everyone was discussing, and certainly never an opinion that varied from his. Lord Winthrop's wife, in short, was supposed to have the character and usefulness of a pretty porcelain vase. Small wonder she'd nearly shattered under the weight of her marriage.

Lord Widmore was a refreshing change. He always treated her with respect and raised topics of conversation as if assuming she had every right to take part in the discussion.

"You're heading for Cumberland, I hear," he said now, falling into step with her as she returned to the ballroom from the card room, where she had helped Lord Eustace trump Lord Thurston. "With Everard, no less."

Claire nodded to a passing acquaintance. "A gentlemanly escort is useful when traversing the wilds."

"Or navigating the *ton*," the marquess acknowledged. "I should hate to see your generous nature put to the test."

Claire smiled at him. "Thank you for your concern, my lord, but I'm certain I will be fine."

"They are Everards, you know." When she looked him askance, he merely shrugged. "Much as I enjoyed Lord Everard's company, I know some consider his family a bit on the scandalous side. And there is, of course, the question about the girl's paternity."

Claire motioned him aside, closer to the pale blue wall and away from any other guests. "My lord, surely you don't malign an innocent child."

His eyes searched hers, as if trying to gauge her inner strength. "It is not her innocence that concerns me. There are issues here you cannot know, secrets the Everards are hiding from you. Are you certain you wish to associate yourself with that group?"

Secrets? Issues? Had Richard withheld information to gain her trust? Oh, those doubts were too easy to blossom, yet she could not risk all she'd tried to accomplish by giving in to them, especially not in front of the marquess, of all people.

"I am an old friend of the family," she said dutifully. "It's my pleasure to sponsor Lady Everard for her Season."

He looked less mollified than anyone to whom she had peddled the tale. "Then you are intent on helping them."

"Quite."

He surprised her by laying a hand on her arm, his long face serious. "If you need anything, if the girl needs anything, let me know. I can do that much for her father."

Claire swallowed as he withdrew his touch. "Thank you, my lord." She very nearly let him go, then realized she did need help, in one area. "There is something, a triviality."

His face was still as serious. "Name it."

"I want Monsieur Chevalier to teach her dancing. I believe your daughter benefited from his instruction."

He smiled then, as if he'd found the answer to his concerns. "Indeed she did. I'm sure I can offer incentive to send the fellow to you. Consider the matter settled."

The other gentleman, however, was not so easily appeased. Everywhere she went, whatever she was doing, Richard was watching. Her husband had always abandoned her the moment he could, preferring the card room or the company of his friends to hers. But tonight she was constantly aware that Richard stood nearby, never interrupting, never threatening, but always ready to do her a service. If he was hiding some dark secret, he didn't show it. His smile remained pleasant, his carriage confident.

He was the one who brought her a fan when the room proved heated. He was the one who found her and Horace Hapheart a table in the crowded supper room. And he was the one who sat at her side when she plopped down on a chair near the end of the night, exhausted.

"Ready to leave?" he asked.

Claire nodded with a sigh. "My task is accomplished."

"Is it?" He cocked his head. "I thought you had one more duty tonight—to dance with me."

Dread fell like a rock into her stomach, but she kept her smile in place. "But you haven't danced all evening."

His mouth turned up on one corner, as if he was pleased at the thought that she might have been watching him as well. "Perhaps I was waiting for the most beautiful woman in the room."

Claire made a show of glancing about. "Ah, I believe you are in luck. Lady Imogene is just releasing her current partner, and no one else has rushed forward yet, for once."

"Lady Imogene can dance with a monkey for all I

care," he said with charming conviction. "Partner me, Claire."

She couldn't. Oh, she couldn't! She'd longed to dance, to move with the music, to smile at her partner across the way in the pure joy of the moment. But she didn't dare trust herself, especially with Richard.

"I regret that I do not feel it proper for a lady in mourning to dance," she told him.

His smile was melting into a frown. "And aren't you planning to give up mourning when we return to London?"

"For your cousin's sake, certainly. I can't go about looking like an old crow if I'm sponsoring her."

"You don't even resemble a young crow," Richard said. "I've been patient. One dance is not too much to ask, madam."

Her mouth was dry. *Father, please! Make him give this up. You know why I can't dance.* Guilt poked at her for fending him off. "Unfortunately, I am quite fatigued. Will you be a dear and call for the carriage?"

He rose, and she nearly sighed with relief. But his puzzled look down at her told her he wasn't satisfied by her answer. "Very well, Lady Winthrop, I'll strike my colors and fetch you the carriage. But you're hiding something, and we have three long days ahead of us for me to discover what that might be. I only hope I can convince you to trust me enough to tell me the truth."

Chapter Seven

She's changed.

The thought kept running through Richard's mind as he saw Claire home and returned to Everard House for his own bed. Claire had always been popular; when he'd been courting her, at some balls he'd had to wade through suitors six deep to reach her side. Then she'd seemed entirely too aware of the power she held over them all; as little as a frown from her would take the wind from their sails. Tonight, she'd been gracious to everyone, from Widmore to the feckless Horace Hapheart. Was it all part of her plan to win them to Samantha's side, or had her proud heart truly softened?

Then there was the matter of her dancing. Claire had danced with a rare combination of joy and grace. He'd found it hard to take his eyes off her as she swung around him, and he'd never known her to sit out a set. Yet tonight she hadn't stepped onto the floor once. He simply couldn't believe she'd forgo the pleasure just to complete her so-called strategy. So, why refuse to dance with him? Was he still so repugnant to her?

He was still thinking about the ball when he left the house the next morning to complete his preparations for the trip north. Mr. Marshall, the butler, had agreed, uncommon gleam in his eyes, to hire more staff and prepare the house for Samantha's arrival, with the help of the decorator Richard had commissioned. Now Richard just had to see that Samantha reached London as planned.

He'd ridden from Cumberland, but he couldn't see Claire making the return journey that way. And Vaughn's chariot, though sporty, wasn't built for travel over long distances. So he hired a post chaise and postilion and made arrangements for changes of horses along the way.

His second task was more grim. At his brother's suggestion, he'd enlisted the aid of a Bow Street Runner to look into the disappearance of Repton, his uncle's valet, and the treacherous footman Todd, who had stolen from them and threatened Jerome and his wife. Richard had no reason to think the footman had returned to London, but the famed thief-takers associated with the Bow Street magistrate's office could travel anywhere in England, on request.

"I've found nothing on your valet," the runner reported that morning, when Richard met him at a public house near the office. A slight, older man with graying, curly hair and a lined face, he wore his red waistcoat, the badge of office, proudly. "But a fellow matching the description of your footman turned up."

"Oh?" Richard leaned closer across the top of the scarred wooden table. "Where?"

The runner cocked a grin. "He was found dead in a rooming house in St. Giles last night, shot through the heart. The constables felt it was a falling-out among thieves."

Richard could see why they'd make that assumption. The St. Giles area of London was rumored to be a cesspool of crime. Though Todd had stolen from them, Richard found it hard to imagine the footman falling so low. And why stay in the rookeries? With a priceless porcelain box to sell, he could have gone anywhere, in far better style.

"Confirm his identity and keep looking for Repton," Richard instructed, passing the fellow another twenty pounds for his efforts. "I'm heading to Cumberland this afternoon. Send word to me at Dallsten Manor in Evendale."

The runner had agreed, and they'd parted company. Richard was returning home via Piccadilly when he saw the man Claire had called Lord Eustace from the evening's ball strolling in his direction.

"Everard, isn't it?" the young lord asked, positioning himself so that Richard could not easily pass him. The way he swung his ebony cane told Richard the fellow was actually considering using it as a weapon.

"Captain Everard," Richard said, widening his stance.

Eustace nodded. "You seem a decent chap. See that you marry her this time. I'd hate to have to call you out." With a tip of his top hat, he passed and left Richard standing there.

What was that all about? Did the fellow actually think Richard was courting Claire? If so, then Eustace was dimmer than he looked. With a shake of his head, Richard continued on his way, but he'd hadn't even reached Hyde Park before he found Horace Hapheart blocking his path.

Today the dandy was dressed in a checked coat of red-and-white material that surely would have looked better draping the back of a horse. His shirt points were so high Richard wondered the fellow didn't poke himself in the eye. He had a sheet of newsprint in one paw and an eager look on his flabby face.

"Intent on capturing her heart, are you?" he asked with

a ready grin Richard might have appreciated on another occasion.

Richard impaled him with his captain's glower. "Have we been introduced, sir?"

Hapheart had the grace to redden. "Well, by your leave, I thought, as you were a particular friend of Lady Winthrop's…"

"And what," Richard said, "gave you that idea?"

Hapheart thrust the paper at him. "It's all there. You can't deny what's in print."

Against his better judgment, Richard took the cheap newspaper and glanced down at it. It was one of many scandal sheets sold on the street corners to entertain Londoners with too much time on their hands. One tidbit immediately caught his attention.

It appears our fair city will shortly be witness to a rarity—a fully grown baroness rising from the wilds of Cumberland. Lord E really was a naughty fellow, wasn't he?

If that wasn't disturbing enough, the item below it set his blood to boiling.

And the apple doesn't fall far from the tree. Captain E refused to leave the side of a certain widowed lady at Lady W's ball, importuning her for a dance, we have it on good authority. He was doomed to disappointment, for it seems the lady has learned her lesson when it comes to the captain's courtship.

He shoved the paper back at Hapheart. "Do not believe everything you read, sir."

"Oh, certainly, certainly," he chirped, pacing Richard

as he set off down the street. "Just last week they claimed I'd increased by two stone and it wasn't half that." He leaned closer. "Just tell me, do you plan to do the pretty this time?"

Richard stopped. "I refuse to discuss the lady."

Hapheart quailed. "Yes, yes. Normally I'd quite agree. But I've had a bit of bad luck at the tables, and I'd really like to get in on the wagers."

Richard frowned. "Wagers? What wagers?"

"The betting book at White's. Someone's already giving two-to-one odds you'll marry her in a fortnight." He must have seen Richard stiffen, because he ducked back and held up his hands in front of his paisley waistcoat as if to fend off a blow.

"Good day, Mr. Hapheart," Richard said. And he pushed past the dandy and left him behind.

This was why he hated London, Richard thought, as he returned home to watch his trunk being strapped onto the carriage he'd hired. All this intrigue, all this subterfuge, for what? Neither Hapheart nor any of the men who chose to waste their money betting on his future knew him or Claire. If they did, they'd understand why he'd never offer her marriage again.

He still remembered the day he'd emboldened himself to speak to her father the first time. He'd danced with Claire the night before at a ball, and she'd encouraged him.

"Do you think you could be happy with a seafaring man?" he'd asked at one point, when they'd promenaded around the room arm in arm, her rose-scented perfume teasing his nose.

Her smile up at him was tender. "I can be happy with you, Richard. I promise." Her pale eyes had sparkled like stars, and he had dared to reach for the heavens.

The very next day, he'd ridden his horse to their family

town house, an imposing edifice off Hyde Park, and followed the footman up a polished mahogany stair to a withdrawing room at the back of the house. Fine paintings graced the light green walls, ancient vases from China and Rome sat on alabaster pedestals, and white-marble statues gazed back from alcoves and corners.

The man sitting in a leather-bound chair near the center of the room regarded Richard just as thoughtfully and still. The earl didn't even extend a hand as Richard approached him across the thick Aubusson carpet, and his gray eyes showed no emotion as Richard stammered out his request for permission to offer for Claire.

"And why," the earl had said, steepling long fingers in front of his gray coat and making Richard feel even more like a student brought before the headmaster for stealing, "should I give you my greatest treasure?"

Then, Richard could only agree with the man that Claire was a pearl beyond price, and he would do anything to have her at his side. Now he couldn't help wondering whether her father had counted her in the same category as his other priceless pieces of art.

"Because I love her," Richard had said, standing tall. Even at seventeen, he'd been able to look over the heads of most men, including Claire's father, had the earl deigned to rise from the chair. "With me, you'll always know your daughter is honored and respected. I will care for her and protect her all the days of my life."

"Fine words," Claire's father had said in that cool voice, face stiff. "But I hear nothing of support. You are not the heir to the Everard legacy, are you?"

Richard swallowed. "No. My brother holds that distinction."

"Then you must have some bequest through your mother's line."

"A small one," Richard acknowledged, thinking of the house in the corner of the Four Oaks estate that his mother had intended for him should he decide not to go to sea.

"A small one." The earl stood, and somehow Richard felt shorter. "I'm afraid you do not know my daughter as well as you ought, Mr. Everard. A small inheritance will never satisfy Claire. If you have no other means of supporting her, this conversation must be at an end."

He started forward to pass Richard for the door. Desperate, Richard darted in front of him. "My uncle hopes to charter a privateer against the French. I could apply for the crew and a share of the prize money."

The memory of the earl's distant, polished smile, so like the one Claire had worn yesterday, still chilled him. "Very well, Mr. Everard. Return with a fortune, and my daughter's hand is yours."

He'd returned with a fortune, two years later, to find that Claire's hand was already firmly in her husband's. Neither Claire nor her father had seen fit to honor their promises. Richard had used the money to outfit his own ship, as a merchant vessel. And he'd refused to give his heart again, especially to a woman like Claire.

Claire could hardly wait for the carriage to arrive that afternoon. Everything was going as she'd planned. Monsieur Chevalier had sent word this morning that his other commitment would be met sooner than expected, and he would be joining them in Cumberland within the week. The Marquess of Widmore truly was a man of his word.

And thank You, Lord, for working for the good of those who love You.

She felt as if she was following His lead instead of

her own for once. Surely that would make a difference in her life.

She was leaving London, as she'd planned, but instead of hiding away in the back of beyond, she would return for one more Season, to sponsor a girl who needed her help. She'd made so many mistakes her first Season. She felt as if the Lord was giving her a chance to help another avoid those disasters.

She'd never been blessed with children, but perhaps she could show her love to Samantha Everard. She could imagine the girl listening raptly to Claire's advice as Claire dressed her in pretty clothes and taught her how to look beyond circumstances to character. What fun they'd have planning her coming out.

She was so eager to leave that everything was ready when Richard arrived. Thanks to her new maid, Josette Mercier, Claire's clothes were packed and the amber cross was tucked into her reticule for safekeeping. A neighbor had agreed to hold the key for the solicitor to pick up for the new owner. Claire even had a new hairstyle under her black satin-lined bonnet.

"Madame has such pretty hair, *oui?*" the diminutive maid had said that morning when she'd come to wake Claire with the last of the bohea on a tray. "She should wear it softer, *non?* A few curls here and here to bring out the eyes, *oui?*"

"Yes," Claire had acknowledged with a smile at the way the dark-haired girl made every declaration a question.

There was nothing questioning about Richard, however. He took command the moment he stepped down from the coach. Gone was the elegant gentleman from the night before. His brown wool coat was practical, his boots below his tan breeches scuffed from long wear. He hadn't donned a hat, but then Claire doubted he'd have been able to wear it, tall as he was, inside the carriage he'd brought with him.

Claire was a little disappointed they wouldn't be taking the chariot to Cumberland, but she knew the yellow post chaise with its shiny black trim was built for travel. A postilion, an older man of slight build, was already astride the lead horse; he tipped his white hat to Claire as she descended the stairs from the house. The yellow waistcoat peeking out from his blue jacket exactly matched the color of the coach.

Claire thought he might help load her bags onto the rear of the chaise, but it appeared he needed to stay with the horses, for when she explained that her footman was gone, Richard stripped off his coat and ported her trunks and bandboxes down the stairs to the carriage himself. She thought the grimace on his face might have something to do with the number rather than the weight, which he seemed to bear effortlessly on his broad shoulders.

He raised his brows only when Mercier made her dainty way past him, a small travel case in her hands.

"You agreed to a French maid," Claire reminded him as he put a hand to her elbow to help her into the carriage.

"I didn't think she'd come with us to Cumberland," he replied, stepping back to shrug into his coat. A moment later, the carriage rocked as he climbed in. He took one look at Claire and the maid sitting side by side on the front-facing seat, then pulled down the catch that held an extra rear-facing seat for himself. Somehow Claire thought he hadn't intended to spend the journey on the narrow, ill-padded bench.

"Surely you didn't expect me to travel for weeks alone with you?" she said.

"Weeks?" He twisted to wave at the postilion through

the wide front window. "We'll reach Dallsten Manor in under four days, madam, or I'll know the reason why."

As the postilion called to his horses and the coach set off, Claire smiled at the goggle-eyed maid beside her. "I expect we'll hear a great deal of bluster from Captain Everard between here and Cumberland. He can't seem to help himself."

"As your ladyship says, *oui?*" Mercier avoided Richard's frown and busied herself with pulling out some sewing from her case.

He sighed. "I beg your pardon, both of you. This will be a long journey, by anyone's reckoning. I'll do what I can to make it easier for you."

His smile was kind, and Claire felt herself smiling back. "Ah, but even weeks isn't such a long journey for a sea captain, I'm sure. Your travels kept you from England for years."

As soon as she said the words, she wanted to call them back. They reminded her of the years that had separated them, forever. But he didn't seem to notice her lapse.

"That much is true," he said, voice warm against the squeaks of the carriage frame, the rattle of tack. He shifted in the seat as if trying to find a comfortable position. "It's funny how you can sail all over the world, and still long for one glimpse of the green fields of England."

Claire settled herself into her seat, too, the well-used leather conforming to her body, her leg at the best angle to avoid a mishap. "Equally odd that one can spend a lifetime in England, dreaming of being elsewhere. Tell me about your travels. I've wondered where you were, what you were doing."

Lord, help me, please. What is wrong with me? That statement to Richard was even worse than her first blunder. She'd made it sound as if she'd been longing for him!

But Richard didn't seem to find her request improper. He launched into a series of tales that soon had her thoroughly engaged. Listening, she fancied she could hear the wind howling in the rigging, the calls of his sailors as they scrambled about the deck, the clash of cutlasses when they met the enemy. Oh, how marvelous to see the flash of bright plumage on exotic birds in strange lands, to inhale the sweet scent of honeysuckle, the dusky aroma of cinnamon. What she wouldn't have given to have traveled to all those places with him.

Immediately guilt tore into her. She'd traded those dreams for what she'd thought was more real at the time—stability and security. Lord Colton Winthrop had had the lineage Richard lacked, the wealth Claire had been raised to expect. He had been dashing and handsome, and her father had pressured her to make a match of it. She'd agreed, and lived with her regret for the next ten years.

She'd wanted her marriage to be a partnership. She'd known she wasn't in love with Lord Winthrop, but she'd hoped whatever feelings they had for each other would grow into love, or at least a comfortable companionship. Instead, it seemed her husband would be satisfied with nothing less than the complete obliteration of the woman he'd married. The very traits she thought others might prize in her—her intelligence, her wit, her spontaneity—he found abhorrent. For a short time, she was ashamed to admit to anyone, she had tried to conform, tried to be a soft little dormouse who meekly acquiesced to her husband's demands. But she'd felt herself being chipped away, little by little, and something inside her had protested.

Thank You, Lord, for that!

She was fairly certain there were men on the *ton* who

were capable of appreciating their wives, who treated their spouses with something approaching admiration and equality. She had every intention of helping Samantha Everard tell the wheat from the chaff. Claire, however, wasn't ready to try her hand again. Perhaps she'd never be ready. She would keep her promise and bring Lady Everard out, but her heart would stay safely hidden. And nothing Richard Everard could say would change that.

Chapter Eight

By evening, they'd reached Dunstable in Bedfordshire, an area of fairly flat farmland, the fields plowed for planting. The half-timbered Bull Inn was just off the London Road, and the many fine carriages thronging its wide, cobbled coaching yard gave testament to its popularity. Richard escorted Claire and her maid inside and made the arrangements with the friendly innkeeper, securing a large bedchamber at the top of the house for the two women, with a private parlor adjoining it, and another room for himself down the corridor.

They gathered a short while later in their parlor. Paneled in warm oak, with elaborate carvings over the fireplace and door, the room made Claire feel settled. Even the carved-back chairs proved welcoming as she and Richard sat at a heavy-legged table to eat. Richard seemed to have thought of everything. He gave Claire the best place by the fire and served her first from the spiced mutton the innkeeper provided. He kept her glass and her plate so full she finally had to wave him away.

"Practicing for your cousin?" she teased him, when the maid had gone to return the empty dishes and tray to the kitchen.

He stretched long legs to the red glow of the fire, and his satisfied sigh, she thought, came more from the ability to relax after the cramped quarters of the coach than from the innkeeper's hospitality.

"I could use the practice," he said. "It's been a long time since I participated in the Season."

"We'll give you plenty of opportunities to help," Claire promised. "Your cousin will need an escort and a gentleman to attend her when she has male callers. Given your description of her, I imagine the door knocker will rarely be silent."

To her surprise, his look darkened. "You're probably right, though the scandal sheets didn't help."

Claire frowned. "Was there something in the papers about Lady Everard already?"

"Just rubbish," he said.

Claire braced her hands on the table. "Rubbish or not, I need to know, if I'm to protect her."

A smile tickled the corner of his mouth as he glanced up at her. "Since when were you the protector?"

Claire blinked. An excellent question. Yet the idea that the wretched scandal sheets would dare to print anything derogatory about her protégée was the outside of enough. She had such hopes for this Season! But surely Richard wouldn't understand.

"Well, perhaps *protect* is too strong a word," Claire allowed, pulling back her hands to fold them in the lap of her black wool gown. "But make no mistake, Richard. We must watch out for her. The Season can be a dangerous place for an untried girl."

"Now you sound like Samantha." He rose to go to the fire, strong fingers wrapping around the brass handle of the poker.

Claire watched as he stirred up the coals. "You said

she is anxious about her Season. Is she so shy and retiring then?"

He snorted as he returned the poker to its place. "There isn't a shy bone in her body."

"Then why dread the Season?"

He kept his gaze on the fire and shifted on his feet, as if weighing his answer. Oh, there was a story here as well; she could feel it. Had Lord Widmore been right? Was there some secret surrounding Samantha Everard?

"She's lived in Cumberland all her life," he said. "London will be different."

"Certainly," Claire acknowledged, a little disappointed in his answer. "Though most girls I knew couldn't wait to trade the country for the city. The shops, the assemblies are far superior."

"You would know."

There was an edge to his voice she could not like. Did he think her such a flibbertigibbet that shopping and dancing were all that mattered to her? "Come now, sir, you cannot disagree. You know that the museums, the theater, the art and science exhibitions in London eclipse anything else in the empire. You've been all over the world. Your cousin's manor in Cumberland, however grand, cannot hold a candle to a city the size of London."

"Dallsten Manor is a decent country house," he replied, grudgingly, she thought, "but you're right that London has more to offer by way of diversions."

"And I shall show her each one, I promise. She will be so happy, she'll never want to leave."

He turned then and met her gaze. "If that happens, we shall have words, madam."

Claire leaned back at his vehemence. "So you expect your little country mouse of a cousin to remain unchanged by her time in the city? Odd. Most families hope that their daughters will gain some sophistication during a Season."

"Samantha needs no town bronze. She's perfect the way she is."

Claire smiled. "Spoken like a doting older cousin."

He strode around the table to her side. "Make no mistake, Claire. I will not have you making Samantha into a copy of you. If that is your intention, I will return you to London tomorrow."

Claire's face tightened, her spine stiffened, and Richard regretted his words. He'd enjoyed the ride to Dunstable, more than he'd thought possible. He'd meant to spend the time engaging Claire in conversation, trying to understand her better, but she'd drawn him out instead.

He'd never been one to chatter on about his plans, to boast of his accomplishments. Yet reliving his travels with Claire had made him appreciate how fortunate he'd been. By the way she leaned forward, nodded in encouragement, widened her eyes at his escapades, he might think he truly had conquered the world. But he mustn't forget his purpose in partnering with her, and turning Samantha into a conniving Society miss was not part of the bargain.

Yet that truly wasn't what Claire had offered. She'd merely been assuring him that Samantha would enjoy London, that Claire could manage the girl's doubts. Once again, he'd let the memory of the past overshadow the future.

He sighed and sank onto the chair beside hers. "Forgive me, Claire. I don't know why I keep doing that."

"Issuing ultimatums or bullying with your height?" she inquired in a pleasant tone, as if she were asking how he liked his tea.

He winced. "I shouldn't use either tactic, especially with you."

"Agreed." Her smile was just as pleasant. "But you do seem determined to try."

"And you seem determined to ignore it."

She rose to go to a table along the wall and fetch the embroidery she'd been working on during the trip. She'd made good progress, he saw. Already a dozen bloodred roses bloomed from the white muslin.

"You engaged me to sponsor your cousin, sir," she said, returning to her seat and taking up her needle. "If you need schooling in manners, I can recommend an excellent tutor in London."

"No, thank you," he said, trying to keep from wincing a second time. "I can master manners. It's my temper that seems to be troubling me."

"I'm afraid I cannot help you there."

No, she couldn't. *But You can, Lord. Why do I want to lash out at her?*

Condemn not, and ye shall not be condemned; forgive, and ye shall be forgiven.

That was one of many verses he'd learned on forgiveness. He knew the Lord expected it of His followers. Yet every moment in Claire's company, he found himself wondering what would have happened if she'd been willing to wait. Would he have stayed in England instead of heading back out to sea? Would they have a daughter by now, perhaps a son with the dark Everard eyes? Would they have been as happy as he'd dreamed?

"Why did you marry him, Claire?" The words tumbled out of him, yet he would not call them back. He needed to know that he'd been supplanted by the better man.

Then he might be able to find the forgiveness that verse talked about.

Her fingers froze on the needle, suspended in midpull, red satin floss trailing across the fabric. "What a strange question after all this time."

"Not so strange," Richard replied, shifting on the hard seat. "You said you'd wait."

"You'd said you'd write." Her head remained bowed, as if she focused on her task, yet the needle did not move.

"We made port rarely. I posted when we did."

At last the needle returned to its course. "The first letter arrived when I returned from my wedding journey. My husband burned it in front of me, unopened."

He wanted to reach out and stop her hand, force her to meet his gaze, show some emotion. "Why? I was no threat to him. I was half a world away, and he'd already won what I most wanted."

The path of the thread grew uneven. "He didn't see it that way. Winthrop expected absolute obedience and utter devotion from his women."

Women? Anger licked up him anew. Had the wretch been unfaithful to her? "Tell me you were happy," he demanded.

She pulled the thread taught and twisted it to make a knot. "As I told you, Captain Everard, I have learned to be content."

He wished he could say the same. And he wished he could believe her. But the more time he spent with her, the more questions he had about her life over the last ten years. Unfortunately, Mercier slipped back into the room just then, stilling his tongue as surely as the discussion had stilled Claire's needle.

But nothing could stop him from wondering.

* * *

Claire had never been so thankful to see a servant. She'd jabbed herself twice trying to pretend she felt nothing for Richard's pain. Another moment in his company and she'd have been crying on his shoulder, lamenting the life they might have had together.

Had she been happy, he'd asked. There were moments, in the early days of her marriage, when she'd been delighted with her life, sure she'd made the right choice in a husband. Winthrop was the perfect partner in Society, at first—handsome, witty, charming. Those characteristics had quickly faded from their home life and then their social life, leaving her wondering whether she'd been blind or simply naive.

Even her astute father had failed to see the problem. He'd gone to heaven before he'd learned the true nature of the son-in-law he'd so admired. And she'd hidden the truth from friends and acquaintances under a pleasant smile that twisted her stomach and bruised her heart. She could hardly admit the circumstances to Richard now. Let him believe she had been content in her life. He certainly seemed as if he'd been content in his.

She thought he must be concerned he had revealed too much of his feelings, for he asked no more questions about her life and told her little more about his over the next three days of travel. He did, however, ask her about her plans for Samantha.

"We have set the stage," Claire replied, as the coach wound its way through the little hamlets of Leicester, north and west into the tree-lined lanes of Cheshire. "The best families are in charity with Lady Everard and should welcome her into their midst."

"Even after the gossip?" Richard pressed, dark eyes narrowed.

"Every play has critics," Claire said. "Many people go to see it because of the criticism. We must use the gossip to our advantage. We will show them that your cousin is a young lady of good breeding and character. Her very presence will prove the rumors false."

She said those words with all the conviction of her heart and the faith in the prayers she had been sending up each night before retiring and each morning before she and Richard set out. Richard looked skeptical.

"In my experience," he said, "people see what they want to see."

Claire smiled. "I share your experience, sir. That was why it was so important for us to paint your cousin in a good light. Now, we must make sure she has all the skills she needs to succeed in London, and we take the town by storm."

"Plays, painting and war," Richard said with a grin. "You make the Season sound delightful."

Yet Claire was certain it would be. She hadn't realized how much she needed a challenge, something worthwhile to make her forget about her own troubles. In Samantha Everard, she was sure, she would finally achieve something of lasting value.

By the time they reached Dallsten Manor, Claire was on the edge of her seat, gazing out over the head of the postilion. The lands started at a quaint stone cottage and ran along oak woods turning green with spring. On a rise stood the house, a lovely reddish sandstone not too distant a color from Richard's hair. As the coach drew up before it, the mountains loomed in the background, shrouded in mist and mystery. Claire was enchanted.

Winthrop had had a pretty place like this, but it hadn't been entailed, and he'd sold it with the excuse that he was not the type to rusticate in the country. As Richard handed her down onto the graveled drive, Claire found it far easier to imagine living here, watching the snow pile high in the winter, the flowers bloom in the summer.

She could also picture Samantha growing up here, unspoiled, innocent, sweet. She couldn't wait to guide her, to shepherd her into the bigger world and help her find her place in it. Even Claire's leg felt stronger, her step more sure, as she followed Richard up the stairs, leaving Mercier to escort her things to the back of the house, where the postilion would be paid before returning the post chaise to its owner.

Richard didn't bother knocking at the stout oak door. He opened it with a flourish and bowed Claire in ahead of him.

The entry hall was wide and parquet tiled, and a medieval tapestry, colors still proud, shrouded one of the tall, white walls. A carved oak stair rose in majesty to the upper story. A shame they could not simply take the house to London with them. She could see herself welcoming guests in a receiving line, introducing the titled and wealthy to a blushing Samantha, helping the girl start her first ball.

But she was suddenly aware of a noise, rising in volume and threatening to dispel her vision. It sounded like a clank and clash of metal on metal, and it was punctuated by cries of "Take that!" and "Again!" Richard, who had been a few steps ahead of her, backed up to her side as if to protect her.

Two figures appeared on the landing above them, rapiers in hand. One was a man in a flowing white shirt over black breeches and boots. She thought she recognized Richard's cousin Vaughn Everard, with his white-gold hair and lean physique.

His opponent was a girl gowned in white muslin with

golden curls tumbling around her slender face. One hand was tight in her skirts, lifting them out of her way like a charwoman. Thrusting and parrying, she forced Vaughn Everard back to the great oak stair. With a cry, he leaped down it to avoid her blows. Grinning, she seated herself on the banister sidesaddle and slid down it to land upright on the parquet floor. Her sword point was at his neck as he reached the last step.

Disappointment dug into Claire, stopped the breath in her chest. This was the shy flower she'd hoped to bring into bloom? This creature the sweet girl who feared to leave the country? What must Richard think of Claire to see her as the woman to bring this, this hoyden, into fashion? Or was Samantha Everard's untamed nature the secret he'd been hiding?

Richard must have seen the look on her face, for he said in a strangled voice, "Claire, I can explain."

Both his cousins turned at the sound, and their dark eyes, so alike, widened.

Claire didn't stop to think, didn't even raise a prayer. She lifted her chin and put on her polite smile. "It appears you've brought me here to no purpose, Captain Everard. I fear I cannot help you. Pray return me to London, immediately."

Chapter Nine

Richard barely smothered his groan at Claire's demand. When he looked at his cousin Samantha, standing there sword in hand, he saw a spirited girl who was eager to sample all life offered. But Claire obviously saw an untamed creature whose actions would reflect poorly on her. Samantha must have thought as much, for she tucked both hands and the sword behind her and curtsied demurely. The sword thunked against the parquet.

"Lady Winthrop," she said breathlessly, "welcome to Dallsten Manor. I'm so sorry I wasn't ready to receive you properly."

Vaughn also swept them one of his expansive bows, head down, free arm making an arc of white linen. Richard was certain the movement had never failed to impress the ladies. "A pleasure to see you again, Lady Winthrop," his cousin said.

Claire's stiff posture did not thaw; every regal line of her black gown shouted offended femininity. "A shame I cannot say the same, Mr. Everard," she replied. "I had heard your wit was sharper than the sword, but here I find proof otherwise."

Vaughn's dark eyes narrowed as he straightened. "Even a lady must needs defend herself."

"Ah, yes," Claire said, smile as icy as her look. "When a gentleman fails to ask for a second dance, Lady Everard can no doubt whip out a blade and teach him a lesson. That will certainly distinguish her from the other young ladies."

"Samantha knows better than to carry a blade in public," Richard felt compelled to say.

"Indeed," Claire said. "Then my work here is clearly done. Lady Everard, I wish you luck. I fear you'll need it."

"Claire," Richard started, but the sword clattered to the floor before he could finish. White-faced, Samantha rushed up to Claire and seized her hand.

"Oh, please don't despair of me, Lady Winthrop!" Those big brown eyes swam with tears, and her lower lip trembled. "I've been raised out here, all alone, with no mother or sister to guide me. Now I'm expected to take on London, and I simply cannot do it without you!" She sucked back a sob and cast herself into Claire's arms.

Vaughn met Richard's gaze over Samantha's shaking shoulders. His poet cousin's pale brows were up, his head cocked as if he couldn't quite believe the girl's performance. Neither could Richard. Samantha was entirely too good at manipulating emotions, using tears and temper to effect her ends. He could not admire the trait. But if she won the day this time, he knew he wouldn't have the heart to scold her.

"There, now," Claire was murmuring, patting Samantha's back. "I'm sure it's entirely too easy to follow your cousin's exciting example, but you must think of your future. A woman's reputation is her most precious possession. You wouldn't want to tarnish it."

"No, no," Samantha said, disengaging to wipe at her

eyes with her fingers. "Of course not. But how can I tell what's merely in vogue and what's downright scandalous without advice from someone who understands such things?"

Richard watched Claire. Emotions flickered behind those cool eyes—interest? Concern? He knew the moment she straightened her shoulders that she'd made her decision.

Please, Lord, let her stay.

The strength of the prayer astonished him. Until that moment, he hadn't realized how much he wanted Claire to stay. Certainly Samantha needed the guidance of a lady, as she'd just proven with her antics. He was more surprised, however, to find that his feelings for Claire had little to do with Samantha.

Claire smiled at the girl before her, so contrite, so concerned. She had no doubt that at least part of Samantha's seemingly heartfelt plea was playacting. Tears still brimmed in her wide eyes, but Claire saw intelligence and cunning underlying the gleam. If the girl truly wanted Claire's help, Claire could do much good here. And the girl was right—with Jerome, Richard and Vaughn Everard as cousins, she certainly needed a female to guide her.

"Very well," Claire said. "I will stay."

Claire thought Richard let out a breath. Samantha certainly brightened, but Claire held up a hand. "On two conditions. First, you will heed my advice, in all things."

"That promise," Vaughn said, "could hide a multitude of evil."

Claire met his thoughtful gaze straight on. Oh, but he was going to be the difficult one. She didn't know him well. When Richard had courted her, Vaughn Everard had been a scrawny fourteen-year-old with a puppylike devotion to their uncle. Since then, he'd made quite a name for himself on the *ton,* with his outrageous poetry and equally mad habit of challenging other men to duels for the least insult. Many women probably went along with anything he suggested, out of eagerness to please or fear of reprisal. She wasn't one of them.

"I find teaching a young lady to use deadly force no better," she countered. "And I'm sure a gentleman would not be so cavalier as to interrupt a lady when she is speaking."

Vaughn clamped his mouth shut, jaw clenching with the effort. Claire tried to ignore the grin on Richard's bearded face.

"I'll do my best to listen, Lady Winthrop," Samantha said, hands clasped before her muslin gown.

Claire inclined her head in acknowledgment. "And second, we will have no more of these histrionics. I prefer honesty and plain speaking."

Richard snorted, then turned the sound into a cough, covering his mouth with his fist. Did he think that Claire used such methods to manipulate? Once, perhaps, and to her sorrow. Well, he would soon learn that she was made of stronger stuff these days. If Samantha was to be her protégée, Claire would take that duty seriously.

"Yes, Lady Winthrop," Samantha said, head bowed in humility Claire couldn't believe she was feeling. Any girl with courage enough to take on Vaughn Everard in a sword fight would not be cowed by a little scold from a near stranger. Samantha would be no more easily led than her father and cousins.

That fact ought to have disappointed her, sent her into the dismals as much as when she'd first seen the girl, like an unbridled colt, leaping about the landing.

Yet exhilaration filled Claire, as if for once she'd been handed a challenge she was perfectly equipped to meet.

That knowledge comes from You, Father. Thank You!

Just then, a little round woman came hurrying from the corridor to the left. She had snowy-white hair bound around her head in a coronet braid, and her gray gown was neat and clean.

"Forgive me, sirs, your ladyship," she said with a humble curtsy, although the look in her gray eyes made Claire wonder whether she herself should apologize for some infraction. "I didn't hear the knock or I would have been here sooner. Welcome back, Captain Everard."

"Thank you, Mrs. Linton," Richard said, going on to introduce their housekeeper to Claire. He took command of the situation then, ordering Samantha to her room to change, and the housekeeper to make sure Claire's room was ready. Interesting how easily he slipped into the role of leader.

Of course, one of the things that had drawn her to him when they were younger was his confidence. At seventeen, Richard Everard had known exactly what he intended to achieve in his life and how he intended to go about it.

"There's a whole world out there, Lady Claire," he'd told her one summer night as they'd stood on a veranda, the sounds of the ball they'd been attending muted through the glass doors behind them. "England needs to be part of it."

"My father says we have colonies across the globe," Claire had said.

His dark gaze mirrored the stars. "And goods and people that must move between them. I mean to help that along."

She was so thankful he'd been given that chance, and so sad she hadn't been a part of it.

But she had no more time for reverie. Mrs. Linton seemed eager to show her up the great stair and across a gallery, to a long corridor that led toward the rear of the house.

Claire saw immediately that Dallsten Manor could prove a problem for her. The house was apparently shaped like an L, with a stone tower anchoring either corner of the shorter branch, and the bedchambers lying along the longer one. All this walking about added to the strain on her knee. She would have to be careful.

The room the housekeeper gave Claire was done in shades of purple, from the lavender silk wall-coverings printed with bouquets of violets, to the aubergine fabric draping the canopied bed. Even the curved-back armchairs by the fire were upholstered with purple velvet. The only other color was to be found in the dark oak of the furnishings and the soft green pattern of the carpet.

"Fit for royalty," Claire mused to herself, as she took off her bonnet.

"English royalty, *non?*" Mercier said, coming from the dressing room with her tiny nose in the air. "We French have more originality, *oui?*"

"All the rooms are like this," Samantha said, fairly skipping into the room. She still wore the muslin gown, though she'd tied a pink bow under her bosom, and the satin ribbon bobbed with her movements. "There's an emerald room, a golden one and a blue one. Mine's pink. Cousin Jerome says the designer was myopic."

Claire couldn't argue that. She also couldn't argue that the girl was already disobeying orders. "What a shame the same can be said for your gowns. I was certain your cousin told you to change, yet here you are in a dress exactly like the one you were wearing."

Samantha flounced over to one of the armchairs and seated herself. "You said you wished me to obey you. You didn't say anything about Cousin Richard."

"Mercier," Claire said, "I am very sorry, but I fear you'll only have me to serve. Lady Everard is obviously not ready for her own French maid. She never changes her clothes."

As Samantha turned to stare at the maid, Mercier waved a hand. "Oh, *quel dommage!* I was made for a greater challenge, *non?*"

Samantha scrambled to her feet. "Did you really bring me a French maid?"

"This is Josette Mercier," Claire said. "She is French, and she is a maid. She is also versed in all the latest fashions, from gowns to hair." Claire patted her own hairstyle, which had been crushed a bit by her bonnet. "Whether I allow her to help you, however, is entirely up to you."

Samantha hurried forward. "I'll just go change. Perhaps Mercier could come with me?"

"You go," Claire said. "I'll send her to you shortly."

Samantha bobbed a curtsy and dashed out the door.

Mercier shook her dark head. "We will have our hands full with that one, *oui?*"

"*Oui,*" Claire said. "Go after her, slowly, and look over her closet. I want to know what she'll need when we get to London."

Mercier dropped a more graceful curtsy. *"Oui, madame."*

As the maid left, Claire set her bonnet on a table by the door and went to look out the window, parting the damask of the aubergine drapes. Green fields stretched away, dotted with the white of sheep. Clouds just as white and fluffy drifted across the sky. Despite her tumultuous introduction to Dallsten Manor, she felt as if her cares were slipping off her shoulders.

Thank You, Lord. I needed this.

As if in warning, her leg spasmed. Claire limped to one of the armchairs and sat rubbing at her knee through her skirts. *I suppose this keeps me humble, Lord, but I'll need all my strength if I'm to do Your will here. Help me, please.*

The pain eased under her fingers, and she could breathe again. She only hoped the peace would last.

Samantha and Mercier returned in remarkably short time. Mercier merely rolled her eyes at Claire before returning to the dressing room to finish unpacking Claire's clothes. Claire took the gesture to mean that Samantha's closet wouldn't bear saving.

The girl was now gowned in a navy wool dress with a white collar and cuffs. Last year's fashion, certainly, but Mercier had managed to tame the girl's curls back from her face in a pink satin band. Claire motioned Samantha to the armchair opposite hers.

"Perhaps we could take a moment to become better acquainted," Claire said.

Samantha nodded eagerly. "I'd like that. I understand you've known Cousin Richard for years."

Claire had said she valued plain speaking, but she wasn't ready to discuss her past. "Since my own first Season, yes," she replied. "And you were born here?"

One of Samantha's slippered feet was tapping on the green carpet as if the girl couldn't bear to sit still with so much happening. "Actually, I was born in Carlisle. Papa bought Dallsten Manor for Mama when I was little. It's the only home I remember."

She sounded almost wistful. Claire didn't want to encourage her to look backward too often, either. "And soon London will be your home. Tell me, what do you wish to accomplish in your Season?"

Samantha rubbed her hands down her skirts. "I want to be presented to the queen, be welcomed by all the hostesses who refused Papa and garner no less than three offers for my hand."

The words came out clipped, as if she were reciting something from memory. And the list exactly matched Richard's. Surely he hadn't bullied the girl into this.

Claire smiled to hide her rising concern. "Then you don't care to see the sights of London—the Tower, the Parthenon marbles, the British Museum and Horse Guards."

She scooted forward in her chair. "Those sound marvelous, actually. Do we really have things that came from ancient Greece?"

"A few," Claire replied. "Others, as I understand, are in transit. Who knows how many more will arrive before we do? You might also enjoy the theater, the opera."

She nodded eagerly, threatening her grown-up coiffure. "Yes, certainly."

"And I suspect you might like to make friends with girls your own age."

The sigh was clearly heartfelt. "Oh, that would be wonderful."

"Well," Claire said, smile broadening, "we shall certainly see what we can do. First we must make sure you are prepared."

Samantha sat back. "Miss Walcott, I mean Mrs. Everard, taught me about deportment and being presented to the queen."

Claire leaned back as well. "Ah, then you did have female companionship."

She blushed and lowered her gaze. "Yes. Forgive me. I just wanted you to stay."

Claire had thought as much. "And Mrs. Everard is your cousin Jerome Everard's wife, your former governess."

Samantha nodded, absently twirling her finger in her hair beside one ear. Mercier would have fainted had she known.

"That's right," the girl said. "She understands all about coming out, but she's never actually been to London. I'm not sure I know everything I should."

"We'll find out over the next few days," Claire promised. "I won't let you step from this house until you're confident you're ready."

Her smile was breathtaking, but it quickly faded. "Well, we are set to go up right after Easter. How I feel has nothing to do with it. The plans have been made."

So she *was* being forced. Why? Had they no understanding of the importance of a Season? Claire felt herself bristling anew. "Plans can be changed. You have asked me to be your sponsor, Lady Everard. From now on, things will be managed to my satisfaction."

"My cousins may have other ideas," the girl warned.

Claire's grip on the arm of the chair was as firm as her convictions. "You leave your cousins to me. I'll have a thing or two to say to Captain Everard if he tries commanding us."

She only hoped her determination wouldn't fail her when she and Richard had to face off over the matter.

Chapter Ten

"I don't much care for your Lady Winthrop," Vaughn said, as he followed Richard into the library. Of all the rooms in Dallsten Manor, Richard liked this one the best. The tall bookcases, dark wood paneling and massive desk reminded him of his cabin aboard his ship, the *Siren's Gold.* He went to the large, high-backed chair by the fire and nodded to his platinum-haired cousin to join him. But Vaughn went instead to stand by the mantel and crossed his lean arms over his chest.

"You don't have to like her," Richard pointed out. "She's here for Samantha, remember?"

"I see little benefit to her crushing Samantha's spirit."

Richard chuckled. "It would take more than a hurricane to crush Samantha's spirit."

Vaughn let his arms fall, a reluctant smile lifting his lips. "You may be right there. I had my hands full the last two days, with Jerome and Adele gone."

"Where are my brother and his new bride?" Richard asked, leaning back against the upholstery. After four days in the little chaise, stretching his legs was a luxury. "I thought they planned to take their wedding trip after Samantha was finished with her Season."

"They did. But we received word that Four Oaks was in danger of flooding from the spring rains. Jerome was concerned."

Richard could understand that. His brother would inherit Four Oaks from their uncle once Samantha navigated her Season. The small estate was to be home for him and his new wife. Jerome would have wanted to make sure it was protected.

Vaughn raised his chin. "You know how he is when he has a problem to solve, like a dog with a fresh bone. I couldn't stand his muttering another moment. I insisted that he go secure the place."

"And Adele went with him?" Richard raised a brow. "Don't tell me you've been here with Samantha for…"

"Two days," Vaughn said. "But don't concern yourself. We weren't alone. Mrs. Dallsten Walcott installed herself in Uncle's old room. She's been serving as chaperone."

Richard was surprised there was a house left in which to chaperone. Mrs. Dallsten Walcott, the mother of Jerome's bride, lived in the dower house at the foot of the drive. Her family had once owned Dallsten Manor before her husband's death had impoverished her and Adele. Though Mrs. Dallsten Walcott had sold the house to Uncle, she had a difficult time remembering she was no longer the lady of the manor. In fact, she had a habit of making off with whatever struck her fancy in the house. She'd obviously been preoccupied that afternoon, or she'd never have allowed Samantha to take up the blade.

"Dare I ask how you passed the time, besides teaching Samantha to fence?" Richard said.

Vaughn dropped into a nearby chair at last. "She has her father's gift for picking things up quickly, Richard. You should have seen her take Lord Kendrick's fence on my gray."

"Swordplay and jumping fences." Richard shook his head. "Remember our purpose—to see Samantha safely through her Season. You do her no favors by encouraging these kinds of pursuits."

Vaughn shrugged. "Very well, but if you make her into a pattern card of virtue I shall be forced to take action."

Even with Claire's guidance, Richard couldn't see Samantha in danger of conforming to Society's dictates. Of course, he'd once thought Claire that strong, and she'd proven him wrong.

"Don't concern yourself on that score," Richard said. "I'll find Mrs. Walcott and convey our thanks. She can retire to the dower house now. Claire will see to Samantha."

"Then I can focus on hunting Uncle's killer." He stood as if wishing to start the process immediately. "What did you learn from Widmore?"

"Not enough," Richard said, and went on to explain his meeting with the powerful lord and the report of the Bow Street Runner.

When he'd finished, Vaughn shook his head, pale hair turning gold in the firelight. "Then we still know nothing."

"Very little," Richard agreed. "I have more questions than facts. For instance, why did Uncle go alone, without asking one of us to second him?"

"Perhaps it wasn't a duel," Vaughn said, his look darkening.

"Uncle called it as much in the letter he left outlining his last wishes," Richard reminded him.

"But there's the code duello," Vaughn insisted, "with rules requiring seconds, agreements on weapons and meeting places." He began his restless pacing, threatening to wear a path across the Oriental carpet between the hearth and the door.

"And we both know Uncle disregarded rules when it pleased him." Richard leaned forward so he could keep an eye on his cousin. "Besides, Widmore implied that Uncle didn't trust us, that he hid the duel and Samantha from us for a reason."

"He trusted me." Vaughn's voice held both pride and pain. "He would never have kept me out unless he was protecting me."

Richard could not be so sure. His uncle's moods had swung from wildly optimistic to fatally pessimistic. And he seemed to have a different relationship with each of his nephews. Jerome had been the heir presumptive who thrashed at not having enough control of the legacy he could see their uncle eroding. Vaughn had been the son that Uncle had never had—so like him in looks and temperament.

Richard had always had one dream—to one day take command of the fleet of ships their family owned. When his parents had been killed and he'd been sent with Jerome to live with their uncle, Lord Everard had taken one look at the ten-year-old Richard and ordered him packed off to school.

"But Father wanted me to apprentice under Captain Carver," Richard had protested. "I was to go this very year!"

"You're not ready for the sea, boy," Uncle had said, not unkindly. Still, the words had dashed Richard's hopes all the same. "You go off to school until you're old enough to be entertaining at least. Then we'll talk."

It had made no sense, then or now. Boys joined the navy as young as six, merchant ships by eight or nine. Only his mother's pleas had kept him home until ten. Though he'd been raised inland, he felt as if the sea was in his blood, and every moment away from it was painful.

Still, he'd tried. He'd done well in school, looked at every subject as a way to excel when he was finally allowed to go to sea. A captain needed mathematics to calculate tides and navigate difficult waters. He needed a good command of the English language to write his log and order his men to good advantage. He needed to be healthy and strong to withstand the blasts of nature, the vagaries of politics that dominated world shipping. Richard had tried to be the man his father, grandfather and uncle had wanted of him.

A shame I didn't realize what You wanted, Lord, until it was almost too late.

When he had returned to London seven years later, his uncle had had to look up at him.

"Well," he'd said with a grin, "now we're getting somewhere." He'd taken Richard down to the Thames that very afternoon, filling his head with tales from before Grandfather had been elevated to baron, when both he and Uncle had sailed. Richard had been ready to sign aboard the first ship they saw, but Uncle advised caution. Together, they'd made plans for Richard's future—a few voyages as a junior officer to learn the ropes and then a captainship.

But that night, Richard had seen Claire across a crowded ballroom, and everything had changed.

"If Uncle was going to confide in any of us," Richard told Vaughn now, "it would have been you. The fact that he said nothing concerns me greatly."

"Agreed," Vaughn said, and his voice sounded lighter, as if Richard had lifted a burden by acknowledging his place in their uncle's affections. "And none of the servants knew anything about Uncle's valet, Repton?"

Richard shook his head. "He's disappeared."

Vaughn paused. "He can't have gone far. He didn't

even collect his pay last quarter day. He must still be in London. He was the last person to see Uncle alive—he must know something of use. Let me return to London, find him and discover the truth."

The request was familiar; Jerome had been refusing it for weeks. Ever since Uncle's death, Vaughn's temper had rested just below the surface, ready to explode. Richard knew his brother feared the form Vaughn's vengeance would take. Yet Jerome's diplomacy and Richard's investigation had led them nowhere. Like Vaughn, Richard wanted the mystery of his uncle's death solved.

"Give me a day or two to get settled," Richard said, rising. "Then you have my blessing to head for London." He met his cousin in the middle of the room. "But if you find Uncle was murdered, as we suspect, go to the authorities. Promise me that."

His cousin hesitated, and for a moment Richard thought he would refuse. Then he held out his fist. "I swear it."

Richard met the fist with one of his own. "And I swear to bring Samantha to you right after Easter to start her Season."

Vaughn grinned as he lowered his hand. "The sooner, the better. There's been a local pup sniffing at her heels since Jerome and Adele left—that Toby Giles fellow."

Pup was the right word. Jerome had told Richard how Toby had recently teamed with Samantha to steal the vicar's wig as a prank. "I wouldn't worry. He's just a lad."

"He's seventeen," Vaughn countered. "The same age you were when you first courted Lady Winthrop. I'll do my best to scare him off before I go, but he may be brash enough to offer for her."

The words were a solid punch to his abdomen, and Richard exhaled. Somehow he'd never seen himself having to refuse a suitor's request. He was too familiar with the pain. "This isn't going to be easy, is it?"

Vaughn clapped him on the shoulder. "Easy as jumping a fence on a spirited horse. Besides, as you said, you have Lady Winthrop to help now. That frown of hers could put the fear into Napoleon himself. Giles will be child's play."

Richard could only hope he was right, but he was certain Claire had an entirely different opinion on what constituted a proper suitor, and he didn't relish going toe-to-toe with her on the matter.

Claire knew she had to discuss Samantha's situation with Richard at the first opportunity. Her own future was also at stake. How could Claire keep her bargain with Richard if the girl didn't have her Season? Once Claire would have ignored her misgivings, plunged ahead to what she thought she wanted. Now she knew the Lord expected better of her. She expected better as well. Even if she was forced to return to her original plan of a rain-cracked cottage in Nether Crawley, she would not force Samantha to London unless the young baroness was ready.

Lord, I'll just have to rely on Your grace. He hadn't left her through her tumultuous marriage. She was confident He wouldn't desert her now. So she dressed with care for her first dinner with the Everards, choosing a black high-waisted gown of lustring that gave back a shine as she moved. It was both elegant and no-nonsense. She wanted to set an example for Samantha, and she wanted to make sure both Richard and Vaughn realized she was a woman of her word. But she didn't expect to have to prove herself the moment she walked out her door.

Another lady stood in the corridor. She was dressed in a fine green gown of the last decade, with its lower waist and wider skirts. Her carriage was regal, her look haughty.

Only the gray of her hair, piled high, spoke of her age. Claire could not imagine who she might be or why she was fingering the marble statuette of a shepherdess that stood in an alcove along the pale blue wall.

"A lovely piece," Claire ventured, moving closer.

The lady started, then drew herself up and looked down her hawklike nose. "Indeed. It belonged to my grandmother. I cannot imagine why it was moved to this remote location where no one can appreciate it."

As every member of the household had to traverse this corridor a number of times a day, Claire could not see the area as so far removed. And how could that statuette have belonged to the woman's grandmother? Was this woman an Everard? She certainly didn't have the dark brown eyes or platinum hair that generally marked the family. And the last female Everard that Claire knew of, besides Samantha, had died thirty years ago.

The woman beside her nodded as if making a decision and snatched the shepherdess from its pedestal. "I'll just take this for safekeeping."

Claire raised her brows. "Of course you'll speak to Lady Everard first."

The woman's eyes flashed a warning. "And why should that be necessary? Do you know who I am?"

Claire smiled sweetly. "How remiss of me. We haven't been properly introduced. Let the roof be our hostess. I am Claire Winthrop, daughter of the former Earl of Falbrooke and widow of the former Viscount Winthrop. I'm sponsoring Lady Everard on her Season."

For a moment, doubt flickered behind the woman's blue eyes. She clutched the statuette closer as if for self-defense. "I am Mrs. Dallsten Walcott. The Dallstens trace our lineage back to before the conquest. My family has owned this house for generations. And my daughter married Mr. Jerome Everard."

The story just kept getting better. So, Jerome's wife, who had been Samantha's governess, was of a respected family that had fallen on hard times. While Claire was immediately in sympathy with her, she still could not see how her daughter's plight gave her mother the right to rearrange the furnishings.

"Good evening, ladies."

Richard's warm voice, so close behind her, sent a shiver up her. Composing her face, she turned to greet him. As if he knew she had intended to start an argument, and was prepared to meet it, he'd dressed in black as well, from his tailored coat to his satin-striped waistcoat and black wool breeches. But was it merely the dark color that made the skin above his beard look paler? It couldn't be that Mrs. Dallsten Walcott discomposed the captain.

Out of the corners of her eyes, Claire saw the lady in question set the shepherdess back in its place.

"Good evening, Captain Everard," Mrs. Dallsten Walcott said with a sniff. "Will you tell this woman that I am welcome in the manor?"

Richard raised a russet brow. "I imagine you can tell her yourself, ma'am. She's standing right beside you."

As Mrs. Dallsten Walcott glared at her, Claire gazed back with a smile she knew had teeth. "Captain Everard, will you explain to Mrs. Dallsten Walcott why it is impolitic to carry off things that do not belong to one?"

"Belay that!" Richard barked in command.

Claire blinked, but Mrs. Dallsten Walcott jumped, lifting her old-fashioned gown right off the carpet.

He offered an arm to each of them with a charming smile. "Forgive me. Habit. The phrase means to hold off. We have more important matters to attend to. It's time for dinner, ladies. Your navigator is leaving. I suggest you latch aboard or find yourselves scuttled."

Claire accepted his arm, trying not to grin herself. "A shame my father never thought to teach me sailor's cant. Another failing in my education, I fear."

Mrs. Dallsten Walcott accepted his other arm without looking at Claire. The lady's mouth was set in a firm line, and Claire thought she was struggling over whether to disagree with Claire and be thought less than a lady for knowing the vulgar language of sailors, or to agree with her and thus consort with the enemy.

Unfortunately, with the lady on Richard's other side, Claire could hardly start the conversation she'd hoped to have with him. She still could not like the woman's presumption, but Mrs. Dallsten Walcott was obviously considered family if Richard was escorting her to dinner with them. Her attitude remained formal, telling Claire she too felt the antipathy between them. But with Richard's escort, they managed to reach the dining room with no more harsh words said.

At least the designer had used some imagination for this room, Claire thought as she entered. The walls were hung with ivory silk, and mahogany chairs stood around a damask-draped table set with fine china, clear crystal and silver candelabra.

Richard took the seat at the top of the table as the resident head of the household, with Claire on his left and Samantha, who hurried in too close behind Vaughn for Claire's comfort, on his right. Mrs. Dallsten Walcott clearly dithered on which seat to take, finally settling on the chair next to Samantha's, leaving Vaughn to sit beside Claire. The smile on his face said he was amused by all the posturing.

Claire was more amused by his announcement, after

Richard had asked the blessing and they started the savory meal.

"I regret, Lady Winthrop, that I will not be able to assist you and my lovely cousin as you journey to London," he said. "I will be leaving for the capital in a few days."

Samantha's silver fork clattered to her plate. "You're leaving? Why?"

Vaughn and Richard exchanged glances. What was that about? Vaughn immediately turned his smile on his cousin. "Someone has to go prepare the house for you, infant."

She stuck her nose in the air. "I'm not an infant, and Cousin Richard just spent the better part of a fortnight in London making arrangements. I don't see why you must go."

He picked up his own fork and gave it a twirl. "And I see no reason to tarry. You'll join me soon enough, if Lady Winthrop is the social genius Richard claims."

His look to Claire was challenging, and Claire put on her polite smile, ready to do battle. But, to her surprise, Richard spoke up first.

"*Genius* is the perfect word. Never you fear, Samantha. You could not ask for a smarter, more talented or more caring sponsor."

Oh, my, was she blushing? How could he praise her like that? And was she so desperate for approval that such a little kindness could set her hopes to blooming? "You are too kind, Captain Everard," she managed.

Samantha glanced between the two of them, smile slowly spreading, as if she liked what she saw. "Then we'll be together in no time, cousin!"

Vaughn smiled at her as he might at a hound pup that had followed him from the kennel. Samantha's mouth trembled, as did her hand as she returned to her meal.

Richard grinned, but Claire could not feel so sanguine. The girl was clearly infatuated with her older cousin. It would bode none of them any good in the days ahead.

And that meant she had one more thing she must discuss with Richard, as soon as possible.

Chapter Eleven

Mrs. Dallsten Walcott excused herself right after dinner, hurrying off while Richard escorted Claire and Samantha to the withdrawing room. Claire made a mental note to check before retiring to see that the shepherdess still guarded the corridor upstairs and hadn't wandered down to the dower house, where Richard had explained Mrs. Walcott normally resided.

While the dining room had been lovely, Claire took one step into the withdrawing room and decided she liked what she saw here even more. The walls were the palest pink, like the inside of a seashell; the ceiling was inlaid with classical paintings and cameos of blush and pearl. The fine wood of the chairs and settee was edged with gilt, the pieces refined. In such a feminine room, she was certain, things must be discussed civilly.

Claire perched on the settee by the white marble fireplace, waiting for Samantha to join her. But the girl went to the piano along the far wall and began playing something so low and mournful it sounded like a dirge.

"Not her usual style," Richard remarked, taking a seat beside Claire. He looked out of place on the dainty furnishings, as if a bear had been invited to take tea.

Vaughn seemed more at home, going to stand beside the girl and turn pages, and Claire noticed Samantha's playing immediately improved.

"She has a *tendre* for your cousin, I fear," Claire murmured.

Richard cocked a smile. "I've noticed he has that effect on the ladies."

And he had no idea of the danger. "You wanted Lady Everard to have three offers for her hand. I doubt we'll get one if it's known the poor fellow may have to challenge Vaughn Everard."

That won a laugh from him. "Not to worry. Vaughn is devoted, but he considers her a little sister."

Claire didn't think his voice had carried, but Samantha hit a false note and hastily corrected it. The girl's face heated when her cousin reached past her to turn a page, and her gaze flickered over him as if hungry for any part of his attention.

Claire was more aware that she must capitalize on Richard's attention. "I know you want her to be presented," she said quietly, "but I'm not sure she's ready for London just yet."

Richard raised a brow. "You've known her a few hours and you can say that with confidence?"

Claire stiffened. The doubts came too easily. Had she been hasty? She used to be so sure of her decisions, but her inability to see her husband's true character at times shook her faith in herself. "You yourself told me she seemed anxious," she pointed out in defense. "I noticed that as well."

"Every girl is a little anxious," he replied, leaning back as if the matter were settled.

"I wasn't," Claire told him.

His smile proved his pride in her. "I imagine you

weren't. You walked through London as if you owned it. But there aren't many like you, Claire."

Again he was praising her, and again her cheeks were heating. But she wasn't a green girl like Samantha, and she could not let him distract her from her purpose. "Be that as it may, your cousin's anxiety seems deeper than usual. It concerns me."

"Samantha will be fine," he assured her, so cavalierly she wanted to shout at him. "Here, I'll show you." He straightened and raised his voice. "Ho, Samantha. Stop a moment and come here."

Claire shook her head to warn him against it, but the girl had already hopped up from the bench and was scurrying to their sides.

As soon as she stood before them, Richard challenged, "Are you ready for London?"

"Tell him exactly how you feel," Claire urged, watching the girl.

But Samantha's gaze was all for Vaughn, who had followed her across the room and was standing by her side as if to protect her. "Oh, yes. I'm ready. I could leave with Cousin Vaughn if you'd prefer."

Over Claire's dead body. She could not like the way the girl's belief in herself had blossomed since hearing her cousin was going on ahead. "We have entirely too much packing to do for you to be ready so soon," Claire countered. "Though I'm delighted to hear you so eager. You must have decided you are ready to make conversation with complete strangers."

She raised her chin. "I've never had trouble talking to people."

Vaughn chuckled. "Not in the slightest."

"And carry yourself with sublime confidence, in any situation," Claire added.

Samantha lowered her head. "I think I can do that."

"Like a true Everard," Vaughn assured her.

"And dance with anyone who asks," Claire said.

"I can dance," she replied, smile growing. "I know the minuet and the gavotte."

Claire was never more thankful that she'd insisted on hiring Monsieur Chevalier. The girl would be expected to be fluent in at least a dozen different dances, some just making their appearance in London.

As if he understood the problem as well, Vaughn raised his pale brows. "The minuet and the gavotte? Tragic, cousin. You were made for better."

Samantha stared at him, clearly dismayed. "You mean those don't count?"

"Perhaps not as much as you'd hoped," Claire said, leaning back. "But never fear. We have the matter in hand. Monsieur Chevalier, the preeminent London dance master, will be joining us shortly."

Richard frowned. "So you managed to tear the fellow away from his other pursuits, then."

"Yes," Claire replied, trying not to take pride in the fact. "Though I had to use the offices of the Marquess of Widmore to do it. I'm just thankful he's so inclined to help Lady Everard."

To her surprise, Richard and Vaughn exchanged glances again. "Widmore spoke to you about Samantha?" Richard said, and she heard something more than curiosity in his voice.

"The night before we left," Claire replied. "At his wife's ball."

Vaughn's hand strayed to his side as if he longed for his blade. "Odd. Why would he care?"

Claire gazed at the two men, trying to determine their

concerns. "But I thought he and Lady Everard's father were good friends."

"Longtime friends," Samantha said, bunching up her skirts to take a seat on a nearby chair. "I've known him my whole life." She made it sound as if that had been centuries instead of a mere sixteen years.

"And he remembers you fondly as well," Claire told her.

Vaughn smiled, a lifting of his lips that held no warmth. "I must thank him for his kindness. It will give me a reason to renew our acquaintance."

"I predict a fine reunion," Richard said, far too brightly. "For now, I think we've had enough of such concerns." He turned to Claire. "As I recall, you play brilliantly. Would you favor us with a song? Samantha, go turn the pages for our guest."

Claire would have preferred to stay where she was, trying to understand the reason for the undertones in the conversation. She also wasn't willing to concede. Samantha, Lady Everard, wouldn't be ready for London by Easter, even with Monsieur Chevalier's instruction. The sooner Richard and Vaughn accepted that, the better.

But she was fairly certain Richard had commissioned her to play because he feared she'd ask questions he didn't want to answer. And now did not seem the time to press him. So she rose and shook out her black lustring skirts. "Of course. Come along, Lady Everard."

She thought the girl might protest; Samantha also looked eager to stay. But, as if remembering her promise to be guided by Claire in all things, her new protégée followed her to the piano with a dispirited sigh and stayed by Claire's side while Claire played the Mozart sonata she found on the music rack. Richard and Vaughn stood, mouths murmuring, heads close together, russet and pale gold, until Claire had finished.

"That was beautiful," Samantha said, closing the music. "I wish I could play like that."

"Don't wish it," Claire said with a smile as she stood. "It requires far too much time to practice, and you have far more important things to do right now."

And so do I, Lord. Help me to find the words.

Richard may have convinced himself that his cousin was ready, and Samantha certainly had convinced herself since this afternoon, but there was more here than met the eye. Claire had learned to her sorrow that subterfuge had no place among friends and family.

Even though Richard would only be in her life a short time, she saw no reason for him to keep secrets, especially if they could affect Samantha or her. Accordingly, when they all adjourned for the night, she lagged behind to speak with him.

He pulled up when he caught sight of her at the foot of the great stair. "Something wrong, Claire?"

"What issue do you have with the Marquess of Widmore?" she challenged.

He glanced up the stairs as if to determine the location of his cousin, but Samantha had already disappeared down the corridor for the bedchambers. "No issue," he replied, returning his gaze to Claire. "As you said, he's an old friend of the family."

"A friend whose name brings tension. Why?"

"There is no reason for you to worry."

The very fact that his gaze darted away from her as he said that made her concerns multiply. "Certainly I must worry if Lady Everard is at odds with one of the most notable men in London Society."

He sighed. "She isn't at odds." He glanced up the stairs again, then took Claire's elbow and drew her back behind them, where a corridor ran down to other rooms at the rear of the house. The lamps had already been extinguished, leaving the place in twilight. She could barely make out Richard standing beside her.

"I'd prefer you say nothing to Samantha," he murmured, "but perhaps you should know. We have reason to believe Uncle's death was no accident."

In the shadows of the stairs, Claire felt chilled. "But I heard it was a duel."

"So the story goes, yet no one will admit to being the challenger or even his second."

She struggled not to see the evil he implied. "Your uncle was not known for honoring the rules. Perhaps he didn't follow code duello."

"Perhaps." He shifted on his feet, bringing him closer to her. "But his valet, who supposedly made the arrangements, has also disappeared."

"And you suspect foul play."

She thought he nodded. "Samantha knows little of this. Jerome felt she should be protected."

Claire had never been more in agreement with Richard's brother. "I will say nothing, so long as Samantha is safe. I trust you have no reason to think that anyone wishes her harm."

He hesitated, and cold pierced her bones. "What is it?" she demanded, ready to defend her charge. "Has someone threatened her here?"

"Not Samantha," he explained. "Someone attempted to kill my brother two weeks ago here in Cumberland."

Claire gasped. "What? Did you catch the villain?"

"No." Frustration simmered in the single word. "A footman named Todd caused several accidents and finally held Jerome and Adele at gunpoint, all to possess a porcelain box. We have no idea why. He claimed to work at the behest of another, but we haven't been able to discover his master. He got away with the box and disappeared."

Claire refused to let him see the tremor that shook her. "What an untidy household you keep, sir, that everyone disappears on you."

She could hear the smile in his voice. "You can see why I need you."

He needed her? She gazed up at him. In the darkness, he was only a tall shape, yet memory painted in his warm grin, his dreamy eyes. Oh, how she wanted to be truly needed, a helpmate instead of an ornament to be trotted out to impress, but forgotten or abused otherwise. Yet, would it be any different with him? Wasn't she even now just a means to an end?

"Claire?" he asked. "What is it? I told you—we have matters in hand. I've commissioned a Bow Street Runner to look into things in London. He may already have found Todd."

"So you think it's safe here?" she asked, wrapping her arms about her waist.

He reached out and touched her cheek, and the sweetness of it made her catch her breath. "No harm will come to Samantha," he said softly. "Or you. I promise."

She had more she needed to say to him, to determine why he was so intent on having Samantha go to London this year. But he was standing so close, his breath caressing the hair at her temple, and she found herself longing to lean against him, let his arms come around her, sheltering her. Instead, she took a step back.

"I shall hold you to that promise, Captain Everard. Now, if you'll excuse me, I should check on your cousin before retiring."

His hand fell, and Claire turned for the stairs.

"Good night, Claire," he called. "Pleasant dreams."

Dreams? Once he'd embodied her dreams of the future. Now she didn't know what to think. For, no matter his promise, she was very much afraid she was in danger at Dallsten Manor—in danger of losing her heart.

Chapter Twelve

Richard knew exactly what it took to prepare his ship to sail, from inspecting every line to securing his cargo and supplies safely in the hold. He had a far hazier idea of what it would take to prepare Samantha to go to London, so he was a little surprised to find the house in turmoil when he returned from his morning ride the next day.

"An inventory she wants," Mrs. Linton complained to him, catching him as he passed the kitchen from the stable yard. "Of the linen, of the china and cutlery. When am I to find time for that? We're already running short staffed!"

Richard didn't have to ask who "she" was. Samantha would hardly have ordered an inventory, and Mrs. Dallsten Walcott likely knew every item in the house, down to the last brass tack. "Have the maids make a list," he ordered the housekeeper.

She drew herself up, which only brought her snowy head to his breastbone. "And since when could either Maisy or Daisy read or write? Besides, she has them busy with packing."

"I'll speak to her," Richard promised, and managed to escape the outraged housekeeper.

After changing from his riding clothes to a green

coat and tan breeches, he tracked Claire down to the withdrawing room. He'd expected to see her with an apron around her, perhaps a baton in hand, directing her unwilling minions.

But Claire did not appear to be busy packing. She seemed to be presiding over tea. Her dress, though black, had enough lace at the throat and cuffs and flounces at the hem to make her look like a member of the royal family. And the silver-edged saucer didn't so much as tremble as she handed it and the attendant teacup to the fellow seated across from her.

Mr. Toby Giles had attempted to dress like a gentleman, with a brown double-breasted coast and fawn breeches. His cravat, however, was already wilting, a cowlick at the back of his head was making a piece of his carrot-colored hair stand at attention, and he squirmed in the little gilded chair as if he were a boy brought before a tutor for a scold.

Richard thought Vaughn's presence might have something to do with the lad's discomfort. Though his chair near Claire's was just as hard, Richard knew from experience, Vaughn managed to appear as if he were lounging. His lean legs stretched across the rose-patterned carpet; his teacup was perfectly balanced in front of his crimson coat. And his smile was far too satisfied.

Claire must have noticed Richard in the doorway, for she smiled in his direction. "There you are, Captain Everard. Come greet our guest."

Richard inclined his head in her direction, then moved into the room. "Giles. Good to see you again."

Toby leaped to his feet with a clatter of his cup against the saucer. "Captain Everard, sir. Good day."

Richard waved him back into his seat and pulled up a chair next to his cousin. Vaughn tipped up his chin in greeting.

"Tea?" Claire asked Richard, as Toby managed to sit without spilling his.

Richard declined, and her hand fell gracefully into her lap. Like everything else about Claire, her fingers were elegant, almost fragile looking. Yet he knew how impressively they could play the piano, how easily they could direct a gelding and how softly they could caress his cheek.

Perhaps he needed that tea after all. His mouth felt oddly dry all of a sudden.

Before he could ask for a cup, Samantha hurried into the room, creamy muslin gown fluttering about her ankles. The damp curl escaping her hair band told of a recent encounter with the washbasin. Toby scrambled to his feet again, sloshing tea on the carpet. Vaughn rose more languidly, and Richard stood, as custom required.

She made a respectful curtsy to Claire, then went to take a seat on the settee next to her. Toby plunked down on the chair and moved one boot to cover the stain on the carpet.

"Forgive me for usurping your place, dear," Claire said smoothly to Samantha, taking up her own cup. "Mr. Giles is here to see you, after all." She busied herself with drinking the tea.

Samantha's gaze darted around the room, from Claire to Vaughn to Richard and Toby. She visibly swallowed. "Yes, well, good day, to—Mr. Giles."

Toby waited, clearly hoping she might say something further that would help him conjure up the appropriate reply. Samantha merely clasped her hands tightly in her lap.

"Good day, Sam—Lady Everard," he finally returned.

"Scintillating conversation," Vaughn drawled. "Sure you don't want to jump in, Captain?"

Toby turned redder than his hair.

Claire must have taken pity on the lad, for she aimed her smile in his direction. "You mustn't mind Mr. Everard, Mr. Giles. He has a great deal on his mind, as he'll be heading for London shortly."

Toby grinned, gaze turned to Vaughn. "Leaving for London, eh? That's good news."

"Lovely," Samantha said with a sad sigh.

Vaughn raised a pale brow. "Good news, Giles? Why do you consider my imminent departure a stroke of good fortune?"

Toby took a hasty sip of his tea, but if he had hoped Vaughn might turn to another, he was disappointed. The poet's dark gaze never wavered.

Richard caught Claire glancing in his direction. The tip of her head told him she expected him to rescue the poor boy this time. He slapped Vaughn on the back, forcing his cousin to break eye contact with Giles.

"It's good news for us," Richard declared. "You're preparing the way for Samantha to go."

Samantha slumped in her seat.

"Surely you require an appropriate setting for your brilliance, cousin," Vaughn said, with a lift of his chin in Samantha's direction. "It shouldn't take long. And then we'll be reunited."

Samantha blushed, but Richard thought Toby looked a bit green.

"Will you be coming to London for the Season, Mr. Giles?" Claire asked, after a smile of thanks to Richard.

Samantha's gaze jerked back to her friend's.

"I've never thought all that highly of London," he answered, though his look was all for Samantha. "But I might go there, if I had a reason."

Samantha's smile was tremulous. Vaughn crossed his

booted feet. "A sprig of your renown would be bored within a fortnight, Giles. I advise you not to waste your time."

Toby deflated, but Samantha frowned at her pale-haired cousin. "Lady Winthrop doesn't make London sound boring at all. I think Toby would have a fine time."

What exactly had Claire been telling the girl? Richard knew Claire thought Samantha wasn't ready, yet it seemed she'd tried to be encouraging. He appreciated that, even if Claire couldn't know what was at stake for the Everards.

Toby set his teacup aside as if making up his mind. "Then I'll go to London. Count on it."

Samantha beamed, but Vaughn rose. With his crimson coat and platinum hair, he was easily the most striking feature in the room, and Richard was certain he knew it. Samantha couldn't seem to take her eyes off him.

"And I'll be there to meet you, Giles," he said. "For now, I suggest we pretend we are gentlemen and take our leaves. I know my cousin has a great deal to do to be ready. We wouldn't want to delay her."

Put that way, Toby had no choice but to decamp. Samantha insisted on walking him to the door, and Vaughn insisted on joining them.

Richard shifted seats so that he was nearer to Claire. "I see why you thought a male escort might be necessary with callers. Do they ever come to blows?"

"Not if you handle them properly," she said, but he could tell she was troubled. "I'm glad you were here, Richard. Surely you can see why I wondered about her maturity."

Richard raised a brow. "Because she had difficulty coming between Giles and Vaughn? Who wouldn't?"

"You or I or any number of others. And it was more

than that. She couldn't even start a conversation, and the boy is well known to her, isn't he?"

"They've grown up together," Richard acknowledged.

Claire set her tea aside and absently smoothed down her dark skirts. She seemed genuinely worried about his cousin, and he wanted to take her hands and assure her the seas ahead would be calm.

Unfortunately, he was starting to think she was right. The hesitant, tongue-tied Samantha he'd just seen was not the spirited girl he knew. She might not be ready for London. Yet, if he knew his cousin, she would go anyway. How could he help her, and, more importantly, help Claire understand why he couldn't honor her wishes?

Richard saw Vaughn off for the city early the next morning. "Are you certain about this?" he asked, as his cousin waited for Nate Turner, the groom, to finish saddling his horse. "You could come with us after Easter—make sure Toby Giles doesn't run off with Samantha."

Vaughn grinned as he mounted. "I'm not worried about Giles. Besides, you know what business I have in London."

Knew it and feared the results. But he couldn't say that with Nate standing nearby. "It could wait a few more days. Today is Sunday. Come with us to church."

"I think not," Vaughn said, settling himself in the saddle. "But be sure to say a prayer for heathens like me."

Richard tilted his head to look up at the poet. "It wouldn't hurt to say a prayer yourself."

Vaughn's smile lifted only the right side of his mouth. "I'm a lost cause, I fear. Take care of Samantha for me."

"I will," Richard promised. "Take care of yourself."

"That's what I do best." With a call to the gray, he

cantered out of the stable yard. Richard raised a hand in farewell, but his cousin never looked back.

He sighed as he started for the house. When he was younger, he'd felt the same way as Vaughn. Oh, his father and mother had been firm in their faith—attending services, caring for the poor near their estate, praying before mealtimes and before bidding Richard and Jerome good-night. He'd never felt his heart stir at the devotions. When Uncle had offered more interesting pastimes that summer, Richard had returned to London from school, all too ready to try them. The vices had come easily— he never lost at cards, and he was never jug bitten in the morning after drinking heavily. Yet, still a voice had whispered inside him, urging that he was made for more.

He'd ignored that whisper until the night he'd learned that Claire was forever beyond his reach. "Why?" he'd raged at the sky, after storming out of her father's house. "Why did you have to take her away from me, too? Wasn't it enough that Mother and Father died?"

And we know that all things work together for good to them that love God, to them who are called according to His purpose.

The remembered verse had sobered him, stilled his grieving spirit. In that moment, he'd realized that God hadn't been the one to abandon him, to hurt him. Richard had walked away; to be brutally honest, he'd run, only too happy to take what the world offered. He had to accept responsibility for the choices he'd made, to leave England after fortune, instead of staying and fighting for Claire's hand.

He'd found a place then, a presence too precious ever to forswear again. He only prayed his cousin would find that peace before some tragedy brought him to his knees.

Richard sent word upstairs that Samantha should be

ready to leave for services promptly at nine. He didn't ask anyone to wake Claire; he fully expected her to ignore church. But she came down the great stair at five minutes to nine, pulling on her gloves, Samantha right behind her. Her head was high, her tread slow and regal, black skirts brushing the stairs.

Richard leaned against the banister with a grin. "I thought you'd be still asleep."

"Good morning to you, too, Captain Everard," she returned, sailing past him for the door. "Do try to keep up. I will not have Lady Everard arriving late."

With a bemused shake of his head, Richard straightened and followed.

As had been their wont, he had the carriage stop at the foot of the drive for Adele's mother. Today, Mrs. Dallsten Walcott was dressed in a blue gown that reminded him of the waters of Jamaica. As she entered the coach, she eyed Samantha, who was sitting next to Claire in the front-facing seat. Samantha raised her chin, straw bonnet bumping into the seat back, as if refusing to give way.

Richard was certain Claire would refuse to move as well. After all, both her married title and her courtesy birth title gave her precedence of place to the lady. To his surprise, Claire stood and shifted to sit next to him.

The older woman sat beside Samantha and inclined her head. "Lady Winthrop."

"Mrs. Walcott," Claire said with equal coolness.

"Dallsten Walcott," she snapped.

So, obviously the animosity continued. Richard still wasn't entirely sure what had started it. "Ladies," he interjected, "shouldn't we be on our best behavior, particularly on the Lord's day?"

Mrs. Dallsten Walcott sniffed. "Certainly. Though I believe I should have been notified when Lady Winthrop arrived at the manor. Things were not run in such a ramshackle fashion when my daughter was in residence."

"Very likely not," Claire agreed, nose equally high. "I've never visited a house where strangers were allowed to wander the corridors at will."

"Strangers!" Mrs. Dallsten Walcott sputtered. "Do you intend to allow her to speak to me this way, Captain Everard?"

Oh, no. He was not about to enter this fight. He leaned back and crossed his arms over his chest. "I'm afraid I've never been good at advising Lady Winthrop, ma'am. I wish you better luck."

They both *humphed* in unison and spent the rest of the trip staring stoically out opposite windows.

Richard was afraid they'd carry their anger into the chapel, but Claire at least seemed to have forgotten it. He could see why. There was something about the little country church, set on the edge of the Kendrick estate. Reddish stone walls enclosed them in warmth; stained glass windows in jewel tones cast rainbows across the oak pews and the worshiping congregation. Being here raised his spirits, made him think the future could only be brighter.

Today, however, he was encouraged for another reason. Though he entered into the readings and songs with his usual focus, always he was aware of Claire beside him. Her hand touched his as they shared the Book of Common Prayer. Her skirts brushed his calves as the congregation rose to sing. When the vicar said something profound, Richard caught her nodding in agreement.

The Claire he'd known at a callow seventeen had been no more interested in communing with her Lord than he'd been. Could it be that she, too, had found a better way?

And did that mean they might have a chance of finding their way back to each other?

Show me Your will in this situation, Lord. You know I am Your man now. I'm finding it difficult to trust her, and I don't dare trust my feelings, but I know I can trust You.

As they rose to leave, he felt a surety inside. Something was going to happen; he could feel it as he felt a shift in the wind. But whether it was Claire or his own heart that was changing, he wasn't sure.

Chapter Thirteen

$\sim$

What a lovely service! Claire sighed in contentment as she walked beside Richard down the center aisle for the door. Oak arches soared over their heads; the dark stone floor was solid beneath her feet. Around them, people nodded in greeting, whispered to their neighbors. They were eager to know the name of the black-clad woman with the Everards. She clung to the joy she'd felt in the chapel.

Funny how attending church meant so much more to her now than when she was a girl. She'd always gone with her parents, but the lessons from the vicar had never transferred to her home. Her mother had spent her days with her friends, her nights at balls that did not always include her husband. She had died when Claire was thirteen. Claire's father had always been busy, with his estate, with matters of government. If he prayed, she'd never seen it. Neither had she seen it in Winthrop. And her husband was often too ill from Saturday night's activities to attend service with her on a Sunday.

So, she'd gone alone, head high, smile pleasant, as if everything in her life was perfect. She'd been so intent on maintaining the fiction of perfection that she seldom remembered what was read or the intent of the sermon. But then, one day, the readings seemed to be meant just for her, the vicar's sermon to speak to her troubled heart, and she'd realized there was more to devotion than mere appearance.

She'd dashed straight to Hatchard's bookstore and purchased herself a Bible, poring through it even as she pored out her heart to God. Though she'd been born in privilege, she felt like one of the poor the Lord had helped—she had been blind; now she could see.

Because of that change of heart, she looked at the people around her differently. So she could not deny that what she saw in Richard was good. He hadn't needed coaxing to attend service; he'd joined in the responses and sang readily. At times, she'd seen him nod in response to something the vicar had said, as if he were paying close attention. Never had she caught him glancing around as if it were more important to be seen here than to worship. Could it be that Richard's eyes had been opened, too?

She didn't have much time to ponder the matter, for Richard and Samantha seemed intent on making her feel a part of the congregation. Richard introduced her to the vicar, Mr. Ramsey, an older man with a kindly face. Toby Giles wished her good-day and used the greeting as an excuse to prolong his stay by Samantha's side.

Samantha, in turn, was seldom still, darting about the tree-lined churchyard to bring several of their neighbors to meet Claire. Here in Evendale, the girl sparkled like a diamond. Why couldn't Claire find a way to make her so comfortable in another setting?

One of the people Samantha dragged up to Claire was an elderly man with a craggy face and an outmoded, long-tailed coat. Beside him was a dark-haired boy who kept tugging at his cravat as if unused to it. Samantha introduced them as the Earl of Kendrick and his grandson James Wentworth.

"I believe I know your son, Lord Wentworth," Claire told the slender fellow as he stood beside her, leaning on an ebony cane. "He's already in London for the Season, is he not?"

"Indeed he is," the silver-haired Kendrick replied with a fond smile. "And my other son, Lord William, is off trying to save Egyptian antiquities from the French."

At the mention of his father, young James sighed.

Samantha nudged him with her elbow. "Egypt, eh? You never know, Jamie. He might bring you back a mummy!"

The eight-year-old boy brightened at that.

"I sense there's more to the story of Lord William," Claire said, after they'd left Mrs. Dallsten Walcott at the dower house and returned to the manor. She handed her bonnet to the dark-haired maid Daisy, who stood waiting.

"If there is, I'm not privy to it," Richard said, with a glance to Samantha.

"I suppose I was nine or ten when it happened," she replied with a frown as if trying to remember such a long time ago. "Lord William eloped with a local girl when they were seventeen. It was terribly romantic. Then she died birthing Jamie, and Lord William went off to have adventures." She sighed. "Quite tragic, really. It makes me so glad I had Papa."

Claire refused to glance at Richard. Would their lives have been similar had they married so young? Would she have been left to bear and perhaps raise their children alone while he sailed the world having adventures? The thoughts were enough to dampen her mood.

Samantha seemed similarly affected. She might have been saddened by the story or the memory of her father, but her attitude only worsened as the day went by.

Packing and practicing to be presented to the queen held no interest. At last, Claire tried setting up a diversion.

She'd noticed some large pieces of parchment in the schoolroom and carried them downstairs to the withdrawing room, where Mr. Linton, the groundskeeper and man-of-all-work, helped her affix one to the wall. Positioning a lamp on a nearby table, Claire showed Samantha how her shadow could be cast onto the parchment. The girl went through the motions of sketching Claire's silhouette, but her dispirited sighs had robbed Claire of any pleasure in the activity.

Lord, please help me to be patient. She's facing changes everywhere, in her family and friends, in her place in the world. Help me lead her through, just as You led me.

She felt some peace after that, but the only time Samantha brightened was when they'd all adjourned to the withdrawing room after dinner that evening. To Claire's surprise, the girl took Richard's hand and tugged him toward the chair where Claire had been seated earlier. "Come along, Cousin Richard. We must have a silhouette of you."

"Excellent idea," Claire said, to encourage her. Richard suffered himself to sit, and the light threw his shadow up onto the suspended parchment.

Samantha pushed on his shoulders to position him properly. "A little to the left. Now raise your chin. Perfect!" She scurried back. "There, Lady Winthrop. He's all ready for you."

Claire raised her brows. "For me?"

Samantha was already halfway to the piano. "Certainly. This is too important to risk on an amateur like me. I'll play to keep him in the mood. You draw."

Richard's smile said he was amused by his cousin's behavior. Claire shook her head. If she didn't know better, she'd think her charge was matchmaking. Samantha seemed to enjoy romantic stories as much as Claire did. Had she been told the tale of Claire and Richard's courtship and found it terribly tragic as well? Was she trying to reunite them now?

Just the thought set her fingers to trembling, and she clenched her fists to still them. This was silly! She had no reason to be nervous. What harm was there in drawing Richard's silhouette? Nothing much could happen while she was sketching.

She went to the wall and removed her gloves, laying them on the tray that held the charcoal Samantha had been using earlier.

"She means well," Richard murmured behind her.

Claire smiled to herself. "I suppose she does. And I'm glad to see her spirits lift."

"I thought she seemed too quiet at dinner. What is it?"

"Your cousin, I fear," Claire admitted. "I told you she was too attached to him." She reached up to follow the curve of his head with the charcoal, down to where his neck met the collar of his coat. Did he know that his hair in the back had a decided wave? Did it feel as soft as it looked? Goodness, but the fire was too warm!

Behind her, she heard him sigh. "Women like a man who can quote them poetry."

Claire focused on penciling in the line of his brow. "Girls like poetry. Women know to look for more than pretty words."

"And you deserved both."

The charcoal slipped, giving him a long, pointed nose. She licked her thumb and hastily rubbed off the mistake. If only the other mistakes in her life were so easily dealt with.

"Every wife deserves both," she said, and her voice

came out entirely too husky. She cleared her throat. "You said he thinks of her as a sister. I would not be so certain. It's possible he may even offer for her."

His shadow bunched as he shrugged, and she tsked at the movement. He repositioned himself. "I suppose he might, but I'm not sure it would be from the kind of love necessary between a husband and wife. He's grieving for Uncle, and it's too easy to transfer that affection to Samantha."

Claire sketched his nose again, a manly shape, long, straight, determined. "Since when were you such a student of human nature, sir?"

"Since I had to captain a ship. You learn to watch the skies, the waves, the denizens of the deep. They can tell you when a storm is coming. You learn to watch your crew for the same reason."

Claire's charcoal reached the curves of his lips, and her hand started shaking again. She set down the stick and rubbed her fingers with her other hand. "Then, this storm in Samantha—do you think it will pass?"

He shifted in his seat again, and she knew he was regarding his cousin, head bowed over her music. "Perhaps. But do we ever truly forget our first loves?"

"No," Claire murmured, before she could think better of it.

His shadow turned, and she thought he was gazing at her. She didn't dare look at him. Still, he said nothing, as if waiting for her to explain. How could she? If she admitted how often she'd thought of him, how she'd struggled over her choices, she would make herself sound unfaithful to her husband. She had done everything to honor her marriage, to make it a success. It was Winthrop who had dishonored her.

"I cannot finish unless you sit still," Claire said.

He waited another few moments, then settled back in his seat. But his mouth was now set in an unforgiving line, his chin higher than it had been. Claire thought the silhouette looked far more like the commanding Captain Everard, and not the Richard Everard she'd known, and loved.

Richard could not understand Claire, and he had ample opportunity to observe her the next few days. Contrary to his earlier fears, she was the perfect sponsor for Samantha. She managed to teach the girl a number of lessons on how to succeed in London, yet all the while her instructions sounded like the advice of a good friend.

She also kept the girl busy with plans. The only time they settled was to take tea or visit with Toby Giles, who appeared at the manor with a regularity Richard found amusing. He remembered Vaughn's prediction that the lad might have marriage in mind, but, when Richard joined them, he could see no more than teasing camaraderie between the pair.

Claire was equally calm and composed. She never lost her temper, even when Samantha was petulant. She never raised her voice, even when Samantha was loudly enthusiastic. She had a quiet confidence that, Richard was surprised to find, was even more attractive than the gaiety he remembered.

But Samantha wasn't the only one she charmed. Mrs. Linton and the maids were obviously won over, as the housekeeper brought no more complaints to Richard. He even went so far as to check on her, but Mrs. Linton shooed him out of her kitchen with a wave of her plump hands.

"Lady Winthrop and I have an understanding," the snowy-haired housekeeper told him. "She's preparing

Lady Everard for her future, and I am to take care of her present. And each of us knows exactly what's to be done."

Claire had given Richard the same impression. She and Samantha bustled about the manor most days, often with one of the maids or Mr. Linton in attendance. Richard was surprised to find them one day in the library, Samantha in an old-fashioned gown with hoops that spread her skirts far beyond her maidenly curves, and what looked like a bedsheet tied at her waist.

"Practicing for her presentation to the queen," Claire explained, when he stood in the doorway, perplexed. "Slowly, Samantha. Those hoops can be unpredictable."

As if to prove it, the front flipped up, and anyone standing in front of her, Richard thought, would have had to hurriedly look the other way to spare everyone's dignity.

Samantha pushed the hoop down to the floor and turned to Claire, red-faced. "How does anyone manage this!"

"With practice," Claire assured her. "And no young lady I have ever met has died of mortification if things went wrong."

"Wonderful," Samantha muttered, facing front again. "I'll be the first."

Richard watched as his cousin took a step back and nearly tripped over her train. Wincing, he lowered his voice to Claire. "You do intend to accompany her, I hope."

"Of course. I only wish you could join us."

Her comment seemed sincere, but it pointed out the differences between them. She was a lady, the daughter of an earl, the widow of a viscount. He was the second son of a second son, and one step away from trade in his role as merchant captain. She had been presented to the queen; he never would.

And neither would Samantha, he realized, if the College of Heralds didn't uphold her right to the title. Mr. Caruthers, their solicitor, was supposed to be working with the august group to confirm Samantha's right, but Richard had yet to hear the results.

"When is the presentation at court?" Richard murmured, as Samantha disentangled herself from her train and set her gown to rights again.

"Shortly after the Season starts," Claire murmured back, gaze on her charge and not a little troubled, Richard thought. "I've written to Lord Morton, the chamberlain, to request that Samantha be included."

"Are requests ever denied?"

"Gently!" she called in encouragement to Samantha. She clenched her fists at her side as if fighting the desire to rush in and help the girl. Richard had to fight his own desire to reach out and hold her hand, feel her fingers cradled in his own.

"Requests are only refused if the petitioner fails to meet the qualifications," she said to Richard. "A lady must be the daughter or wife of a peer or related to a military officer."

She made it sound as if Samantha's qualifications were obvious, but Richard had a sinking feeling that it wouldn't be so easy. He was beginning to see the impediments that could keep his cousin from fulfilling the requirements of her father's will.

Perhaps that was why, when he found Samantha waiting for him in the stable yard as he went down for a ride one morning, his first thought was of disaster.

"What's wrong?" he demanded, striding toward her.

Her smile was bright. "Nothing." A puff of steam rose from the single word into the cool spring air. Though she was bundled in her pelisse, her night rail peeked out from below the quilted fabric. "I just wanted to speak privately with you."

Mindful of the groom leading Richard's horse from the stables, Richard took Samantha's elbow and drew her back toward the house. "What do you need?" he asked, voice lowered.

She dimpled up at him. "I merely wanted to say that if you intend to win Lady Winthrop's heart, you're going about it all wrong."

Richard raised himself up to his full height. "I am not courting Lady Winthrop."

Samantha shrugged. "Not very well, anyway."

"Samantha—" Richard started in warning.

She held up one finger. "I'm only trying to help. She's a very nice lady, and I would think you'd want her to be happy."

Richard frowned. "Is she unhappy?"

"Well, of course she's unhappy!" Samantha put both hands on her hips. "Left alone so young, miles away from home, not sure who to trust. Who could blame her for breaking under the strain!"

Was the girl talking about herself or Claire? Richard reached out to touch her arm. "You aren't alone, Samantha. Jerome, Vaughn and I would do anything for you."

Her smile was soft. "I know, and I love you for it. We are becoming a family. I just want you to extend that devotion to Lady Winthrop. She's a member of the family now, too."

Some part of him pulled away from the thought. "Your kindness is commendable, but she is merely doing us a service."

"Is she?" She cocked her head, the morning light sparkling on her tousled curls. "And why would that be?"

He hadn't intended to tell her about his bargain with

Claire. Claire's reputation would be damaged if the terms of her payment got out, and Samantha might lose some respect for her sponsor. But he could not have her thinking that there was more to Claire's presence here.

"Lady Winthrop will be well compensated for her efforts," he told Samantha. "You need have no concern for her."

Samantha shook her head. "No compensation can make up for being bullied."

"Bullied?" Richard felt his back stiffening again. "Who's bullying her? Name the person, and I'll see him discharged."

Samantha giggled. "Little hard to discharge yourself."

Richard deflated with a chuckle. "I don't bully her. I couldn't."

"You try," Samantha insisted. "You could be a great deal nicer to her. Come now, admit it." She leaned closer and peered up at him. "You still care for her."

His mouth felt dry, and his palms inside his riding gloves were sweating. "She's an old friend."

"She could be more."

Could she? Why did his heart beat faster at the thought? Nothing had changed. Even as the captain of his own ship, the pride of the Everard fleet, his position was less than Claire's. And though he had a good amount invested in the 'Change and his ship, all that could evaporate in an instant now that England had returned to war with France.

"Perhaps," he allowed to Samantha, "but Lady Winthrop will have plenty of suitors once it's known she's out of mourning."

"No other suitor can hold a candle to you," Samantha said.

Richard gave her a smile but turned away. Claire had refused him before. He saw no reason for her to accept him now. He'd do his best not to vex her in her work with Samantha, but he could promise nothing more. He only pitied the fools in London who'd bet on his behalf.

Chapter Fourteen

Richard tried to put Samantha's suggestion from his mind as he took his ride. The sun had pushed through the usual morning mist, and the last drops of silver clung to the greening wood. He inhaled the crisp air and let it fill him as his horse's hooves crunched against the gravel of the riding path. He had few opportunities to ride on his travels; it was one of the things he missed most about life at sea. Feeling the horse's power beneath him, pounding across the fields and lanes, brought a joy to his heart and spirit.

Finding time to ride in London would be difficult. He could see only changes ahead. Samantha would have her Season, fulfill the requirements of her father's will and go on to be the new baroness. Jerome and Adele would move to Four Oaks permanently. Vaughn, well, Richard could only hope he'd make some peace with their uncle's untimely death and go back to his poetry. And Richard would sail off to Jamaica as planned.

Always before, he could feel the anticipation building for the journey. He'd study his course on maps, talk to captains who had recently made the trip to learn about any changes to shipping patterns or weather. He'd look for news in the papers about enemy nations preying on cargo ships. And each step would only make him more excited about the prospects of adventure.

Now none of it held the appeal it once had. He was more likely to think about sitting by the fire with Claire, helping Jerome set up a more efficient system of identifying cargo, wondering if there was a better way to manage the Dallsten Manor estate. Was he getting old? Or was the Lord leading him somewhere else?

Show me Your way, Lord. Show me the path You want me to take.

That they had company was evident the moment he returned to the manor. Female voices echoed from the withdrawing room, followed by a gentleman's reply and the sparkle of laughter. Richard ventured toward the sounds.

Neither Claire nor Samantha noticed him in the doorway. They were seated on the settee, Samantha in her pale muslin gown and Claire in an elegant black dress, and their attentions were fixed on the center of the room, where a slight man with a head of brown curls, purposely disheveled, Richard thought, was prancing about. The collar of his black coat was too high, in Richard's opinion, his cravat tied in an overly complicated knot. In fact, the fellow looked a bit like a long-necked stork promenading about the room, each leg setting the step precisely.

"This room will not do," he declared, turning to meet Claire's and Samantha's gazes. His voice held the hint of a French accent. "It is not the proper setting for a jewel of Lady Everard's brilliance."

Just what Richard needed, someone to rival Vaughn's effusive praises. This could only be the famed dance master Claire had insisted they hire.

"The schoolroom might have enough space," Samantha

ventured with a glance to Claire. "If we moved the table to the wall."

"Ah," he said, shaking a slender finger at her, "but I understood that you had escaped the schoolroom, Lady Everard."

Samantha giggled.

Richard snorted. The popinjay had to turn his whole body to face the door.

"Captain Everard," Claire greeted Richard with a smile. "Our dance master has arrived. Come meet Monsieur Chevalier. Monsieur, this is Captain Richard Everard, Lady Everard's cousin."

The dance master took a mincing step forward and favored Richard with a deep bow. "Captain Everard, a pleasure."

"Chevalier," Richard acknowledged, moving into the room. "I take it you were determining which room to use for your lessons."

The fellow tsked. "I do not call them lessons. It will be my pleasure to partner Lady Everard in the dance, and I am certain we will both learn a great deal from each other."

Samantha blushed. "What do you think of the schoolroom, Cousin Richard?"

Richard went to stand at Claire's side. "Good space, but I don't relish trying to get the piano up the south tower stairs."

Claire looked thoughtful, but Samantha's face fell. "Oh, I didn't think about that. Of course, we'll need music."

"I assure you we can glide to the music of the spheres," Chevalier said, with a bow to Samantha.

"Yes, well, it would help the rest of us to hear more than a celestial choir," Claire said. "I suppose this room will have to do."

Her tone was polite, but Richard thought she seemed a bit annoyed with the notion. Every lady at Dallsten Manor gravitated to the feminine withdrawing room; he supposed she was loath to disturb it.

"We may have another choice," he offered. "Mr. Linton and I should be able to move the piano to the receiving hall."

Samantha clapped her hands. "Oh, perfect!"

"I don't believe I've had the pleasure of seeing that room," Claire said with a slight frown.

"It's huge!" Samantha exclaimed, waving her hands as if to give the impression of height and width. "Papa favored it."

Richard could understand why. At times, he felt as though he was trying to fit into a dollhouse in this dainty room. The receiving hall at the back of the house was paneled in dark wood and floored in stone, and the ceiling was laced with intricately carved beams. Richard thought Uncle must have enjoyed playing King Arthur there.

"It will do," he promised Claire. Then he turned to the dance master. "You can help us move the piano this afternoon, once you're settled in."

Chevalier raised a surprisingly delicate brow and held up his gloved hands. "I regret, *Capitaine,* that I must refuse. My hands must remain unburdened for the task ahead. You will understand, of course."

Richard thought he understood all too well. He'd never tolerated an officer who was unwilling to dirty his hands when needed. He saw no reason to tolerate laziness in a gentleman under his employ now. He strode forward and clapped the dance master on his padded shoulder, nearly oversetting the fellow.

"I imagine you've lifted any number of ladies in the dance. A little piano should be no trouble." He turned to

Claire to find a smile tugging at her mouth. "What about some refreshments before our exertions?"

"Mrs. Linton is already on her way," Claire assured him. "Lady Everard, why don't you show Monsieur Chevalier the music we have available?"

Samantha rose eagerly and led the dance master to the piano. Richard took her place beside Claire on the settee.

"You don't like him," Claire murmured.

"Not in the slightest. What do you know about him?"

She glanced to where Samantha was giggling over something the dance master had said. "He came from France to England as a boy, I understand. He is well known among the *ton*. It seems any family with a daughter of marriageable age has enlisted his services the last few years, and I understand he's tutored a few gentlemen as well. I've never heard the least complaint or whisper of scandal. Frankly, Richard, I think we were lucky to get him."

Richard could not be so sure. "You said Widmore had a hand in it," he mused.

Claire nodded. "He exerted some pressure, no doubt."

Richard couldn't help grinning. "You mean he bullied the man into helping us."

Claire nudged him with her shoulder. "You needn't make it sound so valiant, sir."

"But you will admit the trait came in handy."

She put her nose in the air. "I will admit only that the marquess seems to use the tactic with greater finesse. He even sent a letter of recommendation for our dance master."

He ought to take some comfort in that, but they'd had another servant who'd come with such a recommendation, the footman Todd. That recommendation could have been forged. Certainly Widmore had disavowed all knowledge of the man.

"You're certain the recommendation was legitimate?" Richard asked. "Did the letter bear Widmore's seal?"

Claire frowned as if surprised by his question, but she nodded. "Yes. And I recognize the man. We've never been formally introduced, until today, but I've seen him with his lordship when I've gone to visit Lady Widmore and her daughter." Her look softened. "I can understand why you might take him in dislike. He's rather full of himself, he's obviously too much of a flirt and he fancies himself a wit."

"He's half-right there," Richard said.

Claire's lips twitched as if she fought a smile. "Be that as it may, I see no harm in him. Now we merely have to discover whether his work lives up to his reputation."

They had cause to find out that very afternoon. Richard had doffed his coat and helped the elderly groundskeeper and the dance master shove the piano down the corridor and under the stairs for the receiving hall at the back of the house.

Chevalier had proven stronger than Richard had expected, bearing his share of the weight with an exaggerated grimace that was all show, Richard thought. He also helped them clear the room, pushing the massive table that normally ran down the center to one side and setting the dozens of chairs it boasted along the paneled walls. Mrs. Linton and the maids rolled up the carpet and swept up the stone floor.

Chevalier eyed the room. "Yes, I can see why you valued the room, *Capitaine*. This will be perfect for my work."

Richard shrugged into his coat, which Claire had handed him as she entered the room. Samantha skipped into the space, obviously excited to start her lessons.

Claire moved more slowly. Her usual glide was just as graceful, but Richard saw the tension underlying her smile. Concerned, he followed her to the piano.

"Is something wrong?"

She glanced to Samantha as if to make sure the girl and the dance master were out of earshot, then motioned Richard closer.

"You should see this," she murmured, handing him a piece of parchment blackened around the edges as if it had been plucked from the fire. "Mrs. Linton found it under a corner of the carpet."

Richard glanced down at the brittle sheet. It was obviously part of a larger composition—he could see the bottoms and tops of other letters on the lines above and below, and the words that remained were only part of a sentence. But those words chilled him: ...*how we can hasten the revolution.*

"What does it mean?" Claire asked, gaze troubled.

Richard shook his head. "I don't know, but I don't think it bodes well, for any of us."

Claire watched Richard take up sentinel beside the door of the receiving hall, as if to protect the rest of them from whatever lurked outside. Yet it seemed that something lay hidden inside Dallsten Manor, and she could not know exactly what.

Revolution? Why talk of revolution? So many conversations in London turned to the French fleet massing across the Channel. Napoleon had vowed to take England by autumn. Already reports talked of French spies landing to the south. But here, so far north and inland? What could a French spy want with the remote Evendale Valley? And no true Englishman would support a rising against the Crown, not again.

She could not focus on the music she was playing. Richard seemed just as distracted. He crossed his arms over his chest, but she didn't think the gesture or his frown came from his cousin's faltering steps. The words had concerned him, too, and he was puzzling over the note just as she was. It must be difficult for him to think that treason might have been plotted in this very room, perhaps by one of his own family.

"Oh, I'll never get it right!" Samantha stopped to stamp her pink-slippered foot.

"Au contraire, Lady Everard," Chevalier replied, taking her hand and cradling it in his. "You are as light as a butterfly skimming the meadow. You merely require a little more practice, and you will soar over the mountains!"

Richard grimaced, and Claire hid a smile. Samantha pulled away. "I think I need to see it done properly." She turned to Claire. "Lady Winthrop, will you show me?"

Claire's stomach tightened in protest. In truth, her leg hadn't pained her as much since she'd come to Dallsten Manor, and she'd managed to take several strolls about the grounds with Samantha. Of course, she didn't dare venture from the graveled paths onto the lawn, for fear the uneven ground would trip her up. She'd also taken her parasol each time to make sure she had something to lean upon if she needed it. No, a dance was much too much to expect.

She smiled politely at the girl. "Someone should play the music."

"I'll play," Samantha insisted, hurrying toward her with a rustle of her muslin skirts.

Claire felt stiff all over. "I truly am not a good example in this, my dear. I've been in mourning the last year; I don't know the latest dances."

"Then it will be my honor to teach you, too," Monsieur

Chevalier declared. He held out his hands. "Come, Lady Winthrop, dance with me."

Claire started to shake her head, but Richard pushed off the wall. "I will partner Lady Winthrop. She owes me a dance."

The dance master opened his mouth as if to protest, but one look at Richard's face and he bowed him past. "Of course, *Capitaine*. I will merely call the steps, shall I?"

Richard reached Claire's side and held out his hand. She couldn't accept it. She couldn't dance with him. What if she fell? How could she answer the questions that would follow? She couldn't let anyone know how badly she'd chosen in her husband.

She shook her head, but Richard bent closer. "Please, Claire?"

The tone was gentle, kind. She hadn't seen such a look in his eyes for years—tender, yearning, hopeful. At this moment, dancing with her was the most important thing in his world. She understood the feeling. Nothing would have made her happier than to move beside him, turning to music meant for them alone.

One dance, Lord? One moment with Richard? Is that too much to ask? Will You keep me standing for one dance?

Her longing filled her to overflowing, forced her to her feet. Hanging on to hope, she put her hand on Richard's arm and let him lead her onto the floor.

Chapter Fifteen

The movement that had so frustrated Samantha was merely a figure from one of the newer dances, so moving with another couple was not required. Claire took her place opposite Richard and curtsied to his bow. Though she hadn't even started dancing, her heart was drumming in her chest. She could barely hear the music Samantha was playing, or the dance master's instructions as he said, "Take right hands and circle left."

Her fingers slid easily into the cup of Richard's large hands, her arm supported effortlessly. The floor felt foreign beneath her as she turned with him, as if she was dancing on the warmth of his smile.

"Pass shoulder to shoulder," Monsieur Chevalier called.

Richard released her to move past her, gaze on hers, body inches away. She caught the scent of bright spring air and cool water. Her shoulder only came to the center of his chest.

"And back."

Here came the first test. Claire took a deep breath and stepped back. Her leg held. *Thank You, Lord!*

"Smile, Lady Winthrop," Monsieur Chevalier suggested. "This is a joyous occasion. Two steps forward, two steps back."

"Yes, Lady Winthrop," Richard said with a grin as they met in the middle. "Smile. You are as light as a butterfly soaring up a mountain."

Claire laughed as they parted.

On they went, moving with the music and the dance master's instructions. Yet all Claire could feel was Richard, so close, like a lost part of her she'd longed to find again. For a moment, she was a girl once more, beautiful, strong, carefree. She'd been given a chance to partner the tall, handsome lad with the soulful brown eyes who'd been watching her across the ballroom all night, and she wasn't about to waste it.

He was so much more now. He moved with a strength that spoke of confidence, of being at ease with his conscience. His smile broadened, deepened, as if being with her fulfilled every desire. Why had she been so afraid to take a chance on him years ago? If he should ask it, would she be any braver this time?

They turned, each with an arm behind the other's back, gazes locked, and the world shrank further away. Those dark eyes were pools of admiration and something more, something she ached to hold to her heart. Richard must have seen the answer in her smile, for he leaned closer, and for a mad moment she thought he meant to kiss her.

With a protest that shot pain to her hip, her knee gave and she lurched to one side.

Richard caught her up. "Easy. Are you all right?"

Samantha must not have noticed Claire's misstep, for the music continued. Monsieur Chevalier, however, was frowning at her as if wondering what she was doing. She knew her face must be flaming.

Still, she pasted on a smile and forced air into her lungs

as she kept her weight on her good leg. "Don't let go," she whispered to Richard.

His grip tightened. "Never."

Oh, how she wanted to believe that. But she could not afford the time to sort out her feelings for him. She had to get off this floor. "There, Lady Everard," she called. "I believe that is how it is done."

As Samantha stopped playing, the dance master applauded. "Oh, well done, Lady Winthrop. You are an angel on the floor, granting mere mortals a glimpse of paradise."

Beside her, Richard bent lower as if to praise her as well. He shifted his grip on her waist to take more of her weight. "Can you walk?" he murmured.

"I'm not sure," she murmured back.

"Lean on my arm," he said. Then, obviously for the others' benefit, he added, "I quite agree, Chevalier. And I think we've had enough practicing for today. Go settle yourself in for the duration. Samantha, remind Mrs. Linton that we'll be having one more to dinner."

The dance master offered him a bow. "I am honored, *Capitaine*. Until then." He traipsed from the room, each step delicate, as if he'd been the one to tire from the dancing. With a grin at Richard, Samantha followed him.

"She thinks we're having an assignation," Claire said, leg throbbing.

"She can think anything she likes," Richard replied. "I'm more concerned about you. Try taking a step."

She did, and pain speared up her leg. Despite her control, she sucked in a breath.

Richard shook his head. "Forgive me, Claire."

"This isn't your fault— Oh!" Before she could finish, he had picked her up in his arms and started for the door.

"This isn't necessary," Claire said, her breath now even

more difficult to regulate. His face was so near she could see the red highlights in his beard, like flames licking through satinwood.

"Apparently it is, if you're having trouble walking," he said, starting down the corridor for the entryway. "What happened to your leg?"

"A fall," she said, trying not to think of that awful night. "I broke my leg, and it never healed properly."

"How did you fall?"

He sounded more surprised than censorious. Still, she could not bring herself to tell him the truth. The story she'd fabricated flowed easily from frequent use. "It was silly, really. I stumbled on the stairs, and my foot caught on my hem. The next thing I knew, I was at the bottom."

"Odd," he said as he reached the grand stair. "You were the most graceful woman I knew. You're still as graceful."

At the moment, that woman had never seemed farther away. She trilled a laugh that took every ounce of her strength. "That's why I called it silly."

He started up the stairs. "I suppose after all these years you don't owe me the truth, Claire. But when you're ready to tell me, I'd like to know."

She was glad he saved his breath then. She wasn't all that heavy, but it couldn't have been easy carrying her up the stairs, even for him. She was afraid he'd question her further once they reached her room, but he merely set her down gently on the chair in front of the fire.

Mercier came hurrying from the dressing room. "Lady Winthrop! Something has happened, *oui?*"

"I fear I overtired Lady Winthrop with my dancing," Richard said. "I'll leave you to see to her needs." He turned and left, and Claire did not have the strength to call him back.

"*Oui,* madame?" Mercier asked, dark head cocked as she regarded Claire with wide eyes.

"Ask Mrs. Linton for a cool compress," Claire said, and her maid bobbed a curtsy and hurried from the room.

And Claire burst into tears. The sobs shook her, set her leg to protesting anew. *Why, Father? Why couldn't I have one dance?*

She used to love to dance, had taken such joy in moving to the music. In the dance, she could forget about her father's expectations, his hopes for her future. It was the one time when she felt she could just be herself. Why did she have to lose that, too?

My grace is sufficient for thee, for My power is made perfect in weakness.

Most days, she clung to that verse. Marriage had shown her her weaknesses, and God had helped her find her strength. She'd survived, made it through, at times solely on faith. But today, leg aching, alone, she couldn't feel His grace. She wasn't even sure she felt His presence.

Are You punishing me? Was I such a disobedient child? You say to honor your father and mother. Father wanted me to marry Winthrop.

And she thought she knew why. An Everard would never have satisfied his ideal for a son-in-law. Her father had feared the Everard reputation, feared that Richard would never be able to support her.

I have not given you a spirit of fear but of boldness.

Now, there was a verse she wished she could take to heart. Once she'd thought she was bold, gathering a cadre of suitors that had made most of the other girls on their first Season green with envy. Richard had been one of that cadre, but only for a moment. One conversation, one dance, had proven him different. He had goals that would take him far beyond her limited sphere.

But that sphere was all she knew. And the more he talked, the more frightened she'd become. She'd been all too willing to listen to her father's concerns. They'd matched her own.

At times Richard had seemed, well, rather boyish, with his impossible dreams and ridiculously high hopes. His unbridled enthusiasm was nothing like the cool detachment of the men her father invited to call on her. They were satisfied with their positions in life, sure of their power and prestige. They seemed, somehow, safer.

She'd been rather afraid to accept the future Richard offered. If he suddenly proposed again today, she'd be no more convinced of it. For now she had ten years of experience to show her how dismal a marriage could be. She had no wish to repeat her mistakes.

Claire took a shaky breath and wiped at her eyes. Then she rubbed the dampness into the sides of her gown where her maid would not be likely to spot it. She supposed she would have to explain at least a part of the situation to Mercier, for this would likely not be the last time the girl would have to deal with Claire's injury.

But Richard? He also wanted to know what had happened to her leg. Perhaps someday she'd tell him, some far-off day when she didn't care whether his eyes brimmed with pity or, worse, blame. As for today, she hugged her arms around her waist and sucked in a breath. Today, she would go on as she had for the last ten years, head high, step measured, smile serene.

And only her Lord would know how troubled her heart was.

Richard left the house and stalked down the lawn. He needed air, light, the sight of the waves stretching in front of him. This close to the fells, the nearest water was the pond below the house, so he made for it and stood on the edge, taking deep breaths.

Water still had the ability to focus his thoughts. When it lay flat and still as the pond did now, it seemed he could see his course easily. When it rose in waves above him as it did at sea, it called on all his reserves. The pond was ridiculously small compared to the oceans he'd sailed, and instead of a forest of masts and laden piers to meet him, it was edged with daffodils. Even on the windiest day in the most rickety rowboat, it would hardly test his abilities. But the situation here at Dallsten Manor, he feared, would test every part of him.

He could not like that scrap of parchment Mrs. Linton had unearthed. Who knew how long it had lain under the edge of the carpet? It could have been a Dallsten who'd penned it, though he had a difficult time thinking of someone like Mrs. Dallsten Walcott plotting treason.

Perhaps it had been written in innocence, complaining about revolutions in France or America. Yet he couldn't help wondering. Samantha and his brother's wife, Adele, had said his uncle had held private parties at the manor every summer. While the villagers enjoyed a catered picnic and games on the lawn, other men had sequestered themselves in the receiving hall. The only name he knew among them was the Marquess of Widmore.

Adele had once said that Samantha had woven a fiction about the event, that her father was really a foreign prince in exile and these men were his loyal officials come to plot his return to the throne. What if they plotted against another throne, the very throne of England? Uncle had boasted a romantic streak wider than Vaughn's. Richard could easily see the man caught up in the idea of a revolution as glorious as those that had changed the American colonies and France.

But the Marquess of Widmore? He stood only to lose if the people of England ousted the aristocracy. And surely he was wise enough to see beyond the initial, heady declaration, to the bloodshed and violence that had marred post-revolutionary France. Vaughn had even admitted that, years ago, the Marquess and Uncle had tried to save some of the French nobles from the guillotine.

So, what did the note mean? Had revolution been plotted at Dallsten Manor? And where were the conspirators now? Did they pose a danger to him or his family?

Just as troubling, however, were his suspicions about Claire. She held herself so deep, but at times he saw the girl who'd infatuated him. He'd originally thought the death of her husband had subdued her. Now his suspicions made his fists clench.

He'd heard of women who'd been hurt in their homes—falling down stairs, as Claire claimed, or standing too close to the fire and getting burned. But he could not imagine Claire in such a mishap. She was too sure of herself, too graceful, too aware of her surroundings. Yet, if she hadn't fallen, that meant someone had pushed her.

He'd met men who were abusive to their fellow sailors when in their cups. He did not keep them on his ship. That any man would raise his voice, much less his hands, to Claire raised such an anger inside him he wanted to shout.

He stared at the still water, so blue under the pale spring sky, so like Claire's pale blue eyes. For once, the waters failed to calm him.

Lord, help me. You know how angry I was with her all those years, but I never wished her harm. It seems she's had to pay the price for her choices. I cannot rejoice in that.

Judge not, and ye shall not be judged; condemn not,

and ye shall not be condemned; forgive, and ye shall be forgiven.

Small wonder that verse kept coming to mind. He'd memorized it early on, when he'd been trying to forget about Claire. Now, however, he had a feeling the Lord wanted him to remember, and do something about it.

Chapter Sixteen

Claire managed to make it down to dinner that night, leaning on Mercier's arm. She had explained about her fall and the leg's weakness, but the moment her maid had spied the swelling joint, she had run to pull up a footstool.

"We lift it high, *oui?*" Mercier said, bustling about, fetching pillows from the bed. She tucked them carefully under Claire's leg. "And after you let it sit with the cool compress, I will wrap it tightly. This is how my father cared for injuries."

"Was your father a physician?" Claire asked, impressed with the girl's quick thinking. She was obviously certain of her actions, for she'd only used a question once.

"Non," Mercier replied, stepping back to eye her handiwork, hands on her hips. "He was master of horse for a marquis."

Despite herself, Claire laughed.

Dinner proved to be nearly as merry. Claire was afraid Richard would renew his questioning, but she needn't have worried. Samantha monopolized the conversation, plying her dance master with questions about London.

"Do they still wear ostrich plumes at court?" she asked,

mutton long forgotten on her china plate. "And the big hoops?"

"Of a certainty. And very fetching you will look in them, your ladyship, I am sure."

"What about the regular balls?"

"My dear Lady Everard, if you are invited to a 'regular' ball, you must refuse. Never settle for anything less than the best."

The sentiment sounded entirely too much like something Claire's father would have said. Lord Falbrooke had gone to his grave dressed in velvet and fine wool, surrounded by silver, no more happy than any day of his life. Claire could not see Samantha following that example.

"There are a great many good and kind people in London," she told Samantha, who was seated across the table from her on Richard's right. "Some may not be considered fashionable, but they are the more interesting, and all deserve our respect."

Chevalier, sitting beside Samantha, beamed at her. "Ah, did I not say this very afternoon that Lady Winthrop was closer to heaven than most mortals? You would do well to copy her, Lady Everard."

"Yes," Richard put in. "You would."

Warmth flowed over her. Claire could not meet his gaze. She should not crave the good opinions of others; that way lay danger, she knew from experience. Yet his praise felt good. She wanted him to see her as an excellent example for Samantha.

She wanted him to like her.

Oh, that was just as dangerous! She should not act to please Richard Everard. Yet she could not help her gaze straying to his from time to time as dinner progressed, and after they had all adjourned to the withdrawing room.

Claire perched on the settee by the fire. Across the room, Samantha and the dance master played at commerce, heads bent over their cards at the little teak table. Claire's hands felt empty after so many days of writing. A shame she'd left her embroidery upstairs. She'd had little time to work on the fine pillow cover that would brighten the house she would live in after the Season was over. She had been so pleased with the pattern of roses earlier. She could not understand why her joy had dimmed.

Richard drew up a chair to sit beside her and spoke lowly, obviously for her benefit alone. "Is that why you stopped dancing, because of your leg?"

Claire kept her gaze on Samantha, who had thrown down a card with a confident grin. "I believe you said you would wait for me to initiate this conversation, sir."

"I didn't ask you how it happened," he countered. "I asked you if it's the reason you stopped dancing. You loved to dance."

The sigh of longing escaped before she could stop it. "Very well. Yes, I stopped dancing to prevent another fall. I never know when the joint will give out. I also carry a parasol at times as a fashionable precaution."

He cocked his head. "Do you miss it? Dancing?"

She refused to let him see how much. "I told you, Captain Everard, I am quite content."

"I didn't believe you when you said it the first time," he proclaimed, straightening. "I believe you less now. Answer the question, Claire."

Heat flushed up her. Why did men think that a command must be instantly obeyed? Neither her father nor her husband had been in the military or captained a ship, as Richard had, yet they'd directed her with just as much determination. At times, she'd felt as if she'd been one of their servants. "It is not my custom to answer bullies, Captain," she replied.

She thought that might set him back, but the only sign that she might have annoyed him was a narrowing of his dark eyes. "I'm beginning to think you know that from experience."

She clasped her hands in her lap and pressed them down against the black silk. "Quite a bit in the last week, actually."

"I would never strike you, Claire."

She could not let him know the power those words held. "And do you expect my gratitude for that, sir? Is it not your Christian duty to protect widows and orphans?"

He glanced at Samantha across the room. "A duty and a privilege."

Why was he so good at cutting through all her frustrations? She could only admire the way he championed his cousin. He clearly cared about Samantha. But, on some level, she thought her father and husband had cared about her, or rather what she could do for them. *Please, Lord! Let Richard be better than that!*

"You are very good with her," Claire acknowledged aloud. "It is to your credit."

He smiled. "She's easy to love—all that life, all that joy. She reminds me of you."

Her breath caught even as her hands tightened. "Sir, you grow too bold."

He snorted. "Better bold than maudlin. A captain learns what to say and when to say it."

She forced her fingers to open and rubbed them against her skirts. "Of course. Then you see me as an underling, much as your junior officers."

He frowned. "You persist in being angry with me to no cause."

could not know that anger was her last defense. "And you persist in saying things you do not mean."

He leaned closer. "I mean every word."

She wanted to believe that. She wanted to believe things would be different this time. But she had changed; he had changed. She couldn't go back to being that girl he'd loved. She was thankful that Mrs. Linton came into the room just then and went straight to Richard's side.

"Lord Kendrick's footman brought up the mail, sir," she said, holding out a pile of letters. "He just had time to drop them by." She nodded to the top missive. "That's Mrs. Everard's hand."

Samantha immediately abandoned her game and hurried over, leaving the dance master at the card table. Richard handed her the letter with a smile. "It's addressed to you."

The girl broke the seal and scanned the contents. "She says Derby is beautiful. The house was spared the worst of the flooding, but the tenant cottages were hard hit. Cousin Jerome is studying plans from the magistrate John Harriott to see if he can build a dike to protect them in the future, the way Mr. Harriott drained his lands. Oh, and they hope to join us in London after Easter." She looked up at Richard as if to see what he thought of all that, then frowned. "Cousin?"

While she had been talking, Richard had broken the seal on another letter and glanced over the words. Claire had never seen his face so pale. Still, he managed a smile as he folded the parchment shut. "That's good news. Now Adele can help you shop for your new wardrobe."

Samantha's smile blossomed. "That's right!"

"I would be delighted to offer my advice as well, Lady Everard," Monsieur Chevalier added, strolling up to them.

As Samantha turned to him, Richard excused himself and left the room. Praying her leg would hold, Claire stood and followed.

"Mrs. Linton." Richard's call down the corridor pulled the little housekeeper up short. "Do you recognize this hand?"

The woman gazed down at the letter he held in front of her. "Can't say as I do, sir. Someone from London?"

Richard watched her. "Why do you say that?"

She pointed to the parchment. "Fine paper. I saw some once in a store in Blackcliff. Mrs. Delaney imports it all the way from London, or so she says."

Richard thanked her and let her go about her duties. He hadn't thought this problem would be easily solved.

"Richard?"

He turned at the sound of Claire's voice. Funny how his given name slipped out from time to time. He was certain she didn't even realize it, or he'd be back to Captain Everard. Now she moved out of the withdrawing room slowly, as if her leg still pained her. He met her halfway. "What's wrong?"

"My question exactly," she said. She nodded toward the paper in his hand. "What was in that letter?"

While he would have relished her insights, he felt compelled to protect her. "It's nothing that need concern you."

She raised her honey-colored brows. "Indeed. I suppose most women would be unconcerned by a matter that causes an intelligent, competent man to blanch."

He'd blanched? He'd have to do better. "Will you believe me when I say I can manage?"

"Certainly. Will you believe me when I say I only want to help?"

He wanted to believe her. He could not see her behind this latest threat to their peace. He knew Claire's handwriting; he still had the few letters, carefully packed away, that she'd written him before she'd married. They'd arrived at various ports of call, each one as welcome as a present at Christmas. His cabin boy had wrinkled his nose every time the rose-scented perfume drifted out of Richard's sea trunk.

The bold, arrogant hand on this letter was nothing like hers. And she hadn't been in the village since Sunday, when they'd all been together, so she couldn't have posted anything from there.

Still, how could he drag her further into this puzzle? If he'd truly thought there might be danger, he would never have brought her here. But the letter indicated otherwise, and Claire had a right to know what she was facing.

He held out the letter. "Someone doesn't want Samantha to go to London. Any idea who?"

He watched as she opened the letter and read it. Would she be frightened? Dismissive?

Be warned. Disaster awaits Lady Everard in London. You are only safe in Cumberland. —A friend.

Claire handed it back to him. "A shame the world boasts so many craven curs," she said as if remarking on dismal weather. "How can I help you protect Samantha?"

Her words might have been pleasant, but a cold fury burned in those pale eyes.

He couldn't help the chuckle that bubbled up. "The hen protecting her chick, eh? Even after the last few days, I find it hard to picture you that way."

She lifted her chin. "I should hope not. I would prefer to be pictured as a falcon than some barnyard fowl."

He inclined his head. "My apologies. But I would think you'd want something more grand. Perhaps a peacock."

Oh, there was definitely fire in her, and now it was directed at him. "Indeed. We will ignore for a moment that the peacock is the male of the species. Tell me, does it remind you of me because of my enduring vanity, or the fact that I screech at odd hours?"

Richard laughed, then bent to meet her gaze. "A peacock, madam, is the most beautiful bird of my acquaintance. That's why it reminds me of you."

Her head remained insufferably high, but the fire banked to a warm glow. "In that case, Captain, you are forgiven. And I will be even more pleased with you if you tell me what you intend to do about this letter."

"You don't recognize the handwriting?"

She shook her head. "No. Could this be associated with the problem you mentioned about your brother?"

"Possibly." His skepticism must have been evident, for her eyes narrowed. He could at least lay that concern to rest. "We have reason to believe Todd is dead."

She took a step back. "Dead? How?"

"A falling-out among thieves, the Bow Street Runner told me. This is something else."

She drew her shawl about her shoulders as if the thought chilled her. "You've made no secret of the fact that we'll be leaving for London after Easter. Could one of your neighbors be envious?"

"Doubtful. None of the older people care, and there isn't a rival young lady in miles, according to Jerome's wife."

She looked thoughtful. "But there are suitors. You know the way Toby Giles has been hanging about."

Giles? Richard could see the lad's brash confidence in the bold handwriting, and Giles had certainly made it clear he disliked London. Given his tendency toward pranks, would he have seen this as a lark? Was Richard reading too much into the note?

"Then you think there's nothing more to this than a jest?" he asked Claire.

She shifted on the hard floor as if standing pained her, and he told himself not to be a fool and pick her up again. "Oh, I imagine he is serious," she said. "He knows what could happen in London. He doesn't want to lose her to a superior gentleman."

"If he's a man," Richard returned, "he should speak to me directly about Samantha. I'm willing to listen."

She turned up her nose. "She could do far better."

Something inside him protested. "She has money and position to spare. She can marry who she likes."

She raised a brow. "Would you give her away to a fortune hunter, sir?"

The words only raised the specter of their past once more. "Is that how you saw me, Claire? As a fortune hunter?"

She sighed. "Must it always have to do with us? We were speaking about Lady Everard and the young man who may be threatening her."

"You didn't answer my question. Again."

She gazed up at him. "I never saw you as a fortune hunter. Fortune wasn't important to me."

Anger rushed through him, and the words spilled out. "Important enough that I must leave England to find it. Important enough that you married the first fellow who offered it."

She stiffened. "I married a man who offered me hearth and home, whose feet were planted firmly on the ground in England, not on some far-off isle. And if you think you can throw me off the scent by distracting me with our dismal past, sir, you are mistaken."

"Lady Winthrop?"

Richard and Claire turned at the sound of Samantha's voice, and his hand went immediately to Claire's elbow to steady her. The softening of her look told him she'd noticed.

The girl had come out of the withdrawing room, face puckered in concern. Monsieur Chevalier was right beside her, but something about the spring in his step told Richard he was more interested than concerned.

Claire smiled. "Yes, my dear? Did you have need of me?"

"No," she admitted, venturing closer and glancing between the two of them. "You were just gone so long that I wondered…"

Claire looked at Richard with an accusing frown, as if to say that this was all his fault. "Of course you wondered," she replied, returning her gaze to the girl. "Everything's fine. Your cousin and I were just discussing the best way to see you safely to London."

The story was only a shade of the truth, yet it rolled easily off her tongue. Even though he knew the tale was designed to protect Samantha, he could not like it.

And he couldn't help wondering what other tales she'd told.

Chapter Seventeen

Claire found sleep elusive that night. She believed the note was merely Toby Giles's attempt to scare Samantha into staying. She knew the tactic well. How many times had Winthrop used it on her?

His pattern had been predictable—first denial that he could have struck her while he was drunk, then anguish and guilt when he saw the bruises forming, and finally threats that she would lose her friends, her privacy and her source of income if she petitioned to the church to separate from him. Her own needs for financial security had kept Claire at his side.

Samantha didn't have that problem; she was an heiress. Richard was right that she could marry whomever she liked. But Claire wasn't about to let a bully force the girl into a poor decision.

Still, things went so smoothly the next few days that Claire began to hope Toby Giles had had a change of heart. As if he knew he'd gone too far, he didn't attempt to call at the manor. Samantha didn't seem to notice his defection; she was far too busy. Monsieur Chevalier had identified a set of twelve dances that she must learn, and he and the girl practiced every afternoon in the receiving hall, with Claire at the piano.

Because so many of the pieces required another couple to execute properly, Richard and Mrs. Dallsten Walcott were often pressed into service. Mrs. Dallsten Walcott brooked no nonsense from her partner, bringing him back to his task with a rap of her finger if his gaze wandered from hers. The older woman had a natural grace, and she picked up the steps easily.

Richard was similarly sure-footed. Where the dance master flitted about, Richard took command of every movement. He was as comfortable on the floor as on his quarterdeck, Claire thought. Sometimes she nearly misplaced her fingers on the keys for watching him.

Despite her concerns, he did not press her about her past or her leg. In fact, he seemed to have distanced himself a little. He spent a great deal of time riding, but she thought perhaps he was checking the area to make sure no enemy lurked in the woods. Once in a while at dinner or in the evenings, she caught him watching her with a slight frown, as if he wasn't sure what to do with her. She was equally unsure what to do about him. But her tasks kept her from doing more than ruminating about the matter.

In the mornings, she, Mercier and Samantha worked on packing for London. Clothes and accessories were one thing; Claire was certain Samantha needed furnishings and decorations as well. Claire had never been to the Everard town house, which had been a bachelor domicile ever since Samantha's grandmother had passed away, nearly thirty years ago. She could only imagine the changes that would be needed to make it comfortable for a young lady like Samantha.

Richard was little help. "We have perfectly good

chairs, Claire," he'd said, when she'd approached him one morning over breakfast in the ivory-draped dining room. "I see no need to uproot the ones in the withdrawing room."

"But Lady Everard prefers the ones in the withdrawing room," Claire had protested, knowing she also preferred them. She could imagine sitting beside Samantha, watching her flirt with her scores of suitors, helping her engage in conversation with some of the most important women of the day, such as the new Lady Cowper. She was only a little older than Samantha, yet had married a renowned politician who might well become prime minister one day.

But Richard couldn't seem to grasp her vision. "We don't need to move chairs. If Lady Everard fancies them so much, she can return to them when the Season is over."

Monsieur Chevalier alone seemed to appreciate Claire's purpose. Though he often slept late in the mornings, he generally appeared sometime before noon, dressed in tailored coat and breeches, hair pomaded until it shined, to offer advice and counsel on what was currently in style.

"Not another landscape," he said, when Claire considered a lovely piece hanging in the library, while Samantha selected some books to take with her. "They are so plebeian. Has Lady Everard no ancestors to grace her walls?"

Samantha sat back in a pool of muslin, face scrunched in thought. "Did anyone ever paint Papa?"

"Very likely," Claire assured her. "And it's probably in the London house. We can search for the portrait there."

Samantha nodded and returned to her task. Monsieur Chevalier took one of his mincing steps toward Claire. "Then you intend to see this through?" he murmured.

Claire raised her brows. "Certainly, sir. Whyever not?"

He glanced at Samantha with a fond smile. "She is a delightful lady, but I think perhaps she is a little young. I would not want to see her eaten alive. The lions of London delight in their prey, as I believe you have cause to know."

What had he heard? Claire studied his profile. His skin was soft, his face and features rounded like a boy's. Yet something lurked in those gray eyes, and she wondered whether it was wisdom. He'd certainly seen enough of the aristocracy to know when a young lady was ready. And she felt the same way. Yet she'd made a promise to Richard, and Samantha was certainly eager to go.

"Lady Everard is going to London," Claire told him. "And I will do everything in my power to make her Season a success. I suggest you do likewise."

"Oh, assuredly, assuredly," he returned with a bow, but she saw his gaze flicker back toward Samantha as if he could not find Claire's faith.

So, neither of the gentlemen who should be helping her were as helpful as Claire would have liked. Their lack of understanding frustrated her, but worse was Mrs. Dallsten Walcott. No sooner had Mercier or Claire set aside an item to go to London, than the lady wandered by and declared that she could not be parted from it.

"That belonged to my great-great-grandfather," she insisted, speaking of a velvet lap-robe Samantha had chosen. "I'll just take it down to the dower house for safekeeping."

By Sunday afternoon, Claire was feeling stymied at every turn. Monsieur Chevalier had been given the afternoon off and had headed for Carlisle, most likely to arrange his next assignment when he finished at Dallsten Manor. Richard had escorted the ladies to church and then gone out riding. Claire knew she should spend the day in more contemplative pursuits, but she heard every tick of the ormolu clock on the mantel as if it were tolling her doom.

Today was Palm Sunday. Next Sunday would be Easter. And the Monday after Easter marked the day many families began the trek to London for the Season. One week did not seem to Claire long enough to finish the work remaining. Accordingly, she started checking the boxes and crates Mercier had already packed and left in Samantha's bedchamber to confirm that everything was in order.

Samantha accompanied her, but she was little help. So long as the girl had a purpose, Claire noticed, she remained sunny, but leave her to her own devices and the clouds quickly gathered. That afternoon, she kept wandering to the window and heaving dark sighs, as if being kept away from the spring air was a great burden to her.

"Did you wish to go riding?" Claire asked, folding an evening cloak into a packing case. "You might be able to catch your cousin."

Samantha toyed with the brass loop that held back the drapes. Her room was nearly as feminine as the withdrawing room, with everything pink and white and graced with ribbon and lace. "No," the girl replied. "He's probably to the Kendrick estate by now. And riding isn't any fun alone."

"I'd be happy to accompany you," Claire offered.

She dropped her hand. "No, thank you. It's not the same."

She didn't add, "without Cousin Vaughn," but Claire heard it nonetheless. She patted the chair next to her. "Come here, Lady Everard. We must talk."

Samantha raised her brows in surprise, but she joined

Claire and fisted her hands in her sprigged muslin skirts. "What have I done wrong?"

Claire chuckled. "Must you have done something wrong for me to wish to speak to you?"

"Perhaps not," she said, but her voice betrayed her doubt. "But Mrs. Everard always used that tone when I was about to get a scold or some such."

Claire sat back on her own chair, black skirts spread about her. "I have no desire to scold you. As your sponsor, it is my privilege to ensure that you have the very best Season possible. Remember when we talked about your goals for your time in London?"

Samantha nodded. "Of course."

"I am concerned you may not be able to achieve them."

Her brows drew down. "Why?" She waved a hand at all the boxes. "We certainly have enough supplies for an army."

Claire smiled. "You'd be surprised how much a young lady needs on her Season. But it isn't the supplies that concern me. It's your attitude."

Samantha sighed again. "Forgive me. I do want to go. Truly. Sometimes I just want to jump in the coach and drive away."

"Tempting," Claire agreed, "but you'd only get to the first inn before you'd wish you'd brought a nightgown."

"I suppose," Samantha said, but she didn't sound convinced. "I truly don't need much to be happy—my riding habit, my mother's pearl earbobs and the Bible my father left me."

Claire frowned. "Your Bible? I don't have that on our packing list. Where is it kept?"

"On the side table by my bed," Samantha said readily enough, but she turned and looked. "Only it isn't there."

This was the outside of enough. Claire rose, leg giving

her a twinge. "And I could guess where it's gotten to—the dower cottage."

"She wouldn't dare," Samantha said, eyes wide.

"Oh, I'm quite certain she would. The only question is whether you are content to allow it to remain there."

Samantha looked surprised to be asked. "Well, no. I was rather counting on having it with me in London."

Claire nodded. "Then you must request it back."

"I couldn't," she said, quailing. "For all I know, it belonged to her before Father gave it to me."

That excuse was far too easy. "Then she would have sold it with the house. She cannot have it both ways."

Samantha visibly swallowed. "Perhaps you can explain that to her. No one else has managed to do so, not even Cousin Jerome, and he can talk the birds from the trees."

"Charm isn't called for," Claire replied, heading for the door. "You must stand your ground, Lady Everard, or you will never be mistress of this house."

Samantha followed her with another of her deep sighs. "Very likely I never will, then."

Claire stopped to eye her. She could not let the girl give up so easily. Too many trials in life, she'd learned, called for backbone. She may have had to take Winthrop's blows, for a wife had little recourse against a husband's cruelty under the law, but she had learned to stand up against the pain.

"Nonsense," Claire told Samantha. "You have no idea how many people will attempt to make you less than you know yourself to be. You cannot allow it."

"I thought we were to turn the other cheek," Samantha protested.

"The Lord advised us not to attempt vengeance," Claire explained, "for violence breeds violence. But I cannot believe He intended us to be taken advantage of. Some battles must be fought, and I fear this is one of them. Now, fetch your pelisse. We will face the dragon in her lair and return with the fabled treasure."

"If you say so," Samantha replied, going to her wardrobe, "but I have a feeling the dragon will eat us instead."

Richard also had reason to visit the lady in the dower house. It had occurred to him that Mrs. Dallsten Walcott knew any number of the local families and might be able to identify the handwriting on the note. No other warnings had appeared, and he'd seen no evidence of anyone hanging around the manor grounds, though he'd made it a habit to go riding at varying hours, and had asked Mr. Linton to keep his eyes open.

He was also still troubled about the piece of paper they'd found in the receiving hall the day Monsieur Chevalier had arrived. Richard had taken Samantha aside the day before to ask her what she remembered about her father's party each summer.

"They were plotting," she'd replied with a wrinkle of her nose, as if she suspected the idea had been offered to humor her. "That's what he always said when I asked what he was doing with the other gentlemen."

Richard could not like the idea any more than she did. "And you never knew the others," he pressed, "outside the Marquess of Widmore?"

She cocked her head. "Funny. I know he'd mention other names from time to time, but none of them meant anything to me. Perhaps that's why I don't remember any of them now, except one."

"Oh?" Richard had stepped closer to her as they stood in the corridor near her bedchamber. "Who?"

"Winthrop," Samantha said, face tilted up as her gaze

searched his. "A Viscount Winthrop. Do you think he could be related to Lady Winthrop?"

"Possibly," Richard had said. "But I wouldn't mention it. It might trouble her."

Samantha had nodded and blithely gone about her business, but Richard was the one who was troubled. What business could Claire's late husband have had with his uncle, especially before his uncle had found faith? He knew little of the viscount, but Richard's suspicions of the way he had treated Claire made it hard to see the fellow in a good light.

With that knowledge and his concerns about the anonymous note, he could not be easy. Someone had felt it necessary to warn them of danger. He needed to know whether it was all a humbug.

Maisy opened the door to the dower house at his knock and indicated a room behind her with a wave of her hand. From the sitting room of the little cottage, ensconced in a rose-colored wing-backed chair, Jerome's mother-in-law smiled at him.

"Ah, Captain Everard. What a nice surprise. May I offer you some tea?"

Richard declined. He couldn't imagine trying to eat or drink in this room. He was having a hard time figuring out how to even enter. His quarters aboard ship might be cramped, for his captain's cabin was half the size of this space, but Mrs. Dallsten Walcott's house was bursting at the seams. Tables crowded against one another, made unsteady by the fact that they perched on no less than three Oriental carpets laid on top of each other. Richard had never seen so many gewgaws and knickknacks in his life, even in a busy Jamaican market.

He managed to thread his way through the chaos, though he'd found it easier to maneuver his ship past jagged rocks in a storm, and sat on a gilded chair next to hers. He thought he remembered its match in the withdrawing room at the manor. It shifted under him, and he would not have been surprised had it given out entirely.

"I was hoping you could help me," he said to the lady, holding up the outside of the note. He saw no reason to burden her with its contents. "One of your neighbors wrote to me, and I'd like to reply, but there is no signature on the letter to tell me the sender."

She leaned forward and squinted at the parchment. "That's not from Lord Kendrick. He has an elegant, gentlemanly hand as befitting his station. And it isn't Mr. Lane, the church warden—he writes more precisely. Nor is it the vicar. Mr. Ramsey effects entirely too much folderol in his writing for a man of the cloth." She leaned back. "I'm afraid I cannot advise you, Captain Everard."

"What about Toby Giles?" Richard asked.

She sniffed. "Mr. Giles? Has the boy even mastered the pen?"

Whatever Richard thought of Giles, he was certain the lady maligned him with that question. She continued before Richard could protest as much. "No, those strokes are entirely too bold to be anyone of *my* acquaintance. Except perhaps for that woman."

Richard cocked his head as he tucked away the letter. "Forgive me, ma'am, but who do you mean?"

She hitched herself deeper into the chair as if consolidating her position. "Lady Winthrop, of course. I know she is a particular friend of yours, Captain Everard, but she is entirely too high-handed. You must have seen that."

Far less than he'd expected. In fact, Claire was surprisingly humble. But perhaps she acted differently when she wasn't around him. "She is the daughter of an earl."

She waved a hand. "Yes, so I heard. But that only makes her lack of condescension more astonishing." She raised her chin to meet Richard's gaze. "She threatened me."

Richard leaned back and crossed his arms over his chest, raising a squeak of alarm from the chair. "Did she indeed?"

"Assuredly! She seems to find my access to the manor troubling. And she begrudges me the few trinkets I've gathered, as if she didn't have enough of her own."

Claire had few trinkets, from what he'd seen, and Mrs. Dallsten Walcott had far too many. Yet what harm in humoring an old lady?

"Regardless, ma'am," he said, "there would be no point in her writing to me when she can speak to me at any time."

"Not necessarily," she insisted. "Perhaps the contents are such that a woman dare not say it aloud to a man." She eyed him as if hoping he would offer her a tasty morsel of gossip. He refused. Nor could he see Claire in the role of villain. What reason could she have to keep Samantha in Cumberland? Claire wanted to live in London; Samantha was her reason to return.

"I'll speak to her on the matter," he promised, rising. He thought the chair gave a sigh of relief. "Thank you for seeing me, Mrs. Dallsten Walcott." He bowed over the hand she offered him. One of the side tables toppled to the floor with a tinkle of breaking glass. Richard turned to right it just as Maisy hurried into the room, Claire and Samantha at her heels.

"More company, ma'am," she said. "Lady Winthrop and Lady Everard." She hastily backed past them into the corridor, as if fearing she might meet the same fate Richard had.

Richard straightened as Mrs. Dallsten Walcott stiffened in her chair. Her long face was alight in triumph.

"Excellent!" she cried. Then she pointed an imperious finger at Claire. "There she is, Captain Everard. You can tell her the truth of the matter this very moment!"

Chapter Eighteen

Claire stared around at the dower cottage's sitting room, aghast. That must be the Bible Samantha had missed, perched precariously on a side table already crammed with an ivory-and-ebony chess set, a porcelain candy dish shaped like a lady's slipper, and three crystal inkstands boasting quills of varying plumage. That miniature of a powder-haired beauty, nearly lost among the other portraits on the far wall, had surely been hanging in the withdrawing room only yesterday. And there, draped over one of the polished brass andirons in front of the fire, was her amber cross from Richard!

Claire marched into the room, setting crystal to chiming, tables to knocking against one another. Richard raised a russet brow, and Mrs. Dallsten Walcott shrank to the back of her chair as if seeking shelter from a coming storm.

"Lady Winthrop—" Richard started, but Claire held up a hand to stop him.

"Mrs. Dallsten Walcott," she said, "you are a thief."

The lady shrieked and clutched the chest of her teal gown as if sorely wounded. "Do you see how she speaks to me, Captain Everard, a poor lonely widow?"

Claire put her hands on her hips. "I, madam, am a poor lonely widow, too, if you recall, but I have never resorted to filling my life with other people's things."

"Perhaps you are more fortunate, then," Mrs. Dallsten Walcott complained, pulling a lace-edged handkerchief from her sleeve and dabbing at her eyes. "I have only my memories to sustain me."

Her memories and half of the Everard household. Claire didn't believe those tears for an instant. She turned instead to Samantha. The girl stood gazing about the room in obvious wonder.

"Lady Everard," Claire said, "I advise you to go through every inch of this house and take back what is rightfully yours."

Mrs. Dallsten Walcott dropped her handkerchief and scrambled to her feet. "Never! And who are you to talk of rights? You know nothing about me or my family."

Claire met her outraged gaze straight on. "And you know nothing of me, madam, if you think I would allow you to take advantage of an innocent girl."

"Innocent!" Mrs. Dallsten Walcott put her long nose in the air. "She may be innocent, but her father was far from it. *He* took advantage of *me,* when I was at my lowest."

"That's not true," Samantha protested, stepping forward, quilted pelisse catching on the thick carpets. "Your daughter told me my father had no interest in Dallsten Manor until my mother begged him to purchase it to rescue you and Adele from penury. And Father always said he'd bought it because the Marquess of Widmore fancied it."

Claire frowned. The Marquess of Widmore had wanted Dallsten Manor? But that made no sense. He had any number of properties all over England, and he seemed to have sufficient funds to easily purchase another, had it pleased him.

Mrs. Dallsten Walcott must have thought the same, for she sniffed. "As if that powerful gentleman needed a baron to secure his way. You see what a villain he was, lying to his own daughter!"

"My father never lied to me!" Samantha cried.

Richard pushed forward, towering over all of them. "Strike your colors!"

Samantha visibly gulped, and Mrs. Dallsten Walcott fell back into her chair, skirts fluttering like leaves.

Claire refused to stand down. She swiveled to meet his gaze. "You are quite right, Captain Everard. Things have gotten entirely out of hand."

She turned to Mrs. Dallsten Walcott, whose lower lip was starting to tremble and this time, Claire thought, in earnest. While she felt for the woman, she still could not see allowing her to continue in this manner. Her need to clutch her past close served no one.

"Madam," Claire said, keeping her tone civil, "I can see why you would feel the need to protect your family's history. My father has passed away as well, and I have had to watch his treasured possessions go to a distant cousin who has no appreciation of their true value."

The woman nodded, though she did not meet Claire's gaze. "It is painful in the extreme."

"I knew you would understand," Claire continued carefully, "given your difficult experience with such matters. That's why I'm certain you will agree that Lady Everard has an equal right to remember her mother and father."

Mrs. Dallsten Walcott nodded again, but this time she looked at Samantha with a sad smile. "Poor dear."

Samantha frowned as if she wasn't sure she wanted to

be pitied, but Claire seized the moment. She picked up the Bible, which was bound in black leather with crimson detailing.

"This was a gift from her father, and it will give her comfort to have it with her in London. I'm sure you won't begrudge her that."

Mrs. Dallsten Walcott sniffed. "Take it, then, if it means so much to you."

Samantha scampered forward and plucked the Bible from Claire's hand, then retreated to the doorway as if afraid it might still be taken from her.

Across the room, Richard was watching Claire, and she couldn't be sure of the emotions behind those deep-set eyes. Was he pleased by the way she was handling the situation? Or did he still think her high-handed?

Help me, Lord! Give me the words!

The next part would be harder, but Claire forged ahead. "I have lost nearly everything of value, so what remains is precious to me." She threaded her way through the tables to the fireplace, lifted the cross from the brass and cradled it in her hand. "This belongs to me. It was in my trunk the last time I saw it. I will ask you to respect my privacy in the future."

"It's only a common cross," Mrs. Dallsten Walcott protested, shifting in the chair as if finding the seat suddenly too hard. "I fail to see why you should make such a fuss over it."

"The lady's request is reasonable," Richard said, crossing his arms over the chest of his paisley waistcoat. "You will honor it."

Though the words were spoken with his usual command, Claire could hear the kindness underlying it. Still, she thought their hostess would argue. Instead, Mrs. Dallsten Walcott visibly deflated.

"Oh, very well. Now, if you don't mind, I'll have that girl show you to the door. I find myself quite fatigued."

Samantha ventured closer. "Do you still think we should search the house?" she murmured to Claire, watching Mrs. Dallsten Walcott as if expecting her to leap up and take back her treasures.

"Not today," Claire replied, voice equally soft. "I'm not sure she can take parting with so many of her things all at once." She dropped a curtsy to honor the lady. "Good day, Mrs. Dallsten Walcott. We hope to see you at dinner this evening."

"And leaving with empty hands," Samantha muttered, turning for the door once more. Claire turned as well to follow her on the narrow path to the doorway. An exclamation behind her made her stop and look back.

She thought at first that Richard had caught himself on one of the tables, for the little pie-shaped stand was still quaking. Then she noticed that his face was growing red as he lifted a long brass tube from the mahogany.

"This is my spyglass!"

"Nonsense," Mrs. Dallsten Walcott said, fussing with the hem on her sleeve. "It is a treasured family possession. My father used it to gaze about the estate from the south tower."

Richard tilted the telescope to expose the brass plaque screwed to the worn wooden barrel. "And were his initials also RHE?"

She waved a hand. "Oh, take it! You three have already robbed me blind. At times I quite bemoan my generous nature."

"I'm certain it is a great trial to you, madam," Claire said, trying not to smile. "Now, come along, Captain Everard. Let us go congratulate ourselves on our ill-gotten gains." She managed to hold her laughter until they'd quit the house.

Out on the graveled drive, Samantha giggled as well. "I'm glad you knew what to do, Lady Winthrop. I'm obviously not much of a dragon fighter."

Richard was shaking his head as they walked past the trees edging the bottom of the drive. "Nor am I, I'm afraid. Forgive me for not taking your side immediately, Claire. I had no idea she'd brought so much of the manor home with her. I wonder if Jerome knows what his mother-in-law is up to."

"I bet he doesn't," Samantha said, Bible swinging in her grip, "or he'd have put a stop to it."

Claire held tightly to her cross as well. "It's not that easy, I'm afraid. I thought at first she was just grasping, but she seems to be trying to recapture her family's glory. She doesn't realize the harm she's causing, to herself or others."

"But you did," Richard said. "You handled that brilliantly, Claire."

Why did she persist in feeling so pleased when he praised her? She focused on the problem instead. "It is a difficult situation. I was so angry with her at first, until I realized why she was stealing our things."

Richard nodded to the cross Claire held in one gloved hand. "You kept it."

So he had recognized it. Her grip tightened on the chain. "Yes. It's a lovely piece."

"May I see it?" Samantha asked.

For one moment, Claire wanted to hold it to her heart. How silly! She refused to end up like Mrs. Dallsten Walcott, clinging to the past. Claire opened her stiff fingers and offered the cross to the girl. "It's amber, from the Baltic."

Richard chuckled. "I actually bought it from a naval midshipman before my first voyage."

Samantha glanced between the two of them. "You gave this to Lady Winthrop?"

"A great many years ago," Claire said, accepting it back from her and sliding it around her neck for safekeeping. She felt Richard's gaze on her and tried not to show it.

"I thought a lady never admitted to being a great many years old," Samantha teased.

"Nonsense," Claire replied, facing forward. "As a widow, I'm entirely over such things."

Richard winked at Samantha. "So very set in her ways that she rushed out to purchase a new wardrobe the moment she knew she was sponsoring you."

"Purely to reflect well on you," Claire assured Samantha.

"Well, certainly," Samantha said, so seriously that Richard laughed. "But I still wish I knew what to do about Mrs. Dallsten Walcott."

"We must find a way to wean her off her treasures," Claire insisted.

"And wrest them from her grip," Samantha agreed, cheerfully bloodthirsty now that she no longer had to face the lady.

"And return them gently to their places," Claire countered. "She truly is lonely, and she has a right to our respect and our care."

"But not our Bibles," Samantha said, hugging hers to her chest.

Richard chuckled. "Or the tools of our trade." He tucked the spyglass under his arm. "I'll have need of this in the near future."

"Oh," Samantha said, "are you going back to sea?"

A cold wind blew down from the mountains, a reminder of winter's passing. Claire hugged her pelisse closer.

"Only when you're safely in harbor," Richard promised Samantha with a smile. "My ship's in dry dock for repairs right now, but I have an agent lining up cargo. Once the Season is over, I mean to set sail for Jamaica."

Claire's steps seemed to drag, her skirts to hang heavily. She kept her head up and her smile pleasant, but something inside her seemed to be crumbling, and she feared it was her heart.

Why am I so surprised and hurt, Father? He's a sea captain. Of course he'll sail away. He never said he'd stay. You promised never to leave me or forsake me, but he didn't.

They continued up the drive, Samantha chatting with Richard about what he would find when he reached the far islands. Neither noticed that Claire's steps were faltering. No! She could not let his plans put a pall on her. She must remember that she had Someone who loved her above all things. She didn't need Richard Everard's love to be content in life.

And she didn't need to fall in love with him again, either. She finally had a chance for lasting peace, for true stability. He'd promised to set her up in her own home when this Season ended. Of course, she could tell no one the source of her funds, or she'd risk her and Richard's reputations.

She'd start over, perhaps take back her maiden name. She'd find a little village where she could make herself a valued member of the community despite her lowered station. Her new home would finally be a space all her own, to make of what she wished. No man would order her about, demand things of her she could not give, expect her to be something she wasn't.

Why did that vision no longer give her such comfort? Had she made the wrong choice yet again?

Her leg protested the exercise, and she stopped to rub it a moment. The ache felt deeper somehow, as if more than her joint was hurting. Richard must have noticed her pause, for he stopped as well.

Something buzzed between her and Samantha like an angry bee, even as a sound cracked from the wood.

"Down!" Richard commanded, stepping in front of her. "That was gunfire!"

Chapter Nineteen

Samantha immediately ducked, but Claire knew her leg would never withstand so sudden a jolt. Besides, she could not see the girl hurt. Heart jerking, she motioned Samantha behind her, even as Richard stood in front of them all.

"Stand down!" he ordered into the woods. "There are women and children here!"

"Well!" Samantha cried. "I like that!"

"Hush," Claire said, ears straining for any sound. The breeze from the mountains set the leaves to whispering like an accusatory chorus. She could see Richard's head turning, giving her a glimpse of his tense profile, as he scanned the wood.

"Move toward the house," he instructed. "I'll pace you."

"Lend me your arm, Lady Everard," Claire said.

"I am not a child," Samantha protested. "I don't need your help."

"Certainly not," Claire replied. "But I need yours."

Richard swiveled, face stricken. "What's happened? Were you hit?"

"No, I'm just a little fatigued from the walking," Claire

assured him, hoping he would understand that it was her leg that pained her. "And I forgot my parasol at the house. Lady Everard, if you would assist me?"

"Of course," Samantha said, blushing. "And please forgive me."

Claire nodded, and they set off up the drive, Claire leaning on Samantha's arm. Richard kept a wary eye on the woods. Every sound set Claire's nerves jumping, every flash of color made her heart beat faster. But no more shots rang, and no one appeared to claim responsibility or apologize.

When they reached the door, Richard turned as if to go back. Fear speared her, and Claire caught his arm. "Where are you going?"

"I want to check the woods," he said. "Give me a moment."

Her fingers dug into his coat. "Surely that is Mr. Linton's duty."

"He's an old man, and I'm not even certain he's back from his half day off." He bent to meet her gaze, and she saw compassion and determination in those dark eyes. "I'll be fine, Claire, I promise. Go inside with Samantha, and I'll join you as soon as I can."

She wanted to go with him, to help him, to keep him from danger. But she knew she would only slow him down with her leg already sore, and truly, he had might on his side. Few, she was sure, would take on a man of Richard's size without thinking twice. She forced her fingers to open and release the soft wool of his sleeve.

"Very well," she murmured, "but I will hold you to that promise, sir."

He gave her a brief smile before heading across the drive for the woods.

"You still love him," Samantha said, as they entered the manor.

Claire stopped so quickly her joint gave. Down she went, skirts bunching, and the parquet floor smacked against her. Samantha hurried back to her, eyes wide.

"What happened? Were you hit after all?"

Claire took a deep breath, pushing herself up to a sitting position. All of her was trembling, but she didn't want to frighten the girl any further. "It's nothing. I have an old injury that flares up from time to time." Goodness, but that made her sound like a grizzled soldier, retired from campaign! She put out a hand. "If you would help me rise?"

Samantha took her hand, and Claire managed to climb to her feet. Each step was a knife in her knee. "Please fetch me a chair from the withdrawing room," she said, holding herself still. Samantha hurried to comply.

Claire stood in the empty entryway, pale walls soaring around her, trying to calm her spirit.

Lord, protect him! I don't know what he's facing. But I believe You have the power to keep him safe.

With a squeak of protest from the chair legs, Samantha dragged one of the gilded chairs across the floor to Claire's side and helped her sit.

"Should I fetch Mercier?" she asked, face puckered in concern. "Or Mrs. Linton? Oh! I don't know if they're back!"

Claire shook her head. "It's all right. I'll just catch my breath a moment."

"I'm so sorry," Samantha said, hands worrying before her pelisse. "I didn't mean to upset you by mentioning that you love my cousin."

Claire kept smiling. "Of course I love your cousin, as a dear and trusted friend."

Samantha puffed out a sigh. "You needn't lie to me. I'm on your side."

"There are no sides," Claire insisted, heart starting to pound anew.

"Certainly there are sides," Samantha said, hands on her hips. "He sees things one way, you see them another, and so you argue. My mother and father did that all the time."

There had been few arguments in her marriage. Winthrop ordered, Winthrop raged, and Claire complied. "Some marriages are like that," she acknowledged.

"Adele says they don't have to be," Samantha said, gazing up at the brass chandelier as if remembering. "I think you and Cousin Richard could deal very well together. You have a very good chance of getting him back, if you want him."

Claire shifted on the seat. How could she be having this conversation now, of all times? She wanted to be out with Richard, to assure herself he was safe. But she couldn't let Samantha see her worry; she didn't want the girl to be frightened or to take Claire's concern as a sign of her devotion to Richard.

"There are a number of impediments between your cousin and me," Claire said. "You heard him just now. He is set to return to his ship after the Season. He will sail away with no thought of those he leaves behind."

"That's not fair," Samantha protested, lowering her gaze and dropping her hands. "I'm sure he thinks of his family often while he's at sea. And even if he doesn't, you can still love him. I loved my father, and he left me for months on end!"

"Perhaps you're a stronger person than I am," Claire said, turning to watch the door. Where was Richard? Had he found and confronted the culprit? What if the fellow was a madman? Was Richard so far from the house no one would hear his call for help? Had he been shot and left to bleed among the new grass, those beautiful eyes staring sightlessly at the sky?

Samantha obviously had no such qualms. "You seem uncommonly strong to me. You don't let anyone take advantage of you, and I can tell you're trying to shelter me from things you think might concern me. It isn't necessary, you know."

Another minute she might go mad herself. Claire gripped the amber cross, focused on its shape within her grip. "I am your sponsor," she told Samantha. "Of course I must shelter you." Would her leg hold her if she rose and went to the door? She couldn't just sit here, waiting.

"Well, I suppose there might be a few things I don't need to know," Samantha said grudgingly. "Like the cost of my gowns, or how long it takes to hear back from the chamberlain. But I wish you would just tell me the truth about your feelings for my cousin."

Something inside Claire snapped. "The truth?" She raised her chin, fear for Richard threatening to overwhelm her. "Very well. The truth is that I never stopped loving him. I will probably always love him. Do you know how that made me feel as the wife of another man? Perhaps, if I'd been able to forget him, my husband might have been able to love and respect me. Perhaps he might even have stayed home at night, instead of thundering into the house each morning in a drunken rage that threatened the staff and my health and safety. Is that sufficient truth for you, Lady Everard?"

Samantha's lower lip trembled. "I'm terribly sorry. It really is none of my affair, is it?"

Claire felt tears coming. "Oh, Samantha, forgive me. I didn't intend to burden you with any of that."

The girl bent and hugged her close. "It's all right. People are always telling me things about my mother and father. I gather they weren't very happy, either. But my father was always good to me."

Claire leaned into the hug, let the kindness buoy her. "And you are good to me, my dear."

"Of course!" Samantha disengaged to give her a watery smile. "I'm quite fond of you, you know. I just wish you and Cousin Richard could find a way to be together now."

So did she. "I fear your cousin would say that that ship has sailed."

Samantha made a face. "I'm not so certain. Sometimes I see the most tender look on his face when he gazes at you."

"Perhaps he still has feelings as well," Claire allowed, afraid to hope. "But they are not sufficient to keep him here in England."

Samantha cocked her head, letting her golden curls fall to one side. "Why must he stay in England?"

Sometimes she sounded so young. Claire managed a smile. "Because that is where home is."

"Why?" she persisted, frowning. "Shouldn't home be where the people you love are?"

Claire stared at her, the simple truth revealing more than the girl could possibly know. "How did you grow so wise?"

Samantha spoiled it all with a girlish giggle. "Oh, I've had years to think about such matters. It's fairly easy to see other people's problems." Her face fell. "My own are more difficult."

Claire reached out to pat her hand. "You've helped me more than you know. How can I help you?"

Samantha heaved one of her heavy sighs. "Perhaps you could answer a question for me. When you met Cousin

Richard, how did you know you were in love, that he was the right one for you?"

Once, Claire would have deflected the question with a clever quip. Given their conversation, she could not feel comfortable with that approach now. Perhaps she'd been wrong to try to protect the girl from every concern; perhaps the truth was best. At the very least, the discussion might help her keep her mind off Richard's fate.

"I had many suitors who were handsome and clever," she told Samantha. "There was more to him. He had dreams, and he was working to achieve them. I wasn't sure what to make of him then. Now I would say I admired his character."

The door opened then, and Richard strode into the entryway. His hair was tousled, and a bright leaf lay damp against his shoulder. Yet to Claire he had never looked stronger, more in command. She felt as if she could truly breathe.

Lord, show me what to do. You knew, even though I was afraid to admit it until now, that I love him. Show me Your will in this place. Perhaps here, in Cumberland, we will have a chance to find our way back to each other.

Samantha was running to meet him. "Is everything all right?"

His smile to Claire was weary. "I found no one," he replied, for both their benefits, Claire thought. "Very likely it was a poacher who recognized his error and fled to avoid capture."

Samantha brightened. "A poacher? We should send for the constable."

Richard patted her shoulder as if in agreement. "For now, I'm sure Lady Winthrop needs refreshment. Would you see if Mrs. Linton is back and ask her to serve us all tea in the withdrawing room?"

Samantha nodded and hurried down the corridor for the kitchen. Richard moved to Claire's side, then knelt in front of her, his gaze searching hers. "Are you all right?"

Oh, but Samantha was right. How had she failed to see the tenderness in his gaze, the concern as his fingers brushed her skirts? Richard Everard still had feelings for her. She could scarcely speak with the enormity of it.

He frowned. "Claire? What's wrong? Are you in such pain?"

In another moment, he'd likely take her in his arms and carry her up the stairs again. She could imagine reaching out, stroking the worry from his face, bringing her lips to his in sweet promise.

Oh, such thoughts! Her face felt hot. She smiled at him, a true smile, not her usual polished mask. Her face felt stiff at the little-used gesture, but Richard's eyes widened.

"I'm fine, Richard," she said. "I'm just very glad to see you are home safely. Are you sure *you're* all right?"

"Fine," he said, still gazing at her with a puzzled look, as if he could not understand the change in her.

"Odd," she teased. "I don't recall 'fine' involving such a frown."

He rubbed his brow as if trying to erase any concerns. "After that note the other day, I cannot help but wonder about this incident."

The warmth that she'd been feeling seeped away. "Then you don't really believe it was a poacher."

He made a face. "I don't know what to believe. You said you thought Giles was behind the note. If this is another of his pranks, he's gone too far. As soon as you and Samantha are settled, I'm heading his way, and I may speak to the constable while I'm at it."

The determination in Richard's eyes almost made

Claire pity the boy. But if Toby Giles was taking shots at people, he had to be stopped before someone was hurt.

She covered Richard's hand with hers. "Be careful."

He brought her hand to his lips and pressed a kiss against her knuckles. The gentle pressure was gone before she could catch her breath, yet she felt it inside as he released her and rose and offered her his arm.

"I'll be back before you finish tea," he promised, as he helped her up and escorted her toward the withdrawing room. "You won't even have time to miss me."

Claire smiled at his jest, but she knew he was wrong. She'd been missing him for years. Was she willing to spend the rest of her life missing him, for a few stolen moments like this, between voyages?

A while later, Richard was riding through the valley on his way home from the small farm where Toby Giles lived with his aging mother. Toby's father had apparently been a gentleman farmer, the last of a dying breed. With the spring planting ready to begin, Richard marveled that Giles had had time to visit Samantha so often, much less pen an anonymous note and shoot from cover. He also wondered why the young man had been away from home on a Sunday afternoon. Mrs. Giles had no idea where he'd gone or when he'd return, but she hadn't seemed overly concerned about the matter.

"He's a good lad, my Toby," she'd said as if realizing that Richard had come with a problem. "He always does what's right, in the end."

Richard hoped so. He would have preferred to believe the shot had come from a poacher who had mistaken his prize and then fled when he'd realized he risked being caught. But, growing up at Four Oaks, Richard had heard his father complain of poachers. They preferred the cover of darkness and the safety of the deeper woods. Firing from cover onto an inhabited property seemed the act of a coward, or a desperate man.

But what worried him more was his reaction to the threat. He'd faced down a boarding party of pirates, his blood roaring in his ears. He'd stayed alert for thirty-six hours, shepherding a convoy up the American coast toward Boston. He'd fought his way through a howling gale and waves nearly the size of his ship. The events had tried him, challenged him. Yet only when he'd thought Claire was in danger had he felt fear.

Despite his best efforts, she'd become important to him again. Her concerns, her feelings were strong as bowlines, binding them together, as a ship to a dock. He should pull away, he thought, before he was trapped.

But he didn't want to pull away. He wanted to care about Claire, to care for Claire. He wanted to be the one who held her arm so she wouldn't stumble on the uneven way. He wanted to sit beside her at the dinner table discussing the day's events, planning for the future.

He wanted to court Claire and win her heart.

He urged his horse through the gate at the foot of the drive. Yes, he wanted to court Claire. But what were the odds of success? He'd failed miserably last time. Perhaps he stood a better chance this time, but only while he led the field here in Cumberland. In London, he would have too much competition from wealthier, titled gentlemen. Yet his time in Cumberland was fleeting. His duty lay in getting Samantha to London.

He knew the anonymous note had told of trouble in London, but he rather thought the danger was here. Didn't the gunfire prove as much? Or had it merely been a shot across his bow in warning?

He had never missed his ship more. Where were

his open seas, his endless sky, that pleasure in accomplishment? He felt boxed in, his choices limited and entirely unsatisfactory. His frustration must have been evident, for Nate Turner, the groom, was quick to take the reins to allow Richard to dismount, and quicker to lead the horse away, as if concerned about Richard's displeasure.

Claire was equally quick to speak with him when he joined her and Samantha in the withdrawing room. The dance master had returned, and he and Samantha were looking over the sheet music, probably choosing the accompaniment for their practice session tomorrow. Claire moved toward Richard, her smile welcoming but her steps measured, and he hurried to meet her to save her any pain the effort might cause.

"Did you talk to the constable?" she murmured, gaze fixed on his. The blue of her eyes looked deeper, as if her concerns had darkened it.

"No," Richard replied. "I wanted to give Giles an opportunity to explain first. He wasn't home. I left word with his family that I must talk to him."

"Perhaps this is your answer, then," Claire said, holding out a folded sheet of parchment much like the previous note. "Mrs. Linton found this shoved under the kitchen door. It was addressed to me, but I think you'd better read it."

Chapter Twenty

Claire could barely force herself to stand there beside Richard, near the door of the withdrawing room, watching as his russet brows drew down, his dark eyes narrowed. She refused to give in to the ache in her knee when so much was at stake.

The moment Mrs. Linton had handed her the note, she'd known she was in trouble. There was her name, Lady Claire, bold as brass on the outside of the folded sheet, as if the writer was a close friend. And what was inside was worse.

Captain Everard may not appreciate the danger, but you do. The shot today was a warning. You and the girl will never be safe until you give up the idea of going to London. I count on you to convince him.

"Mr. Giles has never had a conversation with me when you or Samantha weren't present," Claire said to Richard, as his gaze swept over the page. "I cannot conceive why he'd think I'd help him in this odious plot."

Richard crumpled the note in his fist. "This is rubbish." Claire frowned, unsure whether to be relieved or concerned by how easily he dismissed the note. "Rubbish? You can say that after today?"

His gaze met hers. "I say rubbish, madam, because I refuse to be diverted from my course by a phantom. Can you be ready to leave for London tomorrow?"

"Tomorrow?" Claire clutched at her gown to steady herself. "Impossible. I need at least two days to finish packing."

"Leave a list with Mrs. Linton. She can send the items."

"Perhaps," Claire replied, mind reeling with all she'd have to accomplish to honor his wishes. "But just repacking the necessities into smaller cases we can bring with us in the estate's carriage will take the better part of a day."

His mouth tightened. "Are you determined to stay here?"

She should be. The manor, with its stone towers and strong walls, was secure. Besides, what if the notes truly were meant as a warning? What if something dangerous lay waiting for them in London?

"I don't know what to do," she told Richard. "Is it too much to ask to wish to feel safe?"

He paled. Shoving the note in the pocket of his waistcoat, he put a hand on her arm as if to comfort her. The touch was as warm as an embrace. "Forgive me, Claire. You have every right to feel safe. I'd like to pummel the fellow who's sending these notes. Failing that, how can I ease your concerns?"

She rubbed his hand, marveling at the strength, the determination, all for her. "You want to pummel him— I'd prefer to face him down."

He grinned. "You like making bullies bow down, don't you?"

Thank You, Lord! You gave me that strength! Claire

returned Richard's smile. "Perhaps I do. Unfortunately, he may be more right than he knows. If Samantha isn't ready, she is safer in Cumberland. And staying here gives you sufficient time to find this enemy and stop him."

He sighed and withdrew his touch, and she knew his answer before he spoke. "Samantha must go this year. Staying in Cumberland is out of the question. I'll give you tomorrow, Claire. We leave for London on Tuesday morning. Now, if you'll excuse me, I should change for dinner."

Claire watched him leave the room, his head high and proud, then she sighed. What was wrong with him? He claimed the notes were rubbish, yet he was willing to uproot the household in response. What was in London that he felt so compelled to go?

Monsieur Chevalier excused himself and left to change as well, but Samantha joined Claire as they started up the stairs. "What was wrong with Cousin Richard? He looked in a fearful temper."

"He did indeed," Claire replied, hand firm on the polished oak banister. "It seems we're leaving for London sooner than expected. The day after tomorrow, to be precise."

Samantha clattered up the stairs ahead of Claire, then glanced back, excitement dancing in her eyes. "You mean Tuesday?"

"Yes, I'm afraid so," Claire said, trying to keep moving despite the throb of her knee. "Come with me to my bedchamber, if you please. I need to think."

Samantha hurried ahead of Claire, humming a snatch of a hymn they'd heard that morning. Claire found her seated in one of the armchairs by the fire, hands clasped tightly in her lap.

"What must we do?" she asked as Claire sat opposite her.

"The list is long, I fear," Claire replied, adjusting her skirts and using the movement to give her knee a gentle rub. "We'll have to repack, of course, let Monsieur Chevalier know that we will have to dispense with his services, make sure the carriage and horses are ready and send word to Everard House to expect us." She smiled at Samantha. "I imagine your Cousin Vaughn will be delighted with the change of plans."

Samantha's smile broadened. "Oh, I hope so!" Suddenly, she sobered and sucked in a breath, leaning back from Claire. "It's happening rather fast, though, isn't it?"

Claire cocked her head at the sudden change in attitude. "Dearest, what's wrong? We will have to work hard, but we can be ready by Tuesday."

"I suppose," Samantha said, but her lower lip trembled.

Claire leaned forward. "Tell me what's troubling you."

Samantha's eyes were huge in her fine-featured face. "I want to go to London, truly, but it's a bit much." She visibly swallowed. "Perhaps too much?"

"There, now," Claire said, conviction building. She reached out, took Samantha's hands and gave them a squeeze. "Nothing says you must go this year. You're only sixteen. You can come out next year, or the year after."

Samantha brightened, then slumped against the back of the chair. "No, it must be now. My cousins are counting on me."

"I'm certain they will understand," Claire assured her.

"But I promised!" She stood, as if sitting was too constraining, and began to pace about the purple room.

"Promised what?" Claire asked, watching her.

She turned with a swirl of her muslin skirts. "That

I'd be presented and go to balls and attract suitors." She shivered as if the ideas were abhorrent. "That's what Papa wanted for me."

Though her leg protested, Claire rose and went to put her hands on the girl's shoulders. "And what do *you* want?"

Samantha frowned. "I no longer know. Once I wanted to stay here and marry Toby Giles and raise horses."

The vision nearly made Claire smile, for she could see Samantha in the role. But she also knew the vision had been formed from an incomplete knowledge, particularly about the character of a certain young man. Claire had made the same mistake once, thinking her life must be only what she'd experienced so far, fearing to venture into the unknown, relying on someone she thought she knew.

Help her, Lord, to see the wider choices, to see Your will.

"And what do you believe is right for you now?" Claire asked.

Samantha met her gaze. "Now I wonder if there might be more for me, if I tried."

Thank You, Lord! Claire hugged her. "So much more, my dear," she murmured. "I promise we will discover it together." She pulled back to eye Samantha again. "But you needn't rush into it. It will all be there next year, too."

"But Papa's fortune won't."

Claire frowned, releasing her. "Your inheritance is in jeopardy?"

"Not mine," Samantha said. "My cousins'. Unless I am presented, make my coming out and receive offers from three presentable gentlemen, Cousin Jerome, Cousin Vaughn and Cousin Richard inherit nothing."

Claire stared at her. "By whose command?"

"My father's will." She sighed. "He laid it out very specifically. Their fortunes depend on me."

What a burden to place on a young girl! Claire had never felt less in charity with the late Lord Everard. "What a horrid way for your father to treat them, after all they did for him!"

Samantha nodded, face puckered. "I know. But Papa really did it for me. He wanted to make sure I found my place in the world, and that they would help me when they found out about me. He seemed to think they might resent me, because I get the title and the lion's share of the Everard legacy." She smiled sadly. "I truly don't think he should have worried. My cousins are very good to me."

So Claire had thought. It couldn't have been easy learning their uncle had a daughter they'd never known. But Claire had assumed they'd received their inheritances from Lord Everard, that they helped Samantha now from a sense of love and duty.

What if she was wrong? She'd misjudged Winthrop all those years ago, seeing the man she'd wanted to see instead of the man he truly was. Had she done the same with Richard Everard and his cousin Vaughn? Samantha's father had hidden his daughter in Cumberland for a reason. Had he mistrusted his nephews so much? Was that why he'd set up his will in this manner, to ensure that they helped the girl? And were they helping now merely because their own fortunes depended on it? How hard were they willing to push the girl to get what they desired?

Richard had gone to sea years ago to make his fortune, no matter the cost to their future together. She had never heard whether he'd been successful. Certainly he'd never stayed in England long enough to spend a fortune. Was that because he loved the sea so much, or lacked the funds to be elsewhere?

And was he willing to make that fortune now, at Samantha's expense?

Claire laid a hand on the girl's shoulder. "Please know I only want to help. This decision must be yours. If you choose to wait, I will support you."

Samantha nodded and immediately turned the subject to what must be accomplished on the morrow. With only a little time left until dinner, they parted to change. Claire's mind, however, remained fixed. She'd been pushed to make the most important decision of her life. She could not allow Richard to do the same to Samantha.

She was in no mood to appreciate the lovely meal Mrs. Linton served up, ham surrounded by potatoes layered with cheese and mushrooms and accompanied with vegetables fresh from the Kendrick conservatory. The others seemed equally distracted. At the head of the table, Richard chopped into his asparagus as if fighting off Barbary pirates, and Samantha pushed her candied carrots around her gilt-edged plate. Only Monsieur Chevalier seemed unaffected, chatting about gossip he'd heard in Carlisle and helping himself to seconds from the nearest serving dishes.

"We had some excitement, too," Samantha said at one point. "A poacher shot at us."

Chevalier choked on his ham and reached hastily for his glass. "A poacher, you say," he replied when he had caught his breath. "Such dangerous times we live in—poachers in the woods, highwaymen on the roads. Perhaps you should stay in Cumberland, Lady Everard." He laughed as if he'd made a clever quip, and Samantha giggled.

Claire barely kept her hand steady on the silver. Clearly, the dance master also still thought Samantha should wait. Was he an ally?

"Tomorrow we will start on the Sir Roger de Coverley,

I believe," he continued, as Maisy brought in a strawberry trifle and cheeses for the second course. "You will enjoy it, I know."

Richard cocked a grin. "You haven't heard. We make for London on Tuesday."

"Tuesday?" He blinked, paling. "Why?"

Claire glanced at Richard as he selected a slice of cheddar. This was his chance to explain, to say something that would ease her concerns. *Please, Lord, show me I'm wrong!*

But all Richard said was, "I decided we would do better to be in town sooner."

"Oh, certainly," Chevalier said, though his recovery was faster than Claire's. "Mind you, you did request my time through Easter."

"You could come with us," Samantha suggested hopefully.

"Or find another sponsor," Richard said with equal encouragement.

"Unless, of course, you can explain to Captain Everard why Lady Everard isn't ready," Claire said.

Silence fell. The dance master glanced around as if surprised to find himself suddenly the center of attention, then started preening. "I believe Lady Everard will be a shining star in London, after a little more work."

"Nonsense," Richard said as Samantha deflated. "You called her a butterfly on a mountain. That's good enough for me."

"But not for me," Claire said. "I have survived a London Season, sir. I know what it takes to be successful."

"You do indeed," he said with a smile of admiration, but this time his praise failed to warm her. "And I'm sure Samantha will do equally well."

Claire smiled. "A young person blessed with a fortune is always popular, sir. But I'm certain you knew that."

Both Samantha and the dance master were glancing back and forth between the two of them. Richard's frown was focused on Claire, as if he couldn't understand the source of her animosity. "Stand down from quarters, madam. I mean no harm."

She wasn't willing to give up. "Then you agree Samantha may enter the Season on her timing, not yours."

He returned his gaze to his plate. "My orders stand. We leave for London on Tuesday."

Claire set her napkin on the table and rose. Monsieur Chevalier scrambled to his feet. Richard looked up at her, obviously surprised.

"Then, pray excuse me this evening, gentlemen," she said, though hiding her emotions took more effort this time. "I have a great deal to do to be prepared. Lady Everard, please join me upstairs when you're finished."

She swept from the room. Better to spend her time in useful pursuits than mulling over the fact that the man she loved was apparently intent on using a young girl to his advantage.

Richard stayed at the table long after Claire had left, puzzling over her reaction. Samantha had excused herself a short time later. Only the dance master seemed to feel obliged to keep him company.

"The fairer sex, alas, cannot comprehend the times and tides, eh, *Capitaine?*" he commiserated, moving to the seat next to Richard and filling his own glass.

Neither could the dance master, Richard thought. What an interesting profession that all he need worry about was the correct placement of a shoe against the floor.

Chevalier didn't seem concerned by his lack of

response. "A gentleman must remain constant in his opinions," he said after taking a sip. "Else the empire would crumble, I fear."

Richard eyed him. His smile was pleasant, comradely, but his gaze remained focused on Richard as if gauging his response. "Do you call me inflexible?"

Chevalier waved his free hand. "Not at all! I am certain you are the rock on which Lady Everard can rest secure."

"Yet you agreed with Lady Winthrop," Richard said, leaning back from the table. "You feel Lady Everard isn't ready for London."

He smiled ruefully as he set down his glass. "I have tutored many young ladies in the dance. I can tell when they are ready, and when they hesitate. She hesitates."

Richard snorted. "She doesn't hesitate anywhere else. She's been known to jump in where angels fear to tread."

"A lady after my own heart." One finger traced the flower pattern woven into the damask cloth. "Humor me a moment, *Capitaine*. I have some experience in these matters. You may have been told that I came to England to escape the Terror. England was to be the land of sanctuary, you know." He made a face as he pulled back his hand. "But opportunities here are not what I'd hoped. Often I wonder what would have happened had I had stayed and fought. I hope that Lady Everard does not end up living with such regrets."

Richard knew all about living with regrets. How many times had he wondered what might have been had he stayed in England? Was he encouraging Samantha to make the same mistakes? He'd been so young, too young to know what he wanted, too proud to ask God's direction. Yet, surely going to London was the right thing, for everyone concerned.

"I will do my best to ensure my cousin has no regrets," he promised the dance master.

Chevalier drained his glass and set it on the table. "Now, that I am very glad to hear, *Capitaine*. Perhaps you will consider my advice, eh? Now, if you will excuse me, I must pack my things as well."

Richard nodded, and the odd fellow left him to his thoughts at last. Yet his suggestion kept running through Richard's mind. Samantha had to go to London, but was Richard wise to encourage her to leave now? On the other hand, if she stayed in Cumberland, would she be safe from this person who threatened them? Their enemy claimed London to be the more dangerous, yet Richard had never been shot at in the city! If all else failed, he had loyal officers and sailors in London waiting for their ship to be ready. He knew he could keep her safe there.

Besides, Samantha had to go to London for her Season, to fulfill the requirements of her father's will. Too much depended on it. Richard could set sail and bring in an income, and Vaughn had always been able to fend for himself. They might survive another year waiting for their inheritances. Jerome could not. He was counting on it to sustain him and his new wife. These damages from the spring floods made it critical that he have cash at hand, or he would lose all. He'd trusted Richard to get Samantha safely to London. How could Richard let him down?

His brother had always been the one to sacrifice. Jerome had stayed with Uncle and safeguarded the legacy while Richard was at school; he'd helped Richard understand the cargo side of the business when Richard had returned. Richard had sailed away twice, once to seek his fortune and once to try to forget Claire, leaving Jerome to carry the burden of managing the Everard legacy alone. Richard refused to be so selfish again.

I know what You expect of me, Lord. I will not forget it.

Claire was another matter. Why was she so determined to stay in Cumberland? The last note almost made her sound like a conspirator. He hated that suspicion. But he'd been able to bargain for her services; someone else could bargain for them as well, ask her to convince him to heed the note's warning. A smile from her still held far too much power over him.

But why go to such trouble? He found it just as difficult to imagine Giles as his villain. Who else cared where Samantha went? How could her presence in London affect anyone but the Everards? Was someone intent on keeping Jerome, Richard and Vaughn from their inheritances? Or was there something else at play here?

What he wouldn't give for an ally, a trusted friend to help him think through these issues. *Lord, show me. I've lost sight of the beacon; I can't guide my ship through these rocks. I need a navigator.*

Claire's face came immediately to mind, mouth curved in the heartwarming smile she'd worn that afternoon when he'd returned from the woods. The sweet promise called to him. If he wanted to take her up on that promise, if he wanted her help, he had to trust her.

Richard pushed back from the table. Tomorrow, he would find the opportunity to clear the air with Claire, once and for all. She might fall into his arms or order him from her sight. He thought his chances of success were better surviving a hurricane at sea. There he might lose his ship. Now he stood to lose his last chance at love.

Chapter Twenty-One

Claire was up at dawn the next morning. Mercier had nearly dropped a tray of hot cocoa when she saw her mistress, swathed in a ruffled dressing gown, writing desk on her lap, sitting in the chair making lists.

"I'll sip while we work," she told the maid, lifting the cup with one hand and waving the tray away with the quill of her pen. "And I will need all your considerable skills today."

Mercier gave a sharp nod and set to work dressing Claire for the day.

Claire was thankful for the maid's efficiency. She'd had a difficult night, alternating between worrying and praying. But with the light came clarity. She might not be able to convince Richard to wait, but she could do her best to make sure the trip went smoothly. And she could help Samantha and Richard face whatever they would find in London.

Samantha was more than willing to help with the preparations. Together with Mercier, they determined the bare necessities needed for the trip and Samantha's first fortnight in London, located those items in the various trunks and boxes as well as rooms around the manor, and packed everything for immediate travel. Mercier also repacked Claire's things. Mrs. Dallsten Walcott was even sent for this item or that, and Claire thought at least a few things had been "found" in the dower house.

As much as the housekeeper could, given her other duties, Mrs. Linton worked beside them.

"I want to make sure I know how to finish the packing when you've gone," she said with a sniff, her quicksilver eyes shining with unshed tears, "so I can send our Lady Everard what she needs by mail to London. And if I may say so, Lady Winthrop, this house will not be the same without you all."

Claire knew what she meant. She was going to miss Dallsten Manor. Odd how she felt more at home in a house she'd lived in less than a fortnight than in the town house she'd shared with her late husband for ten years.

She wasn't sure how Monsieur Chevalier spent the morning, for he could not have had much to pack, having only been at the house a few days. She did bump into him from time to time, once near the muniments room that held the manor records, and once near the library, and he'd gibbered some flattery before hurrying about his business.

Richard, however, was more determined. Three times he attempted to commandeer Claire's attention, appearing in the doorway of the room where she was working, touching her arm as they passed in a corridor. All three times she dismissed him with a curt, "Not now, sir." She was only surprised he hadn't argued.

Claire, Samantha and Mrs. Dallsten Walcott were in the receiving hall, collecting sheet music and other items that had been used in the room over the last few days, when Mrs. Linton located them late that afternoon.

"Sorry to interrupt, your ladyships," she said, "but there was a letter for Lady Everard."

Claire, on the other side of the room, felt as if the floor dipped beneath her. Turning with care, she saw the housekeeper hand Samantha a folded sheet before bustling out. Even from where Claire stood, she recognized the bold writing.

"Lady Everard," she started, moving toward her, but the girl had already broken the seal and opened it. As Claire reached her side, Samantha paled.

Claire drew her away from where Mrs. Dallsten Walcott was shuffling through sheet music. "What does it say?" Claire asked Samantha quietly.

Samantha met her gaze, eyes dark and troubled. "It says if I go to London, something dreadful will happen to Cousin Vaughn."

Claire took the note from her stiff fingers to read it.

Do not go to London, or someone you love will die.

How could he! Oh, but she'd have a word or two with Toby Giles if she ever saw him again.

"Horrid creature," Claire said aloud, tucking the letter into her sleeve. "He's a great bully, threatening death from the shadows. You mustn't fear it, Samantha. All your cousins are strong, intelligent men who can look out for themselves. I pity the wretch who thinks otherwise."

Samantha managed a smile, but it quickly faded. "But who would hate me so much to say such things?"

"You don't recognize the hand?" Claire asked, watching her. "Perhaps your Mr. Giles?"

Samantha drew herself up. "Toby? Never! Why would he do something so mean?"

Why would any man be cruel to the woman he claimed to love? "You said you once planned on marrying him, dear," Claire reminded her. "Perhaps he feels the same way and wants you to stay here with him."

Samantha tossed her golden curls. "Then he would jolly well tell me to my face. He's never minced words with me before."

Claire still wasn't convinced. In a conversation with the vicar one Sunday, even the church leader had lamented that Mr. Giles was something of a jokester. But Samantha was clearly not willing to accept the fact that her beau might be immature enough to try to scare her into staying.

"Is there another young man who would prefer that you remain in Cumberland?" Claire asked.

"Jamie Wentworth, Lord Kendrick's grandson?" Samantha mused with a frown. "But I doubt he could write so boldly."

Claire remembered the shy eight-year-old from services. By the way he clung to Samantha's side, gazing up at her wide-eyed, it was obvious that he worshipped the ground she walked on. Claire could not imagine him writing such notes, nor daring to threaten harm to the girl.

Samantha touched her arm. "We must warn Cousin Vaughn."

Claire covered her hand with one of her own. "Now, then, I'm sure he's fine. Someone is just trying to frighten you."

"Well, he's doing a good job." Samantha glanced around as if expecting the villain to pop out of hiding and accost her. "Swear to me we'll leave first thing in the morning." She held out one fist.

Claire wasn't sure what she meant by the gesture. "Of course we're leaving in the morning. This changes nothing. You must stand up to bullies, Samantha. You cannot allow them to rule your life."

She dropped her hand, dark eyes stormy. "No, only kill the ones you love."

"It won't come to that," Claire promised. "I'll show this to the captain. In the meantime, perhaps you should go distract Mrs. Dallsten Walcott. She seems inordinately interested in your piano all of a sudden, and I fear Mr. Linton's heart would burst if she convinced him to move it down to the dower house for her."

With Samantha settled, she hoped, Claire stepped out into the corridor. She pulled the note from her sleeve and frowned down at it. Samantha seemed so certain Toby Giles was innocent. But if not Toby, then who? Surely no one in the household would leave such notes. Mrs. Linton was tearful about their departure, she'd brought the notes each time, and she certainly could have had her husband fire from ambush. Yet Claire could not see her as so cruelly manipulative. Maisy and Daisy, the maids, she dismissed out of hand.

Samantha's fears about going to London waxed and waned in proportion with her feelings for her cousin Vaughn. She needed an excuse to stay in Cumberland. She might have engineered the letters and enlisted the aid of her Mr. Giles to post them, and to fire from cover. But she truly wanted to help her cousins, despite her trepidations, and Claire did not think her dismay at this latest note was an act.

That left Mercier and Monsieur Chevalier. The idea that her little maid might have betrayed her hurt. Yet, what reason could she have? Mercier had made no secret of the fact that she preferred the more active life, a more prestigious household. She would want to return to London. And what could the dance master hope to gain by keeping Samantha in Cumberland? At best, they amounted to a fortnight of work for him.

No matter which way she considered it, she could no longer avoid talking with Richard. He needed to hear about this latest threat. She searched for him in the manor and finally located him out by the large pond on the front of the grounds. Though the mist crept down from the mountains, he stood on the grass, looking out over the water. She could imagine him standing by the wheel on his ship, gaze as steadfast, frame as confident. The image caused a pang of regret. He'd be back at his post all too soon, sailing away from her life and taking her heart with him.

But she knew how to put on a pleasant face when confronted with heartache. "A penny for your thoughts," she said, as she drew up next to him.

"My thoughts aren't even worth that, I fear," he replied, gaze focused on the still waters, a deep green today with the darkening sky.

"I doubt that," Claire said, "but what I have to say will hardly help." She held out the note. "This just came, for Lady Everard."

He eyed the note as if she held a snake. "Did it indeed? More of the same?"

"Yes, though this time it promises death to someone she loves."

He closed his eyes a moment, as if to block out the thought. Opening his eyes, he turned to her. His face was lined, weary, and she wanted to hug him close and share the load that burdened him.

"There are too many secrets in this house, Claire."

She dropped her hand. "What secrets?"

"This creature's threats, my uncle's plans. Did you know your husband visited Dallsten Manor?"

Claire frowned. "How can that be?"

"According to Samantha, he joined Uncle and Widmore at the summer party."

Claire shook her head. "I never knew of it, though I suppose it's possible. Winthrop went off to inspect his estates for a fortnight each summer. And he was friends with the Marquess of Widmore at one time, though he distanced himself from the man toward the end."

Richard took a step closer, as if intent on understanding her. "How did he die, Claire? You never said."

The ugliness rushed back at her, and she rubbed a hand along her sleeve. "It doesn't matter now."

"Why can you never answer my questions? You've hidden yourself behind a wall."

Why couldn't he focus on the issue in front of him? She felt as if he were trying to pull out her heart. "Hardly surprising," she returned. "I am convinced none of us shows the world a true face. We keep that safely tucked away. Just as this person who writes the notes wishes to avoid us now."

He waved a hand as if that matter could not concern him. "But why do you hide, Claire? Do you distrust the world so much?"

Do I, Lord? The thought came unbidden, yet she felt the answer inside. Protecting herself from Winthrop's abuses, Society's judgment, had seemed the only choice. Surely God did not expect her to give in, to be destroyed by them. Surely hiding was the best way to keep herself safe.

For I have not given you a spirit of fear but of boldness.

There was that verse again. Had God expected her to be bolder in her marriage? Did God want her to be bold now, to tell Richard everything? Yet how could she admit aloud that her marriage had been a sham, that she was a sham? She couldn't.

"Perhaps I have been in the world too little the last year to know my way around it now," she said instead.

The tension in his face told her he didn't believe the tale any more than she did. "And yet you agreed to shepherd Samantha into that world."

"I did. I suppose I hoped I could help her avoid the mistakes I'd made."

"It seems to me you never make mistakes, madam."

That was the face she'd shown the world. Suddenly the falseness of it made her want to sob. If she had any hope of a future with this man, if she wanted to help him with Samantha, she had to tell him the truth.

I think I understand what You want of me, Lord. I should have asked for Your will to be done all those years ago. Forgive me. Help me be bold now, to take advantage of the chances You've given me.

"I am not perfect, Richard," she said, starting to tremble. "And I make far too many mistakes. The biggest, I fear, was in not trusting my feelings for you, and yours for me. Please forgive me."

Richard stared at her. Her lovely face was drawn, as if each word cost her dearly, yet the light of conviction gleamed in her pale eyes.

Forgive and ye shall be forgiven.

That was what the Bible said; that was what the Lord expected. Richard had done all he could to forget Claire, yet some part of him had still clung to the pain of losing her, as if that somehow could keep his love alive. Knowing her now, learning to love her again, it was all too easy to forgive her, to acknowledge his own mistakes.

"We both bear our share of the blame, Claire," he said.

"I hope you can forgive me as well. You must know that I loved you."

She bowed her head as if to avoid his gaze, finger curling a stray honeyed lock behind one ear. "I believed you loved me. I also believed you'd never stay with me."

Richard frowned. "I would never have been unfaithful."

"Not in that way. I never even considered that. I was so naive." She sighed, as if mourning the death of the girl she'd been. "Winthrop kept a mistress while we were courting. He had several others over the course of our marriage. As if to make sure I knew it, he left them each a bequest in his will. Of course, the solicitor couldn't honor them. Nothing remained after all the bills were paid."

She said it so calmly, with less emotion than if she was discussing the dinner menu for the week, or had long resigned herself to the sad facts. He wanted to seize something, hurl it into the pond.

"You deserved better," was all he could think to say.

"Did I?" She shook her head, gaze going out toward the mountains. "I wanted to think so. The first time he hit me in a drunken fit, I thought perhaps God was punishing me for my choices. One night I made the mistake of meeting him at the stairs when he came home. He struck me, and I fell. He refused to call a physician. I think he feared the gossip. If it weren't for Mrs. Corday, I might never have walked again. She brought in a doctor while Winthrop was out, and he set the bone."

"Oh, Claire." He reached for her, but she held up a hand and stepped away as if fearing his touch. He let his hands drop, feeling impotent and wanting to rage at the sky for it.

"He took his anger out on me, Richard. It would have been easy to take mine out on God. But I learned that God wasn't to blame." Her gaze rose to meet his, determined.

"I chose that marriage, and I learned to live with its lack of comfort."

"By hiding," he said, unable to keep the rancor from his voice.

"By keeping my face composed and my focus on God," she returned. "He was there for me the night I returned from the theater to find Winthrop with a lead ball through his temple. My husband had finally realized he could not hope to pay the debts he'd run up. He chose to flee his responsibilities again. His heir had the matter hushed up so the Crown wouldn't take Winthrop's moveable property, what was left of it."

Richard wanted to rail at the viscount for betraying his duty to Claire, but had Richard done any better? In the pain of loss, he'd abandoned her, never offering friendship, never checking on her welfare. Some might have said he was justified.

But I know You expect better of me, Lord.

"I'm sorry, Claire," he said. "I'd like to think I'd have been the better man, but perhaps you were right about me. I wanted to see the world, to make my mark on it. Your father's edict to earn my fortune gave me the excuse to try."

She sucked in a breath. "Then you would have left me."

"I like to think I would have stayed, but I fear you're right. The sea can be a man's mistress, Claire, make no mistake. She is untamable, yet each sailor is proud enough to think he might be the one to tame her. She offers untold riches, yet always at a price, whether in lives lost or families torn apart."

Her eyes brimmed with tears. "You love her still, I think," she said, voice wistful.

"I admire and respect her," Richard replied, "but she

does not control my life. I could stay on land, if I had reason."

She stiffened. He could tell she'd made a decision, but he was almost afraid to hear what she'd say. She took a step closer to him, tilted her face up to his. The rising mist sparkled on her lashes.

"I'm learning that God expects us to be bold in fulfilling his commands," she told him. "So I will say this—could I be your reason, Richard? Would you stay for me, would you stay with me this time?"

The yearning in her voice fed the yearning inside him, filled a hole that had gnawed at his heart for ten years. He gathered her close, sheltering her against the cool mist, just as he longed to shelter her against the tides of life. He could easily imagine making a home with her, growing old together. Nothing compared to that.

"If you think you could be happy with me," he murmured against the silk of her hair, "I would be honored to make you my wife."

She dropped her head against his chest and sobbed.

Richard blinked.

"Claire?" he asked, unsure whether to pat her back or beg her pardon for his presumption. "What have I done wrong this time? I know I'm unpracticed at courting. I've only done it twice, and both times were with you."

She shook her head, disheveling his thoroughly dampened cravat. "You court beautifully," she said between sobs. "Then and now. I'm just having trouble believing it."

"Then, perhaps," he said, "I should be bold as well and put actions behind my words." As tenderly as he could, he tipped up her chin and kissed her.

Chapter Twenty-Two

Claire trembled in Richard's arms, every sense awakened. She felt his arms tightening around her, heard his breath quicken, caught the scent of the sea that seemed to cling to him even now. The taste of his lips was so sweet, so perfect, that she wanted to cuddle against him and never let go.

Yet, as he raised his head, gaze tender, doubts crept in. *Can I trust him, Lord? Do I dare let myself be yoked in marriage again? Am I strong enough to risk all?*

I can do all things through Christ which strengtheneth me.

She clung to the remembered verse as Richard smiled at her. "Was that sufficient demonstration for you, madam?"

All the emotions of the moment tumbled away, and Claire laughed. "And how shall I answer that, sir? If I say no, I belittle your considerable skills, but you may feel compelled to continue. If I say yes, you may stop!"

He chuckled. "What if I promise many more such demonstrations if you agree to marry me?"

"Is that a bribe or a threat?" she teased.

He pulled her close once more, resting his head against

hers, his beard tickling her temple. "Ah, Claire, we'll deal well together. I always knew we would."

"I wish I could bottle your faith and drink it down."

"Do you still doubt? Haven't we done well the last two weeks?"

"When we weren't carping at each other."

His arms tightened. "I do not carp, madam. A captain merely always wins an argument."

Claire smiled at his confident tone. "Only because your crew is, no doubt, so in awe of you that they seldom disagree. I will not be so timid, I promise."

"I would not wish it otherwise. I have no desire to be an autocrat in my own home. You will keep me humble."

Ah, but she was the one who felt humbled at the moment. He loved her! He wanted to marry her! His declaration filled every need, fulfilled every hope. But was it the right choice, this time?

She touched the silver buttons on his paisley waistcoat, gripping the cool metal. "Oh, Richard, are we mad to consider this?"

"Mad not to consider it," he countered. "We were made for each other, Claire."

"But we have so much to discuss," she said, and the protest sounded lame even to her.

As if he thought so, too, he leaned back to eye her. "More? I thought we'd settled things between us. Or is there something you wish to confess?"

Claire shook her head. "Not me. I was thinking about the reason you're so insistent we leave for London. Samantha tells me she is the key to your inheritance."

He grimaced. "A bald way of putting it."

"Is there another?"

"Yes." He released her at last. "You know Uncle always

said the Everard legacy would belong to his heirs—that was his duty and the law of the land."

"The title to your brother, and the fortune split among the three of you, I recall. But that was before I knew about Samantha."

His chuckle was wry, his gaze drifting out over the pond as if the still waters held answers. "That was before any of us knew of Samantha. Her existence took us completely by surprise. We still don't know why Uncle never told us he'd married and sired a daughter, why he hid her here in Cumberland. Vaughn felt betrayed not to be taken into his confidence. Jerome felt betrayed because he'd lost the title he'd grown up to expect."

"And you?" Claire couldn't help asking. "Did you feel betrayed as well?"

He glanced down at her. "I used to pray Uncle would give me my inheritance early, so I'd have the fortune to marry you."

Claire blushed. "At least you didn't wish him in his grave."

"Oh, at times I did, and I hope God will forgive me. That was before I learned what faith can do. I didn't know my uncle well before he died, with my being away at sea, but his last wishes tell me he learned about faith, too. He wanted the best for his daughter. So he arranged things to be certain of it."

Claire still could not like Lord Everard's reasoning. She shifted on the grass, and her dampening hem brushed her stockings, sending a shiver through her. "Did he truly think you'd abandon the girl without his incentives?"

"You thought I'd abandoned you, and you claim to know me well."

Claire sighed. "You're right. So your uncle left an edict,

and you are all just trying to comply. Does the fortune mean nothing to you now?"

He shrugged, and the carefree motion gladdened her heart the way a dozen words of protest would not. "I have enough fortune for ten men. That's not my reason for assisting her. Samantha's success means that my brother and cousin have a future. I promised them I would do everything in my power to help her, including convincing you to act as her sponsor."

"I suppose I should be thankful then," Claire murmured, fingers brushing the wool of her dark skirts. "Your uncle's will brought you back to me."

He took her hand then, and they walked in the twilight toward the house. The mist surrounded them, cooling her skin, quieting sounds. It was almost as if they were alone in the world. Between the uncertain light and the uneven ground, Claire knew a fall was likely, yet she could not fear. She trusted Richard to hold her up.

Thank You, Lord. I see the door You've opened for me, and I'm trying to walk through it, with Your grace.

"What do you intend to do about these notes?" Claire asked.

She heard him sigh as he helped her over a tuffet of grass. "We leave in the morning. If it is Giles, he won't be much of a threat when he's over a hundred miles away."

"Samantha seems certain it isn't Toby Giles."

He shrugged again, a combination of resignation and confidence. "Nothing would please me more than to find the true culprit. I almost wish *you* were the one, so we could get answers."

She tapped his arm as he walked beside her. "For shame, Richard! Do you think me so craven?"

"No," he readily admitted. "But I did wonder if you were so desperate. You agreed to take my money, Claire, to be here. I thought perhaps you'd taken someone else's, too. It seems you were left with little to support you."

"Why, Captain Everard," she teased, "are you angling for an heiress?"

He took her hand again and gave it a squeeze. "Tell me the truth, Claire."

What harm was there now? He knew her worst secrets. "Winthrop left me the town house, its furnishings that were not from the family seat, a lovely coach and four, and a mountain of debt that required me to sell them all."

"And your father? Surely he provided for you."

"He arranged a marriage settlement. I signed it over to Winthrop. I thought perhaps knowing the money was available to him would ease his drinking, that fear motivated him. I'm sorry to say nothing changed."

The memory still hurt, but she knew she must let it go. "Father also left me a bequest, but Winthrop was through it in a quarter."

She was thankful Richard did not chide her for her choices. "What of his heir, your family?" he asked, stepping onto the gravel of the drive, the rattle muffled in the mist.

"Both invited me to live with them," Claire said, following him. "It was charity. I would be the poor relation, caring for the infirm, the elderly. I couldn't bear it. I was proud, I know. But I was so tired of being forgotten."

She could feel the tension in his hand. "I could horsewhip them," he said, his warm voice equally firm, "but then I'd have to turn the whip on myself. I should have asked after you, Claire. I should have made sure you were safe. Like your father, I made assumptions, and I was too proud to seek you out. Forgive me."

She rubbed her shoulder against his sleeve. "There is

nothing to forgive. I did not expect you to rescue me from my choices. That only I could do, with God's leading."

He brought her hand to his lips and pressed a kiss against her knuckles. "I will be forever grateful to Him for bringing us back together."

So will I, Lord. Help us do things right this time!

They had reached the door to the manor, but Claire found herself loath to climb the steps and enter. "What if the notes are right?" she asked Richard, pausing at the foot of the stone steps. "What if danger awaits us in London?"

"With the Everards, I fear, danger is never far away." His tone was light. With dusk approaching, the lamp had been lit beside the front door, and the glow made a halo of flame around his head. "I'll take my chances in London. Everard House is well built, and my ship should be lying at anchor on the Thames by the time we get there."

She could not help but smile at his confidence. "So, we can withstand a siege or flee in the night, is that it?"

His teeth flashed as he grinned. "See how well you know me?"

She shook her head. "But Samantha cannot fulfill the requirements of her father's will hidden in a town house or the bowels of a ship."

"Granted. But with Jerome and his wife and Vaughn with us, we stand a better chance of protecting her."

Claire put her hands on the hips of her black gown. "We stand the best chance if we unmask our letter writer now."

Richard crossed his arms over his chest. "Very well. Who do you suspect?"

She dropped her hands. "I wish I knew who to suspect. Unfortunately, I've already ruled out everyone in the house."

"Even Mrs. Dallsten Walcott?" he teased.

"Oh, I hadn't considered her!" Claire paused, then

shook her head. "No, it can't be her. She'd like nothing better than for us all to leave so she can pilfer to her heart's content."

Richard laughed.

Claire poked him with a finger. "Take this seriously, if you please, sir! Someone is out to hurt you!"

"Not me," he said, but his voice had sobered. "Nor will I allow anyone in my care to be harmed."

"Easy words, sir, but you cannot be everywhere at all times. This person is someone we know. We're nursing a viper."

He nodded. "You're right, though I cannot like it. And I agree that our suspects are limited. None of the staff would harm Samantha, I'm sure of it. They've known her for years, and they're loyal. What of your maid?"

"Mercier?" Claire frowned. "What reason could she have?"

"Money. You hired her after you knew you were coming here. Perhaps our enemy arranged for you to take her with you."

Claire shuddered. "Then he would have to know which agency I use to hire staff and my preferences in servants. That is unlikely and entirely unnerving."

"What about the dance master?" Richard asked.

"Monsieur Chevalier? Oh, surely not! He has no more reason than Mercier."

"He could easily be in the pay of someone else."

Claire made a face. "I suppose you're right. We have no idea who spoke with him before he joined us in Cumberland. But that arrogant hand. No, I cannot imagine it of him." She sighed. "Which leaves us only with you, and I know you are innocent."

He flashed another grin. "As the day is long, I assure you."

Claire threw up her hands. "Then we are at an impasse."

"I still say it's Giles," Richard replied, taking her elbow and helping her up the stairs. "And I'll be glad when we put him behind us."

Richard had cause to remember those words the next day. They'd had a merry farewell dinner, with Samantha scarcely finishing her sentences, she was so excited. If the note had dimmed her enthusiasm, she didn't show it. Richard caught Claire watching her from time to time and thought she was relieved by his cousin's attitude as well.

He also had reason to hope for the future. While he was acutely aware that Claire hadn't accepted his proposal, she certainly hadn't refused it. Holding her in his arms had been the stuff of dreams. But he thought he had a way to go to prove himself to her. This time, it wasn't her father's edict but her own fears that kept them apart.

Show me the way, Lord, to ease her concerns.

Chevalier decamped after dinner, requesting a ride to the valley inn, where he hoped to catch the evening mail coach to Carlisle.

"Though I wouldn't blame you for staying in Cumberland, too, *Capitaine,*" he said, as Richard handed him the money that was owed him. "London can be a difficult place for a young girl. No one would fault you for avoiding it for another year or so."

Richard had thanked him and sent him on his way. But he knew the dance master was wrong. Someone would fault him if he kept Samantha in Cumberland. His conscience would never forgive him for failing in his duty.

They left for London the next morning. Mr. Linton drove the estate carriage, a great, lumbering beast with velvet-covered seats and room for six inside the padded interior. Samantha and Claire took the front-facing bench, while Richard and Mercier took the rear. At least this time Richard had plenty of room to stretch his legs, and the twinkle in Claire's light eyes told him she knew it.

Though she still wore her mourning black, and her face looked pale inside the black satin-lined bonnet, he thought her smile was happier. He hoped he'd had some part in the change. Beside her, Samantha could barely sit still. Richard was treated to a view of all four sides of her flowered bonnet as she shifted about, gazing out first one window and then another.

"Oh!" she cried as the carriage started down the drive. "We're really going!"

Claire reached out to pat her shoulder and urge her back into her seat. "Yes, we are, my dear. There's no need to outpace the horses to prove it."

Samantha wiggled into her seat with an apologetic smile. "It's going to be marvelous, isn't it?"

"Amazing," Claire promised her.

Richard wanted to believe that as well. But they had only traveled a half mile from the estate before trouble started.

Claire and Samantha were deep in conversation about the ball they hoped to hold for the girl once she'd been presented to the queen, and Mercier was working on her mending. Richard found it hard to concentrate on the discussion of dances and the advisability of wearing different types of slippers. His gaze veered out the window, watching the farmsteads slipping behind.

Where would he and Claire live when they married? He'd be giving up his ship, after all. He felt one corner of his mouth lifting as he realized he could think that without flinching. He still had the house at Four Oaks that his mother had left him, but he thought the estate in Derby might prove too remote for his London-loving lady. And he wouldn't have minded being near the Thames, to keep an eye on Everard interests there.

Something moved behind them. Richard blinked and peered closer. A horse and rider were coming up fast. He could see the dirt flying behind the beast. In a moment, he recognized the carrot-colored hair of the head bent low over the horse's neck.

Giles.

It seemed Samantha's beau was intent that she stay in Cumberland after all.

Chapter Twenty-Three

Claire kept her smile pleasant as Samantha chattered on about hairstyles and ornaments. Claire's gaze, however, remained on Richard. She'd noticed the moment his mind had wandered, his look had shifted. The Captain found it difficult to attend to weighty matters of dancing and deportment. She'd smiled and wondered at the thoughtful look on his face. Was he thinking about their future? She could think of little else.

Could she do it? Could she give her hand in marriage, live according to another man's edicts?

No, Lord! Only Yours!

Suddenly, Richard's eyes narrowed, and his head and body thrust forward. Before she could ask his concern, he turned to her. "Samantha, Claire, do exactly as I tell you."

Mercier froze, and Samantha stopped in midsentence to gape at him.

"You're doing it again," Claire said to him, trying not to bristle. "Issuing orders."

"No time to explain," he said, voice as urgent as the cracking of a whip. "I'm going to stop the coach. Stay in your seats, no matter what happens."

"But what…" Samantha started.

"Trust me," Richard said, gathering himself as if he meant to leap from the coach right then.

There was the rub. Did she trust Richard to lead her, to protect her, to love her? The answer was all too easy.

She laid her hand on Samantha's arm. "We will do what we must to help you, Richard."

He nodded with a quick smile of thanks, then reached up and rapped on the panel above his head. A moment later, Claire felt the coach slowing. As the rumble lessened, she became aware of another sound, a cry from behind them.

"Stop that coach!"

"It's Giles," Richard said, hand on the door. "I won't have him following us to London. This nonsense stops now."

"Of course," Claire said, though she could feel herself tensing as well. "You cannot give in to a bully."

"But Toby's no bully!" Samantha protested.

Mercier's eyes were wide, but Richard held up a hand. "That we will soon see." As the coach rolled to a stop, he pushed open the door and jumped down.

Samantha swung herself across the coach so she could see out the window on that side. Mercier edged away from her as if fearing what lay beyond. Claire's heart was pounding so hard she wasn't sure how she managed to peer out her own window.

"Giles!" Richard shouted. "Stand down!"

Claire could see the boy now, reining in his horse. The chestnut obediently braced itself, and Toby fairly leaped from the saddle.

Richard stood at the side of the coach, feet spread, arms hanging loose and ready. The wind caught his greatcoat and billowed it around him.

"Explain yourself," he commanded. "Why do you follow us?"

Toby raked a hand back through his orange hair as if to make himself more presentable, but he only managed to stand the strands to attention. "She's leaving. I had to say goodbye."

Samantha sucked in a breath. "Oh, Toby!"

"After warning her of the danger?" Richard countered. "Threatening those she loves?"

"Did he tell you that?" Toby stiffened, one hand on the trailing reins. "He's mad!"

"He?" Richard took a step closer. "Who do you work for?"

"No one! I meant Mr. Everard, the so-called poet. I don't care what he's said about me. Sam, that is, Lady Everard, is my friend. I've a right to see her off. I may have been busy lately with the farm, but that's no excuse for sneaking her out of Evendale without my knowledge. Let me speak to her."

Richard shook his head as if he'd deny the request. Inside the coach, Samantha fumbled with the door handle. Mercier squeaked in protest.

Claire stopped the girl's hand. "Leave this to me." She lowered the window and leaned out. Richard glanced her way with a frown that she chose to ignore.

"Mr. Giles," she called, and the boy immediately looked her direction.

Richard stepped between them. "What are you doing?"

"Trust me," Claire murmured, smile aimed at Toby. She counted the seconds, willing Richard to extend to her the same courtesy he expected. Her heart soared when he gave a nod and stepped away again. Such a little thing, yet it spoke so much of his belief in her.

She raised her voice even as her hopes blossomed.

"Mr. Giles, Lady Everard must go to London to help her family. I'm certain, as her friend, you would not want to hinder her."

The boy's face was solemn. "Never, your ladyship."

Claire made sure her own face was stern. "And you do, of course, want the best for her."

"Yes, your ladyship." He raised his chin. "But you'll pardon me if I happen to think I'm the best."

Samantha giggled.

Claire hid her own smile. "Certainly, Mr. Giles. Then you had nothing to do with a set of notes that arrived at the manor promising dire consequences if we left the area?"

He scowled as he closed the distance to the coach, each stride determined. "Someone's threatening Lady Everard? Who'd have the presumption?"

Richard met Claire's gaze, and she thought they were in silent agreement. Toby seemed to be speaking the truth. But if he hadn't sent those notes, who had?

"Mr. Giles," Richard said, turning his gaze to Toby's, "make yourself useful. Someone doesn't want us leaving Cumberland. I know Mr. Linton has a fowling piece up on the box. Take it and be our outrider, at least to the first coaching inn."

His eyes lighted. "It would be my pleasure." He grinned toward Samantha as she waved at him from behind her window. "And who knows, perhaps I can escort you all the way to London. That's what friends are for!"

So they set off once more, Toby riding alongside, fowling piece at the ready. Richard could see him scanning the way ahead, eyes narrowed against the dust kicked up by the coach's passing. Every once in a while, he shot a grin to Samantha, who smiled back. She had refused to return to her seat beside Claire and hugged the window of the rear-facing seat with Mercier next to her.

"So you believe him," Richard murmured to Claire, having taken Samantha's spot beside her.

Claire nodded, one honey-colored curl escaping her bonnet and making him long to stroke its silk. "I saw no anger in him when he rode up, no violent intent. He just wanted to be with her."

"I know the feeling," Richard replied. He lifted her hand where it lay on the seat and cupped it in his.

She blushed but didn't pull away. "Be that as it may, we still have the mystery of the notes."

"Agreed. Someone wants Samantha out of London. Why?"

"You two are smelling of April and May," Samantha interrupted. She grinned at Claire and Richard across the coach, while Mercier pretended not to notice. "Anything you care to confess?"

Richard waited. Here was Claire's opportunity to tell his cousin he had offered for her, perhaps even to announce her acceptance. Surely she knew he would do anything for her.

Claire merely smiled, that polite uplifting of the corners of her mouth that was no true smile at all. "Nothing that need concern you," she told Samantha.

Samantha slumped in the seat with a twitch of her mouth. "Well, certainly it concerns me if you two intend to wed. You're my sponsor!"

"And I will continue to be your sponsor, no matter what happens," Claire said.

That didn't sound promising. Did she intend to refuse him after all? He was tempted to ask, even with their interested audience. The thought of spending the next three days wondering was enough to drive him mad.

With a crack, something struck the side of the coach. The vehicle lurched, tumbling Claire against him and sending Samantha up against Mercier. Outside, Toby gave a shout, and the fowling piece roared.

Richard's blood roared likewise. They were under attack! He scooped Claire up and deposited her across the coach with Mercier and Samantha. The maid held her needle at the ready, as if she'd fence with their enemy, and Samantha was wide-eyed.

"Stay close to me," Claire told her, calm in the face of calamity.

Richard had never been more thankful for her pragmatism. He clung to the seat as the coach rocked and swerved, bumping over ruts, skittering over rocks. Linton must be struggling to get the started animals under control. He'd need help.

Richard reared across the coach and pressed a kiss to Claire's forehead. "Stay here," he ordered as he pulled away.

Her eyes nearly as wide as Samantha's, she nodded.

He crouched beside the door, body swaying with the motion of the carriage. His heart sounded louder than the drumming of the hooves. He was a sea captain. What did he know about stopping a runaway coach?

Yet the buck and roll was not unlike his ship during a storm, and he'd always managed to stay afoot, even when the deck flooded from the waves. For Claire and Samantha, he had to do this. Gathering himself, he shoved open the door and leaned out, twisting to face the carriage. The air rushed past, pushing him. It was no worse than a driving gale. First with one hand, then with the other, he grasped the edge of the roof above him and hauled himself up as if climbing the rigging.

"You can do it, Captain!"

Richard didn't dare look toward Toby. Flat on the rocking roof, feeling as if he rode a deck into a hurricane, he crept toward Linton. The elderly man was bent backward, tugging at the reins, while the horses tore at their bits and plunged ahead. Richard pulled himself forward until he could drop onto the box beside him.

"Give me the reins," he called over the wind and rattle of tack.

With a grateful nod, Linton surrendered the leather strips. The reins in his hands, Richard felt the power of the horses surging ahead. It was no different than a sail tugging against the storm. He wrapped the leather around both fists and pulled back.

Too slowly for his racing heart, the horses calmed, and their frantic pace eased. The coach centered itself and ceased pitching.

Beside him, Linton exhaled and clapped him on the shoulder. "That's the way it's done, Captain."

Richard shot him a grin. Then he glanced over to where Toby Giles was pacing them.

"What happened?" he called.

The boy rode closer and tossed the gun up to Mr. Linton for reloading. "Highwayman. I caught sight of him when his gun flashed. Anyone hit?"

The words hollowed out the inside of his stomach like a cannonball. Claire or Samantha could be bleeding to death below him. He'd failed them.

Jerome was to safeguard the Everard legacy, Vaughn was to solve the mystery of their uncle's death, and Richard—Richard's was the easiest task. All he'd had to do was bring one sixteen-year-old girl to London and unite her with a suitable sponsor. Now Samantha's future and her very life could be in danger because he'd failed to read the charts correctly.

Feeling ill, he pulled on the reins once more, and the horses slowed, then stopped. The coach came to rest at the side of the road. He returned the reins to Linton with hands that shook, then jumped down and hurried to the door, Toby at his heels.

"Everyone all right?" he asked, gazing at the three white faces that stared his way from the window they had lowered.

Samantha nodded to Mercier's *"Oui, monsieur."*

Claire edged forward, one finger reaching out to point to a lead ball embedded in the carriage frame where Samantha had been sitting. "We're fine, just."

Richard closed his eyes and sent a prayer of thanks heavenward. When he opened his eyes again, Claire was waiting.

"It was Chevalier, Richard," she said, pale eyes wide. "I saw him as we passed. Our dance master is trying to kill us."

Chevalier! Richard would have liked nothing better than to hunt the dastard down. But he couldn't leave Claire and Samantha with only the elderly Linton and the brash Giles. If Chevalier was so determined to stop them that he'd shoot at a moving carriage, who knew what else he'd try?

Thank You, Lord, for protecting those I love!

"The best thing we can do is press on," he told his audience. "I'll ride on the top with Linton, and Giles can remain at post. We'll inform the authorities as soon as we reach The George in Penrith."

Claire clasped the edge of the open window as if she wished to hold Richard as close. "You cannot let him win, Richard."

He laid a hand over hers. "I won't. I promise. For

now, stay near the center of the coach and away from the windows."

She nodded, face set in determined lines. He wanted to gather her in his arms, protect her from all harm. But he knew he could serve her best by keeping watch for Chevalier. He let go and watched as she shut the window and shifted away from it.

"Lady Everard." Her voice came softly through the glass. "You sit there, and Mercier there. We have a great deal to plan, and I shall need your complete attention."

Richard smiled as he put his foot into the edge of the box and pulled himself up beside Linton. Claire might complain that he issued orders entirely too much, but she obviously knew the value of a well-placed command in a time of crisis. Now he just had to make sure they all survived the crisis.

Chapter Twenty-Four

Claire kept Samantha talking for the next few hours as the fields of Cumberland passed outside. She felt every second as if it were a day. How had she missed Chevalier's treachery? He'd seemed so feckless—a bit vain and too much in love with celebrity, his own and that of others. But she'd never sensed anything evil in him. Had she learned nothing from her marriage after all? Who else's intentions had she misconstrued? Mercier's? Giles's? Richard's?

Her fingers wrapped around each other in the lap of her black traveling gown, so tightly she felt the leather of her gloves tugging against her skin. *Help me, Lord! I can't afford to make that kind of mistake again! Please, show me Your will.*

Something thumped overhead, and Mercier flinched, gaze fixed on the ceiling.

"Yes, I believe you'd look lovely in blue," Claire said to Samantha, whose gaze had similarly risen. "What exact shade, do you think?"

Samantha's gaze lowered, and the conversation continued. But now Claire's attention was also fixed above them. Had something happened? Was Richard hurt? Was she destined to spend her entire life wondering?

No! She had to trust, trust him to look out for himself and them, trust the Lord to see to them all. She took a deep breath, smiled at Samantha, and continued planning for the future.

"We're slowing," Samantha said a few minutes later. She edged toward the window as if to determine why.

"Back to the center, miss," Claire ordered, trying to fight her own desire to look out. "A lady has no need to gawk."

Samantha made a face as if she sincerely doubted the truth of that statement, but she slid dutifully back against Mercier.

"We are safe, *oui?*" Mercier asked, head cocked as she tried to see out the window without moving. "This is the city, *non?*"

They had rolled into Penrith. Even from her place of safety in the center of the coach, Claire could see the stone buildings rising around them, carriages passing. The dusky red stones of The George Inn slipped past the coach as it came to rest in the yard.

She collapsed back against the seat. "Yes, we're safe. Thank the Lord!"

"Amen, *oui?*" Mercier said with a sigh.

Claire was thankful when Richard climbed down and opened the door for them. He'd lost his hat, and the wind of their passing had blown his hair all this way and that. She reached up and smoothed it down, wishing she could feel the softness of the fiery strands through her gloves.

"You're safe?" she asked, withdrawing her hand.

"All clear here," he answered with a smile. "And you?" He lifted her from the coach, setting her on the cobbled yard beside him. His hands lingered on her waist as if to steady her. Didn't he know his touch made her decidedly unsteady?

"We're fine," she assured him. She wanted to ask him so many questions, but Samantha was already at the door, and he turned to help her down as well.

They stayed at the inn to report Chevalier's attack to the local constable, who promised to keep an eye out for the dance master and to send word to other constables up and down the coaching road to do the same. Then Claire, Samantha and Mercier had tea in a private parlor, while Richard excused himself to speak with Toby Giles. When the ladies returned to the coach, however, Claire saw that Richard had been busy. They had been joined by three more outriders, tough-looking gentlemen in dark coats and hats, muskets poking from their saddles. Two took up sentinel behind the coach, while another joined Toby at the front.

The boy at least looked pleased by the extra help, for he saluted Samantha as she passed and gave her a saucy grin.

"Just returning you to London in suitable style," Richard joked, helping Claire into the carriage and climbing in after her.

"Do you really think it's necessary?" she murmured as he seated himself beside her.

"A wise captain never takes chances with precious cargo," he replied with a smile.

She smiled back, but she found it hard to relax the next few days, waiting for another attack. Still, they caught no further sign of the dance master. She could only hope he'd given up or been cowed by the prowess of their outriders.

"But why would Monsieur Chevalier wish us ill?" she asked Richard one afternoon, while Samantha dozed across the carriage. "We treated him uncommonly well. You paid him a fair wage, I'm sure."

"Perhaps someone paid better," Richard replied, arching his back away from the velvet to stretch muscles that must have been cramped from the long ride. "He said once that the opportunities in England were not what he'd hoped. Perhaps someone offered him something more."

"But that only pushes the issue back a step," Claire protested. "Why would that person wish us ill?"

Richard shook his head. "Uncle made enemies over the years. I suppose one of them might seek revenge through his daughter." He glanced to where Samantha's golden head rested on Mercier's shoulder.

"Some vengeance," Claire said. "Your uncle is already dead."

Richard put his arm about her shoulders and held her against him. "I'm sorry I brought you into this. I can't see you hurt, Claire. If you want to disassociate yourself from us once we reach London, I'll understand."

Disassociate herself? Leave Samantha, leave him? Even if her circumstances had been different, she knew her answer. "I am exceedingly pleased to be Lady Everard's sponsor. This business with Chevalier changes nothing."

He rubbed a hand against her arm, the caress soothing. "Thank you. I suppose I'm a coxcomb for hoping you have another reason to help."

Claire allowed herself the luxury of resting her head against his chest, of feeling herself held and treasured. "You know I do. Only don't press me to give you an answer now, Richard. I scarcely understand my own feelings."

"I would never do anything to harm you, Claire."

Oh, how she wanted to believe that! As it was, the best she could offer him was to wrap her arms about him and hug him back.

A day later, they rumbled into the busiest city in the

empire. Fields and hamlets had given way to towering buildings in stone and brick; dusty roads had become cobbled streets. Samantha's conversation had faltered, then staggered into single words like, "Oh!" and "Goodness!" Nothing Claire could have said, she was sure, would have pulled the girl away from the window now. Samantha had moved to the Evendale Valley so young, she likely had no other memories beyond the manor and the little village nearby. Everything about London left her breathless.

But not speechless for long.

"I didn't know there would be so much space. Whose fields are those?"

Claire smiled as they turned onto Oxford Street. "Those aren't fields. That was the edge of Hyde Park. We'll take a ride there some afternoon. You'll find Mayfair more crowded."

"There's a man juggling plates!"

Richard winked at Claire. "Any number of enterprising people make a living in London."

"Oh my!" Samantha sat back, stunned. "The horses on that carriage exactly matched the lady's gown, and she was driving!"

"Now, there," Claire said with a wink back to Richard, "is style."

Samantha remained enthusiastic as they climbed down from the carriage in front of Everard House. Her family home was set just off the street on the edge of a square, with a carriage portico before the lacquered door. The white stone of the house gleamed in the fading sunlight, and windows like a dozen eyes sparkled back at Claire. Grooms came running to take charge of the horse and carriage, and their hired outriders circled the block for the mews to discharge their duty and retrieve their pay. Toby got down off his horse and glanced about as if unsure what to do.

"Make sure your mount is cared for to your satisfaction, then join us inside," Richard instructed.

Claire was glad for his hand on her arm as they crossed for the door. Her leg was throbbing from the jostling in the carriage and the long times with so little movement. She was ready for a steady seat and a quiet cup of tea.

An imposing footman was on duty in the entryway when Richard ushered her and Samantha inside. Richard had obviously been true to his word about refurbishing the house, for the marble floor glowed, and the scent of lemon hung in the air, whispering of carefully polished wood. The vision of elegance was spoiled by the enormous statue of a naked woman, who held out an apple toward Claire.

Claire glanced at Richard and raised her brows. Samantha, standing behind Richard, merely stared around her in wonder.

"I'm Captain Everard," Richard informed the footman, who was apparently newly hired, "and this is Lady Everard and Lady Winthrop, her sponsor for the Season. We'll all be staying for some time. Find Mr. Marshall for me."

"At once, sir," he said, moving to comply with Richard's orders. Just then a voice called from the landing.

"Ho, my cousin the captain! Aren't you off course?" Vaughn Everard, dressed in evening black, hair pulled back in a queue, descended the stair with a ready grin, which faded as he took in Claire and Richard's travel-worn clothes.

"What's happened?" he demanded as he reached the bottom.

"Oh, Cousin Vaughn!" Samantha darted around Richard and cast herself into her cousin's arms.

Vaughn held her close, patting her back, then carefully

pushed her away from him. "Here now, infant. Why the tears? I thought you wanted to come to London, and early too, unless I've miscounted my days."

Samantha wiped at her eyes and beamed at him. "Were you counting the days, too?"

Vaughn offered her a bow. "Every second, I assure you."

Claire thought the poet had more likely been keeping himself busy with other matters while in London, matters he clearly didn't wish to discuss with Samantha. Had he uncovered the truth about her father's death?

A tall, slender gentleman with thick graying hair came down the corridor just then, adjusting his cravat with long fingers. His nose was formidable, and his smile assured. Now, there was a butler.

"Welcome home, Lady Everard, Captain Everard," he said before offering Claire a bow. "Lady Winthrop, I believe I have you to thank for the augmentation of my staff. How might I be of service?"

Claire didn't hesitate. "Good evening. Mr. Marshall, is it? Allow me to make a few suggestions."

In a remarkably short time, Mr. Linton, Toby Giles and the coach and horses had been settled; Samantha was with Mercier setting up her room; and Claire was seated in the withdrawing room with a bracing draught of tea. Though the room lacked the refined femininity of its counterpart at Dallsten Manor, Claire thought the twin windows draped in heavy brocade, the camel-back sofa upholstered in crimson velvet, and the scroll-back mahogany chairs surrounding it would do.

Richard and Vaughn had not taken the chairs' invitation to sit, however. They stood next to the black marble fireplace, faces tight.

"So you think this dance master is in the employ of our

enemy?" Vaughn asked, one hand gripping the mantel as he leaned toward the heat.

"It's the most likely explanation," Richard said.

Vaughn smacked his hand against the stone and straightened. "Then we must find him, make him tell us what he knows." Anger jetted out of him, like steam from a kettle.

"The magistrates will be delighted to assist," Claire said.

Richard glanced her way with a smile, as if glad for her suggestion. Vaughn shook his platinum-haired head.

"The magistrates have been little help so far. They refused to see Uncle's death as murder. We had to pay a Bow Street Runner to look into the matter. He was here yesterday, by the way. It seems he found Repton."

Claire frowned at the name, but Richard brightened. "Uncle's valet? What did he have to say for himself?"

"Nothing. He's dead. They found him floating in the Thames."

Claire set down her tea with a trembling hand. "How horrid!"

Richard crossed to her side and put a hand on her shoulder. As always, the touch steadied her. "We're safe here," he said.

"Are we?" Vaughn strode to join them. "I don't think we can say that until we determine what we're facing. What do we know about this dance master? Where did he live in London? Who were his associates?"

"Besides the Marquess of Widmore," Richard said.

"Who refuses to see me," Vaughn added.

Claire glanced between the two. She could not encourage vengeance. Yet, if the dance master was the only clue to a greater evil, shouldn't she help them find him? She wanted to live in the spirit of boldness the Lord promised.

"I have his address in London," she offered. "It was on his reference."

Richard frowned, but Vaughn went down on one knee in front of her. "Sweet lady, tell me where to seek him."

Claire looked into his deep brown Everard eyes. She could make out the intelligence she'd seen in Richard's, and the excitement that brimmed in Samantha's. But something else lurked there, a pain, a loss that drove him. He would not be one to lash out, she thought, as her husband had done, but he would strike those he felt had wronged his family. She glanced up at Richard for guidance.

"Tell him only what you wish, Claire," he said. "I trust your judgment."

How amazing! He trusted her judgment when she so often questioned it. She felt her conviction building. "His reference is in my travel desk. Mercier, my maid, will know how to find it."

Vaughn hopped to his feet. "Then I'm away."

"And I'm coming with you," Richard said. "Don't leave without me."

Vaughn nodded and exited the room.

Richard squeezed Claire's shoulder. "Thank you."

She put her hand over his, gazing up at him. His brow was drawn, as if his cousin's pain concerned him as well, but she saw no eagerness for a fight.

"You're welcome," she said. "I just hope you learn the truth. We need answers, your cousin most of all."

"He was Uncle's man," Richard said, "more than either of the pair of us. He won't be able to rest until he understands why Uncle died, and why Uncle didn't turn to him for help."

"Then I'm glad I told him about Chevalier," Claire said.

"So am I." Richard withdrew his hand and went after his cousin.

Alone, she stared into the fire. It seemed she'd made the right decision in this case, and she felt certain she was the right sponsor for Samantha. She had to believe she'd been right about Richard as well.

The contrast between him and his cousin went deeper than their looks. Vaughn was a fire blazing hot, as likely to burn as to warm. Richard had learned to temper his desires, make them do his bidding. Unlike her late husband, he knew how to control himself. And every word, every touch, every action said he loved her.

She closed her eyes. *Thank You, Lord. I know what You expect now. I will return Richard's love, be his wife. And I know he'll be a good husband because of the man You made him.*

A sound behind her, the soft placement of a shoe against carpet, forced her eyes open.

"I am very disappointed in you, Lady Winthrop," Henri Chevalier said, sliding out from behind the drapes. "We could have avoided all these unpleasantries if you had convinced him to stay in Cumberland as I asked."

Chapter Twenty-Five

Richard had not reached the entryway before his conscience nagged at him. Claire had had a trying few days, like the rest of them, plagued by worries, pushed to protect. Leaving her with no more than a pat on the shoulder felt wrong. Chevalier might not even have returned to London. And if he had, surely the truth would wait a few more minutes.

"See to our horses," he ordered the footman by the door. Then he turned to Vaughn, who was pacing the space like a caged lion. "Wait for me. I'll be right back."

Vaughn nodded, gaze dark, but Richard thought his mind was already riding ahead to their confrontation with the dance master.

Richard took the stairs two at a time and hurried for the withdrawing room at the back of the house. He'd hold Claire close, soothe any concerns, assure her of his love. She was a strong woman, stronger now than when he'd first known her, but even the strongest needed an arm around the shoulder from time to time. And, truth be told, he wouldn't have minded feeling her in his arms.

The sound of voices drew him up short of the door.

"What are you doing here?" Claire demanded. "How did you get in?"

"With so many new servants? That part was child's play. Waiting for you to be alone was harder."

Richard froze as he recognized the voice. Chevalier, here? Every instinct shouted at him to protect, to defend, but he knew he had to go carefully, for Claire's sake. For all he knew, the man was holding a weapon on her.

"Why do you need me?" Claire protested. "You aren't a friend. You shot at us!"

"You have only yourself to blame," the dance master said. "I did warn you, repeatedly. I cannot help it if you do not listen."

Richard heard the rustle of Claire's skirts, and relief washed over him. She could not be held at gunpoint if she was able to move around.

"I suggest you leave now," Claire said, her siren's voice dangerously low. "Before I scream."

Good for her! But Chevalier had a ready answer. "You will not scream. Think of poor Lady Everard's reputation."

"Why?" she asked. "You didn't. What's so important you had to keep her from London?"

Richard stilled, holding his breath for the answer.

"That no longer matters. She is here. I have failed. My only hope is to escape before he finds me."

"He?" Claire pressed, asking the question on Richard's mind. "Who is your master?"

"Someone too powerful to avoid. Now, onto your feet. You will help me escape."

"I think not," Claire said calmly, but Richard had had enough. He straightened away from the wall and walked into the room.

"Stand down, Chevalier," he ordered. "You've been caught."

The dance master was standing next to the arm of the sofa, far too close to Claire for Richard's liking. But Claire, his marvelous Claire, was seated calmly, skirts arranged about her, as if taking tea with the queen.

"Good of you to join us, Captain Everard," she said. "I believe Monsieur Chevalier would like to turn himself in."

The dance master shook his head, eyes widening. His hair was no longer purposefully disheveled; now it hung about his pale face in limp locks. His black cloak was rumpled and caked with dust as if he'd ridden hard. He pushed the wool aside to show a heavy dueling pistol in one gloved hand.

"Stay back, *Capitaine,* I warn you. I came here for your help. A ship lies ready on the Thames, bound for Jamaica. It is my only hope."

"For all I know, that's my ship you're talking about," Richard said, edging closer. He had to get Claire away from that gun. "I won't allow a madman aboard."

"Madman?" Chevalier laughed, but the sound was high-pitched and fragile. "I am not the one you should fear."

"Then who?" Claire demanded, rising. "Name this phantom that drives you!"

No! She'd put herself between the gun and Richard. He froze once more.

But Chevalier was intent on Claire, face bunched as if in pain. "You must understand," he begged her. "I had nothing. He befriended me, helped me. Always have I done his bidding, watching from the shadows, and he has paid me well. But I know what happens to those who fail him. They disappear in the night, wash up in the Thames. I allowed Lady Everard to come to London, to risk his exposure. He will not let me live."

"Give me a name," Richard commanded, taking a step

toward him. "Who paid you to spy on us, to send those warnings? If I know, I can protect you."

"No one can protect me!" He grabbed Claire and shoved her in front of him, pressing the gun into her side. Claire clamped her lips together as if to keep from crying out.

Richard felt cold all over. "Put down that pistol."

Chevalier pulled Claire closer, and her gasp was like a knife to Richard's heart.

"I will not answer you," the dance master cried. "Back away! Lady Winthrop will come with me to the ship. If I do not see you, I will leave her safely on the dock. Do not try me, or I swear I will kill her!"

Richard could see the desperation in the dance master's gray eyes. His fears drove him harder than a rising tide. Chevalier had already shot from cover twice. This time, Claire was his target.

Richard took a step back, looking for any sign of weakness he might exploit. The most important thing was to get Claire away from the dastard. "Leave her here. I swear you won't be followed."

"Ha! You know nothing!" He edged toward the door, dragging Claire with him. Her head was down as if she despaired of her life. Anger and dread raced along Richard's veins as well.

Please, Lord! Don't take her from me!

"Already he knows I have returned in failure," he said, backing for the door, gaze on Richard. "People watch me. I see them darting into alleyways to avoid notice. But he is fond of the lady, I know. 'She is the key,' he told me. 'With her on your side, you cannot lose.' I enlisted her aid in Cumberland. I will do so again now."

Claire's head came up then, and her gaze met Richard's.

Instead of the panic he'd expected, righteous indignation blazed like cold fire from her pale eyes.

"I'm afraid your patron is incorrect," she said. "I refuse to have any part in this." She brought the heel of her shoe down on his instep. Chevalier winced, but Claire's face twisted as her leg gave out. Down she went, right out of his grip into a puddle of black wool on the floor.

Richard didn't stop to think. He slammed into Chevalier, knocking the man backward. Even as Richard regained his balance, fists rising to defend, the pistol clattered to the floor. Claire snatched it up and leveled it at the dance master as he struggled to his feet.

Richard rose over Chevalier. "Talk. Now."

Chest heaving, he glanced between Richard and the pistol. Claire raised it higher as if to prove her intentions. Seeing her narrow-eyed look, sharp as daggers, Richard wouldn't have wanted to chance her. Chevalier must have thought the same, for he slumped with a sigh.

"Why not? Whatever happens now, I am a dead man. What do you wish to know?"

"Who hired you?" Claire asked. "Who dares implicate me in this mess?"

Richard could only admire her fire, but he fully expected more prevarication from Chevalier. Yet it seemed the dance master was beaten, for he answered readily enough. "Widmore."

Richard recoiled. "Widmore? The Marquess of Widmore? Why?"

Chevalier spread his hands. "This you will have to ask him. I merely do as he orders. I only know that he despised the lady's husband for his weakness and admired the lady for her strength."

Claire's hand didn't tremble, though the gun had to

be heavy. "Then do not try me, sir. Tell Captain Everard the truth."

"You will not like it," he warned, but when she only raised the gun higher, he continued on. "I can tell you this—the English, they have their secrets, and who would think a harmless dance master would steal them?"

Richard frowned, lowering his fists. "What kind of secrets?"

Chevalier's smile was grim, yet Richard felt the pride in it. "Political secrets. Are they not the most lucrative? Plans for war, intentions of alliances. The members of Parliament seldom leave all traces of their work in Whitehall. Often my instruction requires me to stay in their homes. Listening behind closed doors, picking the locks on their desks, it is all too easy."

"But the marquess should be privy to those secrets," Claire protested, hand shifting on the pistol. "He's one of the most powerful men in Parliament, outside a cabinet position."

"And how do you think he rose to such power?" Chevalier shook his head. "Always they underestimate him."

"As they underestimate you, I think," Claire murmured. She glanced up at Richard. "What shall we do with him?"

"Give him to the magistrates," Richard said, knowing his disgust was evident in his tone.

Chevalier clasped his hands together, once more the weak-willed fop. "No, I beg you! His fingers are everywhere. I will not survive my trial. Let me go, to the ship. I will sail away and trouble you no more."

Richard wasn't sure which was the true Chevalier, the effeminate dance master or the cunning thief and marksman, but he knew he couldn't trust the fellow. "You've admitted to theft, espionage and treason," he said.

"We could add attempted murder to the charges. I cannot see you escaping without paying the consequences."

Chevalier took a step forward, eyes lighting. "And what if I tell you another secret? That his power extends beyond England to France! That he is aligned with Napoleon to bring England to its knees. I could name names, offer plans."

"You lie," Richard spat. "No Englishman would help the Corsican monster."

His smile was twisted. "Only one who hoped to surpass him."

Claire held out the pistol to Richard. "Shoot him. I cannot abide his babble another second."

Chevalier darted back, paling. "*Capitaine,* you would not…"

"I might," Richard told him. "And if I don't, my cousin Vaughn Everard would be glad to have a go at you."

Chevalier licked his lips. "But I cannot speak to your magistrate if I am dead."

"True," Richard allowed. "But you can sing to the magistrates just as well with only one leg, though I warrant it will be harder to dance." He gave Claire his free hand to help her rise. "I'll have Marshall send for the watch. Let's see if they're as interested in your stories as we are."

Claire was more than happy to release the pistol to Richard's care. The thing was cold and heavy, and she didn't think she'd have the stomach to fire it. But it had served a purpose. Chevalier sat on one of the mahogany chairs, his head in his hands. And Richard and his family were safe.

Thank You, Lord!

She was also thankful Vaughn Everard had been out

with the horses, waiting for Richard, during the fracas. As it was, he came barreling into the room with the elderly constable hot on his heels.

"Tell me the truth," he demanded, grabbing the dance master by his lapel and jerking him to his feet. "What do you know of Lord Everard's death?"

"Nothing!" Chevalier cried, hands up to ward him off. "I swear it!"

"You lie!" Vaughn spat, but Richard stepped between them.

"Stand down, Vaughn. We've no reason to think he was involved."

Vaughn's chest rose and fell as if he had run hard. "You can't know that. I have to understand, Richard."

Claire's heart went out to him. How many times had she cried out, longing to understand why Winthrop had been so cruel, why he couldn't love her? Yet the fault had rested in him.

"Mr. Everard," she said quietly, and Vaughn's head snapped around to meet her gaze. "We have an answer for you, but we will need to discuss it in private."

He frowned, then glanced at the grizzled constable, who stood listening raptly to everything they said. Vaughn's shoulders came down, and he released the dance master to step back. "Very well. Thank you, Lady Winthrop."

Claire offered him a smile, wishing she could do more. *But You'll have to do that, Lord. He needs You.*

"It's settled then," Richard said. "Constable, I'll go with you to take this fellow to the magistrates. Lady Winthrop, wait here."

"Certainly not," Claire said. Though her knee still protested her movements, she made her way toward the door. "I prefer to see this through." She glanced back to find Richard shaking his head in obvious admiration.

"Madam, will you not take an order, just this once?"

"And set a precedent, sir? Never." She headed out the door. "Now, come along, and do try to keep up."

The magistrate was keenly interested in what the dance master had to say. However, the large-bellied fellow, who received them over his dinner, was clearly skeptical of Chevalier's claims to be working for the Marquess of Widmore.

"Besmirching his betters," he sneered, after sending Chevalier to be locked up for trial. "I've seen it often. Count on it, it's all a humbug."

Claire wanted to believe that the marquess was innocent. It was easier to think that a near stranger like Chevalier was spying on the aristocracy for his own gain. Yet, if Chevalier was stealing secrets on his own, what value could he have found in Dallsten Manor? As far as she knew, Richard wasn't involved in anything that would gain the dance master a pretty penny to pass along. The Everard family had never been particularly interested in political matters, nor were they in positions privy to state secrets.

"And why should the marquess care if Samantha came to London?" Claire protested to Richard, as they headed back to Everard House at last. Night had fallen. Lanterns blazed beside fine town houses, and Claire caught glimpses of ladies in evening cloaks, and gentlemen in top hats from the windows of the carriages passing them.

"No reason that I can see," Richard mused, leaning back against the cushions as if tired of it all. "Samantha thinks fondly of him. I know Uncle trusted him."

"And he seems to remember your uncle and Samantha

fondly as well," Claire said, thinking back to their discussion at his daughter's ball. That seemed so long ago now. She'd changed; Richard had changed.

Thank You, Lord, for that!

"Is any of it true, then?" Claire pressed. "It seems so far-fetched. How does your cousin have anything to do with French or English politics?"

"I wish I knew," Richard said. "And I wish I knew how to protect her in the future."

Claire agreed, and her body felt suddenly heavy, her energy drifting out into the dark night. Her leg throbbed; her stomach protested that she was late for her own dinner. Though they had triumphed for the moment, she wanted to lay her head down on the cushions and cry.

As if Richard knew it, he put his arm around her, and she leaned into him.

"We'll keep her safe, Claire," he murmured against her hair. "I promise."

Faith in him eased her fears, and she took a deep breath, gathering her strength. His lips brushed her temple, soft, gentle, full of equal promise. She could have stayed like this forever.

But the carriage was slowing, and she knew they'd reached Everard House. Time to face Vaughn Everard. Time to face the future.

Richard climbed down readily, but when Claire hesitated to follow, he swept her up in his arms and carried her to the door.

"Richard! What will your neighbors think?"

"That the Everards are once again set on scandal," he replied. But he didn't put her down until the footman had opened the door and ushered them into the entryway.

"Where's Mr. Everard?" he asked the footman as Claire got her balance.

"With Lady Everard in the study, sir," he replied.

"Go," Claire said when Richard looked at her askance. "I'll catch you up."

He strode down the corridor. Claire followed more carefully, each step painful. She could hear voices as she approached—Samantha's higher pitch and two deeper voices, each strident. But she was not prepared for what she found when she reached the door.

Chapter Twenty-Six

Richard must have been just as surprised, for he waited silently inside the doorway of the study. Claire thought the room must bear the stamp of his organized brother. The books and journals were neatly arranged on the pale white bookcases; the square, brass-appointed desk in the center of the room was well stocked with quills, ink and parchment. Heavy armchairs, upholstered in leather, sat before the white marble fireplace, where Samantha was standing, the red glow of the fire making her muslin gown turn as pink as her cheeks.

Two men stood opposite her, like equal points of a triangle. Tension called from every line of their lean bodies, their raised chins.

"Did you never think," Vaughn demanded of the red-haired fellow, "that you might ruin her chances of a future? What of her reputation?"

"Now, there's a first," Richard murmured to Claire, as the other man, Toby Giles, stiffened. "Vaughn's usually the one accused of ruining reputations."

Claire wanted to smile, but she was concerned for the poet. Denied an outlet for his frustrations, would he now turn them on Toby?

For the moment, Toby was holding his own. "Anyone with sense would know otherwise," he insisted. "I was just saying goodbye before heading home to Cumberland."

"It's all right, cousin," Samantha said earnestly, gaze darting between the two of them. "The door was open. We weren't really alone."

"You had no gentleman to protect you," Vaughn maintained.

"Stuff it!" Toby exclaimed. "She had me!"

"And by your own admission you were intent on saying goodbye," Vaughn sneered.

"Fine," Toby said. "I know what's expected. I'll just marry her, shall I?"

Claire gasped, and all three gazes turned to the pair in the doorway. Toby's blue eyes were wide in surprise, Samantha's dark gaze wider in shock, and Vaughn, Claire thought, actually looked relieved.

Samantha recovered first. "Oh, Cousin Richard, Lady Winthrop! I'm so glad to see you!" She rushed forward and threw herself into Claire's arms, nearly oversetting them both. The girl must have felt it, for she disengaged hastily and put a hand on Claire's elbow to steady her. Her look was worried, but not, apparently, for Claire's discomfort.

"I don't have to marry him, do I?" she begged.

Claire was not about to allow her to be forced into a loveless marriage. And she wasn't sure the girl had done anything that required a hasty wedding to avoid scandal.

"Certainly not, dear," Claire said with a look to Richard, who nodded.

"But I want to marry you!" Toby protested, hurrying closer. "I know I'm doing it badly, but I thought you felt the same way."

Samantha clung to Claire. "Well, I…"

"Puppy," Vaughn declared, passing the youth to stalk to Samantha's side. He went down on one knee before her, handsome face tipped back, dark eyes deep and beseeching.

"Dearest lady," he murmured, as if he and Samantha were the only two in the room, "never have I been privileged to meet a more pure spirit, a brighter light than yours. I am not worthy of your love, yet I crave it as the tide craves the moon. I would be honored above all things if you would consent to give me your hand in marriage."

Claire wondered how any woman had the strength to refuse him. She glanced at her charge, hoping she might be proof against his charm. *Lord, I don't think he's the right one for her, but show her Your will, not mine.*

Samantha stared at him, lips trembling. "Are you just giving Toby an example of how it's done, or do you mean that?"

He cocked his head, pale queue falling to one side of his black evening coat. "Do you wish me to mean it?"

To Claire's surprise, Samantha glanced at her. "I don't think so."

Vaughn raised his snowy brows. "Madam, you wound me."

"I'm sorry," Samantha said, straightening as if finally sure of her answer. "But I've been thinking a lot lately about London and what Papa wanted me to do. He didn't want me to follow his example, he said, and wait too long to wed. But he set another example, and Lady Winthrop helped me realize what it was. He looked at my mother and saw a pretty woman. He didn't look deeper or he'd have known they'd never suit. If I'm to marry well, I must be sure of the gentleman's character."

Thank You, Lord! Claire pressed her lips together to keep from crying her praise aloud. She'd hoped she might help Samantha avoid the mistakes she'd made. It seemed she'd been successful, and her heart swelled with the knowledge.

"You've known me most of your life," Toby said, venturing closer even as Vaughn rose. "Surely you know my character."

"To my sorrow," Samantha said with a teasing grin. "You're a good friend, Toby, but I'm not in love with you."

"You could be," he insisted.

Claire watched her charge, but she saw no sign of weakening.

"Perhaps," Samantha allowed. "But I won't take a chance of marrying on that basis." She turned to Vaughn. "I've only known you a few weeks, cousin, but you seem a great deal like Papa."

Vaughn's grin was sure. "Then you should know my character well."

"Only enough to fear it. Papa learned faith and patience later in life, it seems. I'm not sure you've learned those lessons yet."

He swept her a bow. "Then I shall have to prove it to you."

Samantha took a deep breath and glanced at Claire again. "And that's my decision. Do you think I chose wisely, Lady Winthrop?"

Claire beamed at her. "Exceedingly well."

"Agreed," Richard said, stepping forward. Beside him, his cousin and Toby Giles looked like mere boys to Claire. "The matter is settled, except for one issue."

"Only one?" Claire couldn't help teasing. "And what would that be?"

"They both missed the mark on how to propose properly," Richard said. "Allow me to demonstrate."

Claire caught her breath as Richard took her hands and cradled them in his own.

"We have known each other for years, Claire," he started, dark eyes serious, "yet I feel in the last few weeks that I have truly begun to appreciate you. You care deeply for those lucky enough to be called your friends, and you do not hesitate to sacrifice your needs to meet theirs. Your determination in the face of difficult circumstances humbles me. The beauty of your face and form are only surpassed by the beauty of your soul."

"My word," Toby muttered.

"Hush!" Samantha insisted.

Claire could not find the words to speak. He was so intent, so sure of himself and of what he saw in her. She felt as if a rose blossomed inside her, opening its face to the sun.

"I have long wondered whether I could be content on land," he continued. "Even though my faith is strong, I've felt rudderless, adrift at times. Now I see that you are my anchor. With you, I can be truly at rest. I may never have the size of fortune or prestige your father wanted in your husband, but I will love and honor you all the days of my life. I want to be the one who stands beside you, supporting you, encouraging you, whatever storms arise. And on the days God blesses us with sunshine, I want to be the one to rejoice with you. Marry me, Claire."

A laugh bubbled up. "You just can't stop issuing orders, can you?"

He looked toward the ceiling a moment as if realizing what he'd said. "You're right! Let me try that again. Will you do me the honor of marrying me, Claire?"

There he stood, so close beside her, this man she'd loved so long. She had no doubt in her mind what her answer must be. She felt as if the Lord had sent His blessings, that this union was what He'd intended all along. She was the one who had had to realize the wonder of it.

"Yes, oh yes," she cried, and Richard drew her into his arms. Held in his embrace, his lips on hers, she knew she had come home as well.

Samantha's applause brought Claire back to the present, and the fact that she and Richard had an audience.

"Oh, how marvelous!" the girl enthused. "Congratulations!"

As Richard released Claire, Vaughn clapped him on the shoulder. "Not bad, for a sea captain."

"A sea captain no longer," Richard said. "I'll be content to manage the fleet from shore."

"Taking the role of a pirate king, eh?" Vaughn joked, but Samantha started.

"Oh, Lady Winthrop, I nearly forgot!" She seized Claire's arm, gaze bright. "All those letters you've been writing—we have answers! Fittings scheduled, calling cards left from people who want to meet me. Me!" She dropped her hold. "And the chamberlain sent the note with my credentials. I'm to be presented to the queen in two weeks!"

Pleasure rippled through her as Claire realized she'd made a difference here as well. *Thank You, Lord!*

"Wonderful news, dear!" she told Samantha. "What did he say about the dress—wide or narrow hoops?"

"Narrow, I think." Samantha frowned as if trying to recall.

"How many feathers?"

"Feathers?" Richard asked with a frown to match his cousin's. "On a dress?"

"In her hair," Claire explained.

"I don't remember," Samantha admitted. "I'm afraid

I didn't pay much attention after reading that I was to be presented."

"That means the College of Heralds must have approved your lineage," Richard said, brow clearing. "That's a relief, though we'll likely have a visit from Mr. Caruthers shortly over the matter."

"Another gate behind us," Vaughn agreed.

"More importantly," Claire said to Samantha, "it means we must go shopping, first thing in the morning."

Richard groaned.

Samantha sobered. "Is it that bad? Do you think I'm not ready?"

Vaughn tapped her on her nose. "You'll do fine, infant."

That raised her head. "Infant! Well, I like that! A moment ago, you were proposing!"

"A moment ago, I thought young Toby was about to steal a march on me," Vaughn countered, with a narrow-eyed look at the youth. As Samantha frowned and Toby grinned cheekily at him, he turned to Richard and Claire. "But that doesn't mean there isn't danger. You said you had news."

"We do," Richard said. "Mr. Giles, I must ask you to excuse us. Everard family business. You're welcome to stay in London with us as long as you like."

"I may take you up on that offer," Toby said, with a nod to Vaughn. Then he boldly kissed Samantha on the cheek and strolled from the room. As Samantha rubbed her cheek in wonder, Vaughn glared after him.

"Perhaps we could all be seated," Claire suggested, and Richard escorted her to a chair near the fire. The others drew up chairs around her. Firelight played on faces growing relaxed at last after the dramas of the day. Yet Claire knew it was only the calm before the storm. Neither

Samantha nor Vaughn would be pleased with the story Richard must tell them.

When they were all settled, Richard went on to explain what they'd learned from Chevalier and about the scrap of paper they'd found in Cumberland that told of revolution. By the time he'd finished, Vaughn's glare seemed permanently affixed to his face.

"Widmore," he growled, as if the name had become poisonous. "Then he betrayed Uncle's friendship."

Claire glanced at Richard and knew by his frown that he was also concerned about his cousin's need for vengeance.

Samantha must have been just as concerned, for she immediately protested. "We don't know he betrayed anyone. He was Papa's dearest friend. Perhaps he only sent those warnings through Monsieur Chevalier to protect me."

"Protect you from what?" Claire felt compelled to put in. "And don't forget the shots Chevalier fired at you. Those could hardly have come from a good motive. I also can't believe the marquess would have truck with revolution. I still say our dance master is lying."

Vaughn pursed his lips. "Todd the footman nearly killed Jerome, and he also claimed to have worked for the marquess."

"Which the marquess denies," Richard reminded him.

"And the Widmore family has never had the least scandal attached to its name," Claire added. "Lord Widmore has always been kindness itself to me."

"Me, too," Samantha agreed.

Still Vaughn looked unconvinced, head cocked as if studying the problem from all angles. "Uncle's dead, his valet's dead, the footman hired to rob us is dead. And you say Chevalier feared for his life. We need to know why."

Richard kept himself still, a calm sea against his cousin's stormy passions.

"We may know more when Chevalier goes to trial," he said, bracing his hands on his thighs. "In the meantime, I suggest we give the marquess wide berth."

Vaughn's eyes narrowed. "I disagree. I think we should seek him out, demand answers."

"No." Claire had never seen Richard so formidable. He rose from the chair and looked down his long nose. Even the light in his eyes commanded obedience. "We do nothing," he said, each word sharp, as if to embed it in his cousin's mind, "until Samantha has been presented to the queen. She doesn't need a scandal attending her."

Vaughn gazed at him. "Jerome may think otherwise."

"Then he can take it up with me. He's still the leader of this family. I'll accept his orders."

Vaughn's defiance was palpable. But Claire reached up and squeezed Richard's hand. "I can hardly wait. It will be a delight to see you take orders for a change, my dear."

He grinned down at her.

Samantha popped to her feet. "It's settled, then. Come along, Cousin Vaughn. Let's see what Toby's gotten up to."

"In a moment," Vaughn said, rising slowly, as if intent on making his case to Richard.

Samantha winked at Claire before sashaying toward the door. "Very well. I'll just go find him on my own, then. I wonder if he'll be so bold as to kiss me again?"

Vaughn bowed his regrets to Richard and Claire and hurried after her.

"She will be a handful," Richard said, with a shake of his head. "Are you certain you want to sponsor her?"

"Of course," Claire said. "She is a clever girl. She isn't

even out, and she's well on her way to achieving one of the stipulations in the will."

When Richard frowned, she laughed. "She's already received offers of marriage from two eminently suitable gentlemen. Only one more to go."

Chapter Twenty-Seven

Two weeks later, at half past one in the afternoon, the Everard carriage arrived at St. James's Palace and made its way to the appointed entrance.

"I can't do this," Samantha fretted, fussing with the lace edging her velvet overskirt. Her gown was white satin, crossing at the high waist, and hemmed with the same lace. Her mother's pearl bobs dangled at her ears, exposed by curls piled high on her head, and pearls, a gift from Richard, graced her neck. "What if I fall?"

"Then you will pick yourself up like the lady you are and carry on," Claire replied. She was thankful she still fit in her court presentation gown, and it was still in fashion. The pale blue skirt with the white satin overskirt went well with Samantha's. Claire took a moment to adjust one of her ostrich plumes. Four for this drawing room, and wide hoops. What was Her Majesty thinking?

"I wish I could go with you," Richard said, watching them from the interior of the coach. "But I'll be waiting outside to hear all about your triumph."

Claire smiled at him. In the last fortnight they had only grown closer, and her doubts had faded more with each passing day. Though they had decided to wait to wed until after Samantha navigated her Season, Claire was satisfied she'd made the right choice this time.

The long gallery before the presence chamber was crowded as they entered. Young ladies and their mothers in finery as sweeping as Claire's and Samantha's, new brides of titled gentlemen with their doting husbands. Some had been waiting a while, if the wilting of their ostrich plumes was any indication.

A lord-in-waiting in a black coat with tails to his knees and a powdered wig on his head read their names one by one, and the lady and her sponsor disappeared through the doors indicated, letting in a burst of conversation from the other side.

Samantha tugged up her creamy, long gloves. "What if she hates me on sight?"

Claire smoothed a wrinkle in the girl's sleeve. "No one could hate you on sight, Samantha. Whatever happens, remember who you are, who God made you to be. Be true to that vision, and you need have no regrets."

Samantha nodded and visibly swallowed, catching her train up over her arm.

"Samantha, Lady Everard," the lord intoned.

Claire dropped her hand with a smile and went ahead of her through the door.

Inside, the queen and her attendants waited in their sumptuous gowns under a canopy of crimson satin. As Samantha came through the door, she allowed her train to swing free. Several lords-in-waiting spread it behind her with long wooden wands. She glided across the marble floor, and Claire's heart swelled.

Another lord leaned toward the queen. "Samantha, Lady Everard," he read from the card in his gloved hand.

Claire held her breath. The queen's soft face was wreathed in sadness, as if she knew the burden this young lady had inherited. Samantha curtsied, deep, low, until her knee must have almost touched the floor. The hoops bowed with her, and she tilted her face up to Her Majesty.

"My dear," the queen said, bending to kiss her forehead. "Welcome to London. I look forward to hearing many wonderful things about your time here."

Samantha's lips twitched as she rose, and Claire thought she was fighting a grin. "Thank you, Your Majesty," she murmured. Slowly, elegantly, she backed from the queen's presence.

Claire waited to cheer until they were safely in the corridor outside. "You were brilliant!"

Samantha grinned at last. "I was, wasn't I? Let's go tell Cousin Richard!"

And so it began, Claire couldn't help thinking as they returned to Everard House. Samantha's Season had started, along with her quest to accomplish all her father had wanted for her and his nephews. Claire could only marvel at the girl's determination. She gladly shouldered the role that had been given her, and Claire thought she had a bright future.

She was still glad to shed her court finery and put on the apricot day dress she'd ordered before going north. Mercier hummed to herself as she cared for the beautiful clothes. Claire hoped she'd never have to wear black again as long as she lived.

She found Richard in the study, finishing some orders for the new captain who would be taking the *Siren's Gold* to Jamaica. Seeing her, he rose from the desk and came to take her in his arms. She nestled against him, glorying in the strength of him, a strength she knew she could borrow as well as lend to as the days went past. They were together, and nothing, she felt, could pull them apart again.

"Two marriage proposals down and the queen conquered," she murmured. "Now we make sure she's welcomed everywhere."

He sighed. "That will take some doing, given her father's antics."

"It might. But my opinion still carries some weight in Society. I'll do all I can to see she is treated well."

"Still thinking of others, I see."

"Did you not praise that trait when you proposed to me?"

Richard's arms tightened as if to prove his admiration. "I did. But my concern remains for you. You deserve a glorious wedding, Claire, whatever you like."

She lifted her head to smile at him. "Whatever I like? Wedding gowns are not fripperies, my love."

He grimaced, then chuckled as she cuddled closer once more. "Choose whatever gown you like. If it pleases you, it will no doubt please me. I trust your judgment in all things."

So did she, and the confidence that feeling inspired settled over her like a warm blanket. "Then you've truly put our past behind you."

"The dark parts," he assured her. "We both grew into the people we are today, so I cannot completely wish that time away. And there's so much I want to share with you now." His hand touched her hair, softly, sweetly. "For our wedding trip, I'd like to take one last sail, anywhere you wish to go."

Claire's smile only grew. "Anywhere?"

He chuckled again. "Anywhere. I want all of London, all of the world to know that this time the captain's courtship was successful."

"You were successful the first time, too, my love," Claire said. "I just never had the opportunity to show you."

And they spent the rest of their lives delighting in proving it to each other.

* * * * *

Dear Reader,

Thank you for choosing *The Captain's Courtship,* the second book in the Everard Legacy miniseries. The first book, *The Rogue's Reform* (February 2012), introduced the Everard family and the legacy left by Lord Arthur Everard's life and will. I hope you enjoyed the story of how Richard Everard and Claire Winthrop found their way back to each other. The third book, about Vaughn's vengeance, will follow.

I loved writing about a sea captain. I'm fascinated with tall ships, the masted sailing ships from the nineteenth century or earlier. I've been fortunate enough to sail on our state's tall ship, the *Lady Washington,* as well as its sister ship, the *Hawaiian Chieftain.* It wasn't hard to imagine Richard standing on the quarterdeck, sun warm on his face, wind ruffling his russet hair, issuing commands.

You can learn more about tall ships on my website, www.reginascott.com, where you'll also find information on upcoming releases.

Blessings!
Regina Scott

Questions for Discussion

1. Claire questions the choices she made when she was younger. Have you ever made a choice and thought better of it afterward? What did you do about it?

2. Claire also fears for her ability to enter into another marriage because of the abuses of her first husband. How can we help women in abused situations move forward with their lives?

3. Richard has tried to forgive Claire for breaking her promise to marry him, but he struggles with forgetting the hurt. How easy is it for you to forgive? How can we forget past hurts?

4. After captaining a sailing ship for years, Richard is used to issuing commands and having them obeyed instantly. Where are you an authority figure in your life? What kind of obedience should you expect? What do we owe our heavenly Father?

5. Vaughn Everard longs to answer the questions surrounding his beloved uncle's death, but vengeance lurks in the back of his mind. When should we take matters into our own hands, and when should we wait for God to act?

6. Samantha struggles to understand how she will know the man she's supposed to marry. How can we know a person's character?

7. Both Samantha and Claire begin to learn that God has answers to many of our questions. Why do we often wait to ask His guidance? What happens when His guidance seems contrary to what we desire?

8. Chevalier spies on Englishmen to sell their secrets. When does watchful care become spying? What's the difference between spying and reporting?

9. Mrs. Dallsten Walcott gathers things to fill the loss of family. When do possessions reach a point that they possess us? What can we do to avoid this?

10. Reputation was an important part of knowing who to trust in the Regency period. What does reputation mean today? How can we cultivate a good reputation?

11. For a young lady like Samantha, presentation to the queen marked her entrance into adulthood and society. What rites of passage did you go through as you were growing up?

12. Sometimes Samantha seems wise and other times a naive girl. When do we truly gain wisdom? What can we do to reach that point in our lives?

COMING NEXT MONTH
from Love Inspired® Historical
AVAILABLE AUGUST 7, 2012

CHARITY HOUSE COURTSHIP
Charity House
Renee Ryan

When a misunderstanding puts Laney O'Connor at odds with hotel owner Marc Dupree, the truth endangers Laney's beloved Charity House orphanage—but silence could ruin her chances with Marc forever.

THE SOLDIER'S WIFE
Cheryl Reavis

Bound by a promise, Jack Murphy heads to North Carolina, and war widow Sayer Garth. If only he could be certain that his past won't put them both at risk....

GROOM WANTED
Debra Ullrick

The plan was for best friends Leah Bowen and Jake Lure to select each other's mail-order spouses. As the postings pour in, will they spot happiness waiting close to home?

INSTANT PRAIRIE FAMILY
Bonnie Navarro

Will Hopkins's new housekeeper was supposed to be matronly and middle-aged. Young, beautiful Abby Stewart is determined to win him and his sons over—in spite of Will's best intentions!

Look for these and other Love Inspired books wherever books are sold, including most bookstores, supermarkets, discount stores and drugstores.

LIHCNM0712

REQUEST YOUR FREE BOOKS!

2 FREE INSPIRATIONAL NOVELS
PLUS 2
FREE
MYSTERY GIFTS

Love Inspired
HISTORICAL
INSPIRATIONAL HISTORICAL ROMANCE

*When a baby is left on the doorstep of an Amish house,
Sheriff Nick Bradley comes face-to-face with his past.*

*Read on for a preview of A HOME FOR HANNAH
by Patricia Davids.*

The farmhouse door swung open before Sheriff Nick Bradley could knock. A woman with fiery auburn hair and green eyes stood glaring at him. "There has been a mistake. We don't need you here."

The shock of seeing Miriam Kauffman standing in front of him took him aback. He struggled to hide his surprise. It had been eight years since he'd laid eyes on her. A lifetime ago.

"Good morning to you, too, Miriam."

After all this time, she wasn't any better at hiding her opinion of him. She looked ready to spit nails. Proof that she hadn't forgiven him.

"Miriam, don't be rude," her mother chided. Miriam reluctantly stepped aside. He entered the house.

His cousin Amber sat at the table. "Hi, Nick. Thanks for coming. We do need your help."

Ada Kauffman sat across from her. The room was bathed in soft light from two kerosene lanterns hanging from hooks on the ceiling.

He glanced at the three women facing him. Ada Kauffman was Amish, from the top of her white prayer bonnet to the tips of her bare toes poking out from beneath her plain dress. Her daughter, Miriam, had never joined the church, choosing to leave before she was baptized. Her arms were crossed over her chest.

Amber served the Amish and non-Amish people of Hope Springs, Ohio, as a nurse midwife. Exactly what was she doing here?

He said, "Okay, I'm here. What's so sensitive that I had to come instead of sending one of my perfectly competent deputies?"

"This is why we called you." Amber gestured toward the basket. He took a step closer and saw a baby swaddled in the folds of a quilt.

"You called me here to see a new baby? Congratulations to whomever."

"Exactly," Miriam said.

He looked at her closely. "What am I missing?"

Amber said, "It's more about what we are missing."

"And that is?" he demanded.

Ada said, "A mother to go with this baby."

He shook his head. "You've lost me."

Miriam rolled her eyes. "I'm not surprised."

Her mother scowled at her, but said, "Someone left this baby on my porch."

Will Nick and Miriam get past their differences to help little Hannah?

Pick up A HOME FOR HANNAH by Patricia Davids, available August 2012 from Love Inspired Books.

─TEXAS TWINS─

Follow the adventures of two sets of twins who are torn apart by family secrets and learn to find their way home.

Her Surprise Sister by Marta Perry
July 2012

Mirror Image Bride by Barbara McMahon
August 2012

Carbon Copy Cowboy by Arlene James
September 2012

Look-Alike Lawman by Glynna Kaye
October 2012

The Soldier's Newfound Family
by Kathryn Springer
November 2012

Reunited for the Holidays
by Jillian Hart
December 2012

*Available wherever
books are sold.*

www.LoveInspiredBooks.com

LICONT0812